TENNESSEE
WHISKEY

By the Author

Healing Hearts

No Boundaries

Love's Redemption

Unbroken

Captive

Tennessee Whiskey

TENNESSEE WHISKEY

by

Donna K. Ford

2019

ISBN 13: 978-1-63555-556-1

This Trade Paperback Original Is Published By
Bold Strokes Books, Inc.
P.O. Box 249
Valley Falls, NY 12185

First Edition: November 2019

CREDITS
EDITOR: RUTH STERNGLANTZ
PRODUCTION DESIGN: SUSAN RAMUNDO
COVER DESIGN BY SHERI (HINDSIGHTGRAPHICS@GMAIL.COM)

Acknowledgments

Writing, like all art, is an author's attempt to turn experience, emotion, sensation, and curiosity into something that can be shared. Once we discover our writer's voice, the need begins. Writing becomes an addiction, a compulsion, a need. But in this need, there is great power, power to create, power to influence, power to understand. We authors are collectors. We collect emotions, experiences, and events that we then weave together into stories that help us make sense of it all.

This book is one of those stories. Appalachia is a place, a culture, a people. It is made up of old traditions born out of desperate need, commitment to family, despair, hard work, and resourcefulness. I have never experienced another place or culture with more heart and perseverance. Appalachia is my home, my history, and most often my inspiration.

I offer many thanks to you the reader for joining me in this sharing. I hope you enjoy the adventure as much as I do. I have had the pleasure to meet some of you along the way, and your kind words and encouragement mean more than you could know. Special thanks to my beta reader, Brianne, for her gentle prodding, keen eye, and willingness to keep going even when her plate is full. Boundless thanks to my editor, Ruth Sternglantz, for her guidance, patience, and her contagious enthusiasm. And thanks to Radclyffe, Sandy, and all the Bold Strokes team. You have my deepest gratitude.

Dedication

In loving memory of Cordelia Kennedy Lowe

CHAPTER ONE

Dane Foster tossed her camera bag over her shoulder and pulled her luggage off the airport carousel. She'd been in more airports in the last few months than she could count, and the routine left her disoriented. She'd usually have to find a guide to get her feet on the ground, but this time was different. This was home, or at least it used to be. For years she had pushed memories of East Tennessee out of her mind. It was a bit ironic that the one place she had spent years trying to get away from ended up being the one place she needed to be the most.

She stepped outside McGhee Tyson Airport and looked out at the Smoky Mountains looming in the distance, the mist rising in its iconic way, blanketing the tapestry in white clouds. It was a view she had never tired of seeing. She kicked herself for waiting so long to make the trip home. But the world had a way of eating up time and spitting out a used-up life like a dog's chew toy.

It was certainly that way for her. After years roaming around the globe documenting one vicious atrocity after another as a freelance photojournalist for various print magazines, sacrificing everything, and losing everyone she'd cared for, she found herself jobless and right back where she'd started. But she'd made a promise to her best friend that one day they would come here together, and Dane would show her the splendor of the mountains and the unique culture of Appalachia. Michelle never got that chance, but Dane was determined to fulfill the promise just the same. In the months since Michelle's death, Dane had been adrift, unable to find direction in her life. She spent days thinking of the past and longing for those she had lost. Losing Michelle had opened Pandora's box, leaving Dane haunted with questions about her past, regrets for too many mistakes, and uncertainty of what to do next.

Dane grabbed the first cab waiting at the curb. She tossed her bag in the back seat and climbed inside.

"Where to, man?" the driver asked, barely looking up to see who had gotten into his car.

Dane smiled, the slow Southern accent taking her back to her younger years when life was easier, and time moved at a different pace. "Do they still have all those car dealerships along Alcoa Highway?" she asked.

As soon as she spoke the cabbie's head snapped up, his eyes apologetic in the rearview mirror.

"Oh yes, ma'am. Sorry about that. I didn't realize...But yeah, the whole strip is lined with 'em."

"Good," Dane said, leaning back against the seat. "Take me to the first one you come to."

The cabbie nodded and put the car in gear. "Sure thing."

An hour and five thousand dollars later, Dane pulled out of the Chrysler dealership in a 1995 Jeep Wrangler. There was no back seat, but she wouldn't need that anyway. It was a far cry from the BMW she was used to driving, but it was exactly what she needed for now. Besides, she'd enjoy playing a little rough for a while.

Dane pulled into a gas station to fill up the tank and grab some snacks for the road. She picked up a copy of the *Knoxville News Sentinel* and a couple of smaller papers to catch up on the local news. It didn't take long to pick up the theme of the drug epidemic ravaging the rural Appalachian communities.

A spark buzzed in her ear. No matter where she went in the world there was something tearing the people apart. In most places she had been it was war and religion. Why would this place be any different? It seemed the whole human race was out to destroy itself. She had done a pretty good job of destroying her part of it too. She was burned out, fried, washed-up. Those were just some of the phrases used to describe her as she was given her walking papers.

She'd been back from Iraq six months before her boss finally pulled the plug on her. It was for the best. She had no interest in going back. It didn't matter how much money there was to be made—nothing was worth that kind of hell.

She knew her boss had tried to give her a chance. Simon wasn't a bad guy, but too many nights drinking and too little sleep hadn't been the best remedy to chase the demons away. When everything caught up with her, her career was just one of the casualties left in the dust and debris.

Dane squeezed her eyes tight to black out the nightmares that forced their way into her waking life. She turned up the radio to shut out the sounds of the bombs exploding around her. She could still feel the heat of the blast. Her ears rang, a signal the headache was on its way.

A horn blared, and Dane jerked the steering wheel, narrowly missing the car next to her. She had been so caught up in the past, she had drifted into the other lane. She waved her apology to the other driver.

She sighed. At least the excitement had cleared her head. The headache would come no matter what, and the memories would be waiting. Dane looked to the mountains looming in the distance and wished Michelle could see them. She smiled to herself, imagining the trouble the two of them could get into together. Her smile faded as she thought of this as their last journey together. She had come here to lay Michelle's memory to rest. Her body was miles away, but Dane had the overwhelming need to fulfill that last dream they had together. She hoped this would be the one thing that would quiet her nightmares and allow her to let Michelle go.

Dane hadn't bothered to let her father know she was coming, but she wanted to see him. They hadn't exactly been close, and they'd barely spoken in years. But she wanted to change that. She wasn't a kid anymore. She had to stop running from her father and the loss of her mother. Her father had no idea what was going on in her life. But he had never cared about anything but the job, which she no longer had. How would she explain? She dreaded the look of disappointment she knew she would see in his eyes.

Dane shook her head, second-guessing herself. Why had she come here? What did she hope to find in the mountains and valleys of her past? She had been smothered here. She had been miserable. She hadn't been able to wait until she could graduate and get as far away as possible. She had spent years wanting to leave and never look back, and that had been exactly what she had done.

Doubt grew in her mind until it was hard to think. She sat at a stop sign, staring down the road that led to her father's house. Her heart raced as her anxiety grew. What was she so afraid of? Her father wasn't a bad man. She wanted to believe they could find a way to talk to each other. She drove to the house and parked along the road. It was just as she remembered. The trees had grown, marking the passage of time, but everything else was the same as she remembered.

The front door opened, and a woman walked outside. Her red hair instantly had Dane's blood boiling. Her stepmother was only seven years older than her. She had made Dane's life a living hell since she was fourteen years old. She could hear her stepmother's condescending voice pointing out a myriad of things she had done wrong, making sure to guilt Dane so she wouldn't complain to her father.

Dane watched the woman as she got into her Mercedes. Her stepmother drove past without even a glance at her. Dane ground her teeth and gripped the steering wheel, fighting the urge to ram the Jeep into the side of the car. The moment passed, and she let out a long slow breath. Whatever she was looking for, she wasn't going to find it here. She had nothing to say to her stepmother. She only wanted to see her father.

Dane scrolled through her phone, locating her father's office number in her contacts. She took a deep breath and dialed.

"Foster Investments, how can I help you?" a woman's lilting voice sang through the phone.

Dane took a deep breath. "I would like to speak with David Foster, please."

"I'm sorry, Mr. Foster is out of the office right now. May I ask who's calling? I would be happy to pass on a message."

Disappointment hit Dane like a punch to the gut. She contemplated leaving a message but didn't know what to say. *Hi, Dad. It's only been five years since my last visit, but I thought we'd have lunch. Call me.* "No, thank you. I'll try again another time."

She ended the call, wondering if this was all a sign she should just move on. What did she really expect? Part of her wanted to tell her father the truth about everything, needing his reassurance that despite everything, she would be okay. She returned to her contacts and called her father's cell.

"Dane?" Her father's voice sounded uncertain and held a hint of surprise.

"Hi, David. Yeah, it's me."

"What's wrong?"

Dane took a deep breath. "Nothing. I'm in town for a couple of days. I hoped we could get together for lunch or something and catch up. There are some things I wanted to talk to you about."

"You're in town?" She heard a shuffling sound as if he had shifted the phone between his ear and shoulder as a strangely mechanical voice spoke in the background. She imagined him checking his watch. "Are you working on a story here?"

"Yeah, just for a couple of days, like I said, but it's not work."

There was more rustling on the line. "Not work. Is something wrong?"

"No. I just wanted to talk. It's been a while."

"I really wish I'd known you were coming. This is not a good time. I'm at the airport and my flight leaves in twenty minutes. I won't be back until late next week." He hesitated. "Maybe we could make some time then. Will you still be around?"

Dane closed her eyes. She shook her head. He'd likely been at the airport when she'd landed. If she'd bothered to call, she could have made the connection there. "I don't know. I wasn't planning on it."

She heard more rustling on the line. "Like I said, this is a bad time. What did you want to talk about?"

Dane didn't want to get into it over the phone and her questions couldn't be answered in just a few rushed minutes. "Some things have happened." She stopped herself. "I want to ask you some things about Mom."

His sigh was thick. Even through the phone she could hear his disapproval. "What now?"

"I just need some answers, David."

"Look, I have to board the plane. I don't have time to get into this."

"I guess I'll just have to find out for myself," Dane snapped, unable to hide her frustration. Since her mother's death, David had been unwilling to talk about her. He always had an excuse not to answer Dane's questions.

"Leave it alone, Dane. I don't know what else you think there is to know. Don't go looking for trouble."

"Trouble? I just want to know about my family."

"Look. We can talk about this another time. I have to go."

Dane gritted her teeth. "Yeah, it was good talking to you." She ended the call before he could respond. She blew out a frustrated breath. There was no point sticking around town. She'd promised Michelle they would see the mountains. Now was as good a time as any.

She put the Jeep in gear and drove away. She had no idea where she was going, but traveling and drinking seemed to be the only things she had going for her these days. She decided to head north. She had always wanted to see the place where her mother had come from. Maybe she'd find some of the answers at the beginning.

Dane had been driving for two hours. Fatigue and restlessness were getting the better of her. She hadn't seen much more than mountains, run-down houses, and fields of hay for the past thirty miles or so. An old sign by the side of the road caught her attention as she neared the Kentucky state line. The sign was simple and to the point: the Cozy Corner Bar. Cold beer and cheap cigarettes. She doubted she would have many more chances to stop along the rural stretch of road. She guessed this place would be as good a place as she would get.

The building was small. It looked more like an old garage than a bar, but Dane decided to take a chance. She was thirsty and hungry and needed to stretch her legs. She circled the lot. All but two cars were parked in the back. She guessed this was the kind of place most people didn't want to have their car seen from the road.

Dane parked in back and pulled an old cap from her duffel. As she stepped out onto the gravel parking lot, she scuffed her boots through the dirt to dull their polish. At least her jeans were worn and rough after too many miles through too many countries. She threw her bag over her shoulder, not bothering to lock the Jeep. Anything she wanted to keep, she'd take with her. There was no point in asking a thief to cut the top of the Jeep to take a look around.

The moment she stepped into the bar she knew her efforts to fit in had been pointless. She stood out like a pink flamingo at a rodeo. Every eye in the room followed her across the bar, an ominous silence following in her wake.

She took a seat at the end of the bar and turned on her stool so that her back was against the wall. She dropped her duffel on the floor at her feet along with her camera bag. She rolled her eyes. The bags were a dead giveaway that she didn't belong in this place. Oh, well, it could be worse. At least she spoke the same language this time.

A tall woman with auburn hair pulled through the back of a Tennessee baseball cap greeted Dane. She had winter blue eyes, tan skin, and a look that said she was in charge.

"What'll it be?" she asked, as if this was a test.

Dane glanced around the room. "Bud Light," she said eyeing the bottle of Tennessee Whiskey on the wall just behind the woman's head. Her mouth watered. She could almost taste the amber liquid on her tongue. But that was a demon she couldn't afford to let out of the bottle tonight.

"Anything else?" the woman asked.

Dane swallowed. "No. That's good for now, unless you're available later."

The woman looked Dane up and down. When their eyes met again, Dane could see the distrust as clear as shutters being drawn over fragile windows. Dane felt a shiver climb up her spine. The woman didn't say anything in response, but her look was enough to stop Dane cold in her tracks. This might have been a bad idea.

Dane glanced back at the bottle of whiskey that seemed to whisper to her across the counter. Yeah, this was definitely a bad idea.

Dane sipped her beer and watched the bartender, letting her imagination conjure images of her long lean body, her tan skin and muscle telling the story of hard work and quiet passion.

She jumped when a young man theatrically plopped down on the barstool beside her.

"Hey, Emma," he said to the bartender with a wide innocent smile.

She smiled back at him. "Hey, kid. You hungry?"

"Yep. How about a beer and a bologna sandwich?"

"Pimento cheese and pickles?" she asked.

His smile widened. "Yep."

"Be right back," she said before disappearing around the corner into the kitchen.

He drummed his fingers on the counter keeping time with the music playing from an old jukebox in the corner. He sang along to the tune, his head bobbing gently.

Dane smiled. She was amused by the young man. He seemed untouched by the evils of the world. He still carried the joy of a child. Dane tapped his shoulder. "Hey, you know her?" Dane asked, nodding behind the bar to where the woman had just been.

The young man smiled. "Of course. Emma's my sister."

Dane raised an eyebrow. "Really? What's your name?"

"Curtis," he answered as if she should already know who he was.

Dane raised her beer in salute. "I'm Dane. Dane Foster."

Curtis grinned.

Dane looked up as Emma came around the corner and placed a plate of food and a beer in front of Curtis. She studied the two, trying to put the pieces together. There was a huge age gap between them, and Dane wondered if Emma was really the young man's sister.

"What have you been up to today, Curtis?" Emma asked, wiping her hands on a bar towel.

He shrugged. "Nothin' much," he said through a mouthful of sandwich. "I went down to the river with a couple of the guys. There's an old bus parked down there near Parson's Creek. We nosed around there for a while, but we never saw nobody around."

Emma leaned over the bar. "You didn't bother anything, did you?" She'd dropped her voice, but Dane could hear the urgency in her tone. "You know better than to mess with other people's things."

Curtis shook his head. "We didn't do nothin'. Promise. We was just lookin'."

Emma relaxed a little. "Okay, I believe you, but don't go back around there, okay. I don't want those boys getting you into trouble."

Curtis smiled. "You worry too much. I ain't doing nothin' wrong."

Emma placed her hand over his. "I know, sweetie. Just promise me you won't go back there again."

"All right, I won't go," Curtis agreed, sounding disappointed.

"Thank you." Emma pointed to the empty plate. "Want another one?"

Curtis smiled again. "Can I have onions this time?"

Emma rolled her eyes and disappeared into the kitchen again.

Dane was amused by the whole interaction. "Sounds like your sister looks out for you quite a bit."

Curtis turned to Dane, his eyes bright and cheery. "Emma's always there for me."

"Why is she so worried?"

"Aw, she's always afraid I'll get into trouble. She doesn't like a lot of my friends. They get into a lot of trouble sometimes."

"What kind of trouble?" Dane asked, curiosity getting the better of her.

Emma appeared with another sandwich for Curtis before he could answer. Emma glared at Dane. It seemed her distrust wasn't just reserved for Curtis's friends.

Dane held up her empty bottle. "Could I have another, and how about one of those sandwiches?"

Emma held Dane's gaze without blinking. "Anything else?"

"No, ma'am. I believe that's all for now."

Dane talked with Curtis until Emma called for last call at midnight, learning all about his love for bologna sandwiches, peach cobbler, and riding through the mountain trails. She learned he and Emma lived together and she looked after him, and that his secret wish was to go to Alaska and pan for gold like the miners did in the old Westerns he still liked to watch on Sunday afternoon.

When Emma turned out the neon signs hanging around the room, Dane picked up her bags and paid her bill with cash, making sure to leave a generous tip.

Curtis eyed her duffel. "Where are you goin'?"

Dane shrugged. "I'm not sure. I'll probably just sleep in my Jeep tonight."

Curtis frowned. "You could stay at our place. Emma won't mind. She rents out one of the rooms sometimes when people need a place to stay for a while."

Dane glanced across the bar at Emma. She was stocking the coolers and didn't seem to hear what Curtis had said.

"I don't know. She didn't seem to like me much," Dane said, honestly.

Curtis laughed. "Don't worry, I'll ask her." He leaned over the bar. "Hey, Emma. Dane here doesn't have a place to stay tonight. It's okay that she stays at our place, right?"

Emma looked up, obviously caught off guard by the question. "Curtis, we've talked about you bringing strangers home."

Curtis laughed. "Dane ain't no stranger—she's my friend."

Emma sighed.

Dane lifted a hand and waved Emma off. "I don't want to be a bother. If you could just tell me where I could find the nearest hotel, that will do."

"No way," Curtis protested. "You don't wanna stay there. It's a bad place. You'd be better off sleeping in your Jeep."

Dane wondered what made the hotel so bad but really didn't want to find out. She looked at Emma. "I'd be happy to pay for the room."

Emma sighed again. "Fine, but I don't allow drugs or any other illegal activity in my home. If that's what you're into, you may as well go on to the hotel."

Dane shook her head. "No, ma'am."

Emma stared at Dane, still making up her mind. "Oh, all right. You can stay."

"Yes," Curtis cheered.

"Can I help you finish up here?" Dane asked Emma.

"No, thanks, I'm perfectly capable of doing it myself," Emma snapped.

"I'm sure you are, just thought I'd offer a hand." Dane was determined not to flinch, but Emma had a way of making her feel like she was facing a guard dog who was showing its teeth.

Emma tugged her hair tighter through her ball cap and tucked the loose strands behind her ears. She looked tired, the kind of tired that said she hadn't had enough sleep and had carried that chip on her shoulder for way too long.

"I'd like to help," Dane tried again. "It's the least I can do."

Emma reached into a closet and handed Dane a broom.

Dane smiled, taking the olive branch.

Curtis joined in and they had the place closed up within an hour.

"I'll ride with Dane," Curtis announced as Emma locked up.

Emma pursed her lips in disapproval but didn't say anything. She got into an old black Ford F-150 that looked like it had seen better days. It had rust around the fender wells and patches of Bondo dotted the side of the door and truck bed. By the look of things, there was no wonder why Emma rented out a room when she could. Dane didn't imagine Emma made much money working at the bar.

"Thanks for getting your sister to let me stay tonight," Dane said to Curtis.

"It's no big deal. Don't worry, Emma isn't as scary once you get to know her a little. She takes care of everybody. You'll like the house. My favorite part is the barn. I like to hang out in the hayloft and watch the birds build their nests. Did you know that barn swallows don't land on the ground? They just fly through the air catching mosquitoes and flies and stuff. But they like to live in the barn."

Dane was getting a pretty clear idea why Emma worried so much about Curtis. She imagined it was easy to take advantage of his childlike nature.

"Maybe you can show me the barn tomorrow," she said, hoping he wouldn't want to give her the tour tonight.

"Sure. Hey, that's us up here on the right."

Dane followed Emma's old truck down a long winding dirt and gravel drive. An old farmhouse stood like the petrified bones of an ancient dinosaur. There was a large yard in the front, and the old barn was to the left. Its entry had no doors and looked like a large gaping black mouth swallowing up the night. The whole property was surrounded by trees. Floodlights flashed on as they approached, illuminating the weathered old porch. An empty porch swing swayed gently at one end.

Dane shivered. If she was the paranoid type, she'd imagine she had just stepped into a horror flick. She followed Curtis up to the house. An old dog lay on the porch with his back against the door. The boards of the steps creaked under her feet as she walked up onto the porch.

Emma reached down and touched the old dog to wake him. His fur was mottled, black and brown with patches of yellow. His face and muzzle were completely gray. He looked as if he had been here as long as the house.

Curtis reached down to pet the dog too. "Samson can't hear anymore, so he lies against the door so he knows when we get home."

Dane smiled. "Smart dog."

Emma unlocked the door, glancing back at Dane. "How long will you be staying?"

Dane shrugged. "I don't know. I'm not even sure where I am exactly. I'm trying to find my mother's family. They live around here, I think."

"Well, it's twenty-five a night, or one twenty-five a week. That will include meals if you're here when we eat. Breakfast is at nine, lunch is at one, and dinner is at the bar every night except Monday. I'm closed on Monday, so we eat here at the house at six."

"Okay. I'll just go ahead and pay you for the week, and we can see from there."

Emma gave a single nod in agreement. She pushed the door open and led them into the house.

Dane noticed the smell of lavender in the air the moment they stepped into the room. The place was old, and the furnishings were well worn from years of use, but the place was clean and homey in an old-fashioned way. It was like everything else she'd seen so far. The whole place was like a page out of history.

Emma waved a hand, pointing around the house. "The kitchen is to the right and there's a bathroom at the end of the hall. Your room is upstairs, the third door to the right."

Dane looked up the stairs, counting the doors at the top of the landing.

"I'll show her," Curtis said cheerfully.

"There's another bathroom at the top of the stairs, so you don't have to come all the way down here," Emma continued.

Dane fished her wallet from her back pocket and handed Emma the payment for the room. "I had considered trying to get you to take me home with you, but this isn't exactly what I had in mind. Thank you for letting me stay."

Emma rolled her eyes and took the money. "Don't make me regret it."

Dane frowned as Emma turned and walked into the kitchen. She almost changed her mind about the room. Emma was beautiful, but the cold shoulder had a bite. Dane wasn't happy about staying where she wasn't wanted. She'd had warmer welcomes in third world countries, where people barely had what they needed, let alone something to share.

"You comin'?" Curtis asked, already halfway up the stairs.

Dane looked up at his eager smile. At least Curtis was happy she was there. One night couldn't hurt. "Sure. Lead the way."

❖

Emma closed the door to her room and secured the lock. She never liked having strangers in the house. Why hadn't she just said no? She closed her eyes and sighed. Dane, who ever she was, was trouble. She could feel it. She saw it the moment Dane walked into the bar. She was a stranger here, and strangers in these parts meant they were looking for trouble or bringing trouble. Leave it to Curtis to bring trouble home. Dane certainly didn't fit in here. She wore her hair short, and her clothes looked a little worn, but Emma would bet they were professionally cleaned. The Jeep Dane drove still had dealer tags and didn't quite fit Dane's tailored look. Emma didn't know why Dane was here, but it was clear she didn't belong.

She looked up at the ceiling, listening to the creak of the floorboards as Dane walked overhead. Emma wondered what she was doing. There wasn't much in the house worth stealing, but she doubted Dane would take anything—she had her own money. Dane didn't need the worthless trinkets left behind by their mother. There weren't any pills to find in the medicine cabinets, and no other drugs in the house. But Emma doubted drugs were Dane's game. She was a hard one to figure. Maybe she was a cop. Emma frowned. That could be it. If Dane was a cop, she wouldn't last long here.

Emma tracked the sounds of Dane's movements until she was certain Dane had gone to bed, before kicking off her own boots and clothes and crawling beneath the covers. It had been another long day, and tomorrow would be no different. She'd have to talk to Curtis about Dane. She didn't want him getting too attached or mixed up in whatever Dane was up to.

Dane might talk the talk of a country girl, but she looked like city with a little dirt on her shoes. She was a little too thin, and there were shadows lurking in her eyes. She had a weariness about her that told Emma she was running from something or hiding something. She had been quietly attentive to everyone in the bar, and her confidence kept the predators in their seats, content to stalk her from a distance. If Dane stuck around, that distance wouldn't last long. If she was a cop, she was in for a world of trouble from the locals. No one liked outsiders here, but cops from elsewhere were hated above all. This was the kind of town that didn't trust the government, and even the local cops didn't like to share with strangers.

Emma sighed and burrowed deeper under the covers. It seemed she'd only just closed her eyes when she heard the rooster crow. She squeezed her eyes tight and pulled the quilt over her head. "One more hour," she pleaded. Was just one more hour too much to ask?

The rooster crowed again. "Guess so," she mumbled as she threw back the quilt and pushed her legs over the edge of the bed. She sat there for a moment, putting off the day. A familiar smell began to fill the room. She frowned. Coffee?

Emma pushed her feet into her slippers and pulled on her father's old robe. She stopped at the dresser and ran a brush through her hair before making a quick trip to the bathroom.

Dane sat at the kitchen table sipping a cup of coffee. The shadows beneath her eyes said she hadn't slept much, and her hair stuck up slightly on one side. She wore a black T-shirt and loose-fitting black sleep pants.

"Good morning. I hope you don't mind that I made the coffee," Dane said as Emma walked into the room.

Emma poured her coffee and took a seat across from Dane. Dane was staring at her. "What?" Emma asked.

Dane shrugged. "Nothing. Just getting an idea what it would be like to wake up with you in the morning."

Emma scowled. "Are you always this obnoxious?"

Dane gave a look of mock surprise. "Come on, the coffee isn't that bad."

Emma rolled her eyes. "Look, you can rent the room, but that's all you get. So give it up. I get enough of those stupid pickup lines at the bar."

Dane grinned. "I bet." She nodded to Emma's cup. "How about more coffee then?" She stood and brought the carafe to the table, filling Emma's cup and then her own.

Emma watched Dane, her eyes riveted to the scars marring Dane's left hand, snaking up her arm in a mass of twisted flesh as if the skin had been melted. She wondered what had happened to cause the burns. She stifled the urge to reach out and touch Dane's arm, as if the scars on her skin would give up Dane's secrets.

She looked away when Dane sat the carafe on the table. She scolded herself for letting curiosity get the best of her. She sipped her coffee, searching for something to cover for her wandering thoughts. She wasn't used to having anyone in the kitchen, and no one ever bothered to make coffee. "Thank you." She blew across the steaming brew, studying Dane. She met Dane's gaze, deciding on a direct approach. "Why are you here?"

Dane looked confused by the question.

"Jellico is a small place. We don't have a lot to offer people here. There are no jobs, and there's nothing to do here aside from hunting, fishing, driving around the woods, and drinking. It's not exactly a vacation hub if you know what I mean."

Dane shrugged. "I don't know the answer exactly. My mother and her family were from around here. She died when I was young. I've been traveling for a while. I needed a change. I thought it would be nice to learn more about her, where she was from, what her family was like. I was tired and just happened to stop at your bar. End of story."

Emma wasn't convinced. Dane might have stopped here by chance, and maybe her story was true, but there was more—she could see it in Dane's eyes as clear as her own reflection in the still waters of the pond. "A change from what? What are you running from?"

Dane shook her head. "Haven't you ever wanted to push the pause button on your life and take a minute to find out what else is out there, what you're missing?"

Emma pushed away from the table, avoiding the question. "Whatever you're up to, leave Curtis out of it. He's a good kid. He's been through a lot and he doesn't need to be drawn into whatever trouble you're in."

Dane met Emma's gaze. "I'm not here to hurt anyone. I just needed a break from my life for a while. If you don't want me here, I'll go."

Emma considered telling Dane to leave, but she really needed the money for the room. And if Dane was going to be in the area, Curtis would find her anyway.

"You don't have to leave. I'm just asking you not to drag my family into any trouble. There's enough of that going around already."

"What kind of trouble?"

Emma sipped her coffee. "Never mind that."

Footsteps on the stairs alerted them that Curtis was up. He bounded into the room like a child on Christmas morning.

"Hey, Dane, are you ready to see the barn?" he said as soon as his head was inside the door.

"Slow down, mister, since when do you get up this early?" Emma asked as he leaned down and kissed her cheek.

Curtis grinned. "I don't know. I just woke up."

"Well, since you're up, you can go gather the eggs and feed the chickens."

"Aw," Curtis whined.

"Don't give me lip, or I'll have you do the dishes too."

Curtis grabbed a Dr Pepper from the fridge. "Come on Dane, let's get out of here before she gets ugly."

Dane laughed. "Give me a minute to change. I'll meet you outside." She drained her coffee and rinsed her cup. She stopped at the door before leaving. "Thanks for letting me stay."

Emma nodded, looking at Dane over the rim of her cup.

A few minutes later she heard the screen door close and looked out the window to see Dane walking across the lawn toward the barn. Curtis met her at the gate of the chicken coop, his hands moving as fast as his mouth as he talked. She smiled. He was such a little kid sometimes. He didn't really have friends. Most people were cruel to him or used him in some way. He had always been a happy kid, but Emma knew he was lonely and just wanted to be liked.

Dane was playful and patient with Curtis, but Emma didn't trust her. She couldn't afford to trust.

Dane was eager to find out what she could about her mother. She had done a quick search online and had even looked through the old phone book lying next to the phone on the table in the living room. She had tracked down what she could on the ancestry sites and was beginning to wonder if any of her family had survived. She had some old records, but no current addresses. Most of the names she located were deceased.

"Hey, Curtis, do you know of anyone around here with the last name Stewart?"

Curtis thought for a moment. "Well, I went to school with Michael Stewart and his sister Stacey. They live in Coalfield now."

"Coalfield." Dane wasn't familiar with the area and had never heard of the place. "How far is that from here?"

Curtis shrugged. "Not far, an hour or so, maybe more. Something like that."

"What about their family? Do you know anything about them?"

"They used to live in Rugby, but I don't know where."

This wasn't the answer she had hoped for, but at least she knew there were Stewarts in the area. Maybe they were her relatives.

"I have a buddy I go see sometimes in Rugby. If you want to go with me, we could ask him if he knows where we could find 'em."

"Sure," Dane answered. "Can you call him?"

Curtis shook his head. "I'll get in touch with him. I'll see if he's around."

Dane wanted to push, but Curtis had his way of doing things. She had to do this his way. Maybe she'd turn up something soon. She planned on going to county records as soon as they opened on Monday morning.

"So, you're lookin' for your momma?" Curtis asked.

Dane shook her head. "No, her family."

"Why don't you just ask her?"

Dane looked at Curtis, surprised by the question. "She died when I was young. I barely remember the stories she used to tell me about growing up around here."

"My momma died too. I miss her sometimes." Curtis looked up at Dane and smiled. "But now I have Emma." He seemed to think about things for a while before asking his next question. "Is your daddy dead too?"

Dane frowned, remembering the way her father always avoided her questions about her mother. It was like he wanted to forget her. "No. He's alive, but he won't talk to me about her."

"Yeah, I get it. Emma gets real sad when I talk about Momma and Daddy too. After Daddy died, Momma got real sad for a long time and she died too. Emma said Momma loved Daddy so much she just couldn't live without him." He was quiet for a moment. "Do you think that's true? Can somebody love someone that much?"

Dane looked out over the farm from their perch in the hayloft. She thought of Michelle. They had been through a lot together. Michelle had been her best friend, the one person she could go to with anything. Michelle was the one person who always put up with her shit. Other than her mother, Michelle had been the only person she had ever loved. But here she was, alive and well, but Michelle wasn't. Her parents were out of the question. Her father had remarried only months after her mother's death.

"I don't know, Curtis. I've never seen that before, but that doesn't mean it isn't true."

"Yeah, I guess." Curtis stood and dusted himself off. "Want to drive me into town? I have somethin' I have to do today."

Dane shrugged, surprised yet relieved by the change of subject. "Sure."

Curtis smiled. "Cool. I have to get somethin' first. I'll be right back."

Dane watched Curtis come out of the barn below and move to an old storm shelter or cellar. She shook her head. Curtis was an odd kid, but she liked him. She stood and dusted herself off. She didn't mind driving him around. It would give her a chance to get to know her way around, and maybe she could ask some of the locals about her mother. If she was with Curtis, maybe someone would be willing to talk to her.

Town turned out to be a row of small stores and a couple of fast-food joints. They stopped at a run-down mobile home with bags of trash piled outside the front door. An old Toyota Corolla sat on cinder blocks. The wheels and engine were missing, and the hood was propped up against the side of the house. A few chickens ran loose in the yard, and a brown dog tied to a tree next to the house barked as they pulled into the drive. An orange cat sat on the roof of the car casually licking its paw.

Curtis knocked on the door and waited. A gaunt looking young man with pale skin answered the door. His black hair looked like it had been pasted to his scalp with motor oil. He blinked against the sunlight as he peered down at Curtis.

"Hey, man," Curtis said cheerfully.

The man rubbed his face with his hand. "Where the hell have you been, Curtis? I expected you yesterday."

Curtis shrugged. "I was busy."

The guy looked at Dane. "Who's this?"

"That's my friend Dane. She's stayin' with us for a while."

"She looks like a narc."

Curtis laughed. "Naw, Dane's cool."

"You better be right," the thin man warned as he opened the door and walked away.

Dane took this as an invitation to enter and followed Curtis inside. The smell was the first thing to hit her. She cleared her throat and tried to get a grip, but the smell of body odor, vomit, and something she couldn't quite place was assaulting. Her eyes watered.

Curtis sat next to the man on the couch. Dane wasn't sure she wanted to touch anything in the room and chose a plain wooden chair after clearing away discarded sales circulars.

"You have my shit?" the man asked Curtis.

Curtis pulled a small bag out of his pocket and handed it over. The man opened the bag and smelled inside before handing Curtis money.

Dane couldn't believe what was happening. She was sitting in the middle of a drug deal. She was going to kill Curtis.

"Hey, do you know where Michael Stewart's staying?" Curtis asked.

The man frowned. "I haven't seen him since school. Who wants to know?"

Curtis nodded to Dane. "Dane's looking for the Stewarts."

The man turned his gaze back to Dane. He looked distrustful as he scrutinized her more closely. "What's it to you? Are you a fucking cop?"

Dane cleared her throat again, trying not to gag from the filth she felt attaching itself to her clothes. "No. I'm not a cop. I'm sorry, I didn't catch your name."

"Mark," he snapped.

Dane went on as if she wasn't about to climb out of her skin. "I have family around here I'm trying to find."

"Mark!" a woman called from another room.

"What?" he answered.

"Where are my fucking cigarettes?"

"How the hell would I know?"

Mark turned back to Dane, the flash of anger in his eyes and the bite in his voice telling her he was quickly losing his patience. "Mike went to the pen last year. It sounds like he'll be there awhile."

Dane frowned. This wasn't what she wanted to hear.

"Mark?" the woman called again.

"Look, man, this isn't a good time. You guys need to go."

Dane stood and turned to leave. The man grabbed Curtis by the arm. "This better not be a problem, Curtis. And don't be late next time."

"It's cool, Mark. Don't worry."

Dane slammed the door to the Jeep. "What the hell was that?" she asked, her voice raised. "What the fuck are you thinking, taking me to a damn drug deal?"

Curtis laughed. "It's no big deal, Dane. It was just a little weed. Everybody around here does it."

"Not me. Got it? Not me."

"Fine. I just thought you wanted to find your family. Mark knows everybody. I thought he could help."

Dane opened the window, hoping the breeze would blow out some of the stench clinging to her skin and clothes. She didn't think Curtis had meant any harm, and it was hard to stay mad at him for long. "Look, man, you've got to be careful doing that shit. It's illegal in Tennessee. You could go to jail. And thanks to you, I could have too."

"You sound like Emma. But really, it's no big deal. Besides, I have to do it sometimes."

"Why? Why would you have to? Do you need money or something?"

"Naw. It's nothin' like that. Emma gives me money every week, and I get a check from the government."

Dane was frustrated. "Then what do you mean, you have to do it?"

Curtis looked uncomfortable. "I'm not supposed to talk about it to nobody."

"Curtis, are you in some kind of trouble?"

"No. I just have to. That's all."

Dane could see this wasn't going anywhere. "Look, Curtis, if you're in trouble, you can tell me. I'm your friend, remember? Friends talk about things. They tell each other secrets."

Curtis wouldn't answer.

"All right, at least promise me you won't involve me in any more of your drops or deals or whatever you call it."

Curtis bowed his head. "I'm sorry I made you mad."

"I'm not mad, Curtis. I was scared."

He nodded. "Sorry. I just wanted to help."

"I know. Thanks for that part," Dane said, relenting. She patted Curtis on the back, making their amends.

The familiar smile returned to his face and Dane's heart softened. Curtis was a good kid, but he had no idea what he was doing.

"I'm hungry," Curtis announced.

Dane smiled. "Good, I'm thirsty. Let's go see how Emma's day is going."

Dane took a seat at the bar. There was only a handful of people mingling about, which made the room seem too quiet. Emma smiled at Curtis as he took the stool beside Dane.

"What's up, kid?"

Curtis shrugged. "Not much. We've just been ridin' around. Can I have a beer?"

Emma looked at Dane. "And you?"

Dane got the feeling Emma wanted to know more than her drink order. The distrust in her eyes was as thick as the rust on her truck. Emma wore the same baseball cap she'd had on the day before, her hair pulled back, exposing the gentle curve of her face and the strong set of her jaw. Despite Emma's earlier warnings, she couldn't help but notice how beautiful Emma was. She bit back the suggestive remark that was on the tip of her tongue.

"Bud Light and a shot of Jack."

The storm clouds in Emma's eyes darkened. She placed two beers on the counter and poured the whiskey. "It's a little early for the hard stuff, isn't it?"

"Not by my watch. What's the point in waiting?"

Emma slid the glass in front of Dane. "Suit yourself."

Dane disposed of the whiskey with one swift toss. She shook her head as the firewater burned its way through her system. The cold beer chased the fire to the pit of her stomach, freezing out the last embers of memory.

"It's too quiet in here," Dane said on her way to the old jukebox in the corner. The player was a relic. As the music filtered through the room, Dane inhaled the smell of stale beer that mingled with the cleaner Emma used on the bar. Like always Dane surrendered to the isolation that came from being a stranger. Most people would find it lonely, but she found comfort in the disconnect. Being an outsider meant she could see the world as it was without being tainted by expectation or disappointment.

She turned as a soft hand touched her back. A young woman with hair the color of midnight stepped beside her.

"Hi."

"Hello," Dane answered.

"You mind?" The girl pressed a couple of numbers on the keypad. "I love to dance to this song."

Dane straightened. "By all means."

The woman took Dane's beer from her hand and took a drink. "I haven't seen you in here before."

"Nope," Dane replied, amused by the woman's daring.

The woman swayed her hips, drawing Dane's gaze to the exposed skin of her midriff. A gold bar pierced the skin of her belly button. She looped her thumb into the waistband of Dane's jeans and gave her an inviting tug.

"Want to buy me a drink?"

Dane glanced around the room, taking in the faces as if reading signs on the wall. A man and woman were making out at the back table. Two old guys played cards in the corner. A man in dark jeans and black cowboy boots sat at the end of the bar nursing a beer. Dane studied him. He was in the perfect position to see her through his peripheral. His left foot was on the floor turned slightly in her direction. She shifted her gaze to Curtis at the end of the bar chatting to Emma. Emma glanced nervously at Dane, meeting her gaze with a slight shake of her head.

Dane wondered if Emma was warning her or just disapproving. Either way she wasn't in the mood to play this game.

"Sorry, doll. I already have a date tonight."

The woman stuck her bottom lip out in a pout. "Come on, just a little dance won't hurt."

Dane took a step back. "Maybe your boyfriend over there will take you for a spin."

The woman straightened.

"Enjoy the drink and the music. But like I said, I already have a date tonight."

Dane walked back to the bar, watching Emma's eyes as she turned her back on the girl. Emma hadn't taken her gaze off the man at the end of the bar. Her hand rested on the small bat she kept by the cash register.

The woman turned to the jukebox, swaying her hips from side to side. Dane shook her head. She nodded to Emma and tapped the bar. "Another round if you don't mind."

"How did you know?" Emma asked.

Dane took a drink of the beer. "Oldest trick in the book. I'm not that drunk or that stupid."

Emma smiled.

"How often do they come in here?" Dane asked.

"They make the rounds. I see them in here a couple of times a month."

Curtis turned to see what the fuss was about. He grinned. "Dang, Dane, how'd you say no to that?"

Dane slapped Curtis on the back. "Not my type, buddy." She turned to Emma. "But how about you, Emma, want to dance?"

Emma shook her head. "I'm not that drunk or that stupid." She picked up the empty bottles and walked away.

Curtis laughed.

"What?" Dane asked with a smirk.

"Nothin'."

Dane lifted her drink to her lips as she cut her eyes at Curtis.

He laughed harder.

"Cut it out," Dane warned, giving him a playful shove with her shoulder.

CHAPTER TWO

Dane sat in the hayloft watching the farm wake up. She was restless and hadn't been able to sleep. She pinched the bridge of her nose between her thumb and forefinger, trying to push back the headache. No matter how tired she was or how much she drank, the dreams always came. She wondered if she was doomed to relive that day over and over for the rest of her life.

The rooster crowed, signaling the time for the day to begin. It was a good thing she was an early riser. It wasn't long before she saw Emma come out of the house to begin the morning chores. She started with feeding the chickens, and then she gathered the eggs, fed the pig in the pen beside the barn, and spent some time working in the garden. She used an old-fashioned blade to cut back overgrown weeds around the edge of the fence. She used a back and forth swing of the blade that sliced through the growth like a scythe in both directions of the swing. Grass and weeds were sliced and tossed aside, leaving a rough but effective cut. Dane was getting tired just watching her. Did she ever take a break?

Emma picked up an ax from the shed and headed for the back of the house. The dull thud of the ax sounded moments later. Dane knew Emma still hadn't warmed to her much and didn't have much to say to her, but if she was going to stay here, she needed to start pulling her weight. The money she gave Emma wouldn't go far, and she was drinking her coffee and eating her food.

Dane decided it was time to intervene. She rounded the corner of the house just in time to see a dead pine tree fall away from the other corner of the house. The tree bounced once when it hit the ground, and branches snapped under the weight of the impact. The top of the tree was so brittle it broke into three pieces along the trunk. Dane jumped at the thundering sound of splintering wood.

Emma leaned on the ax handle as she wiped sweat from her brow. Her skin glistened in the morning sun as the light danced across the perspiration coating her neck and chest. Dane's heart fluttered, and she felt a flash of warmth rush across her skin.

She gathered herself and walked toward Emma.

"Hey," she said, not wanting to startle her. "Good job with that. Looks like it was ready to take out part of the house."

Emma looked up as Dane approached. "You're right. I should have done this a long time ago. I got lucky this time." She took the ax and began chopping off branches along the trunk of the tree.

"Would you like some help?"

Emma stopped and handed the ax to Dane. "Suit yourself."

Dane took the handle, placing her hand over Emma's, trapping her fingers. "I'd be happy to help out with things around here. It would be good for me to stay busy, and I'd like to help. Maybe if you didn't have to do everything around here you could get a little rest, relax a little."

Emma pulled her hand away. "I can take care of myself. If you want to help, then help, but don't expect any favors."

"Ouch," Dane said. "That isn't what I meant. I'm just trying to help. I don't want anything from you, Emma." That wasn't exactly true. Emma was beautiful. Dane would have to be crazy not to notice her.

Emma's cheeks and neck turned red. Dane braced herself for the next round, expecting Emma to explode.

Emma squared her shoulders, steadying herself. "I'm sorry. I know I've been rude to you, but all I have is Curtis and this farm and that bar. I've lost everything and everyone else. I can't afford to lose this too."

Dane took a step closer to Emma. "I'm not the bad guy. I'm not going to hurt you."

"I hope you're right, city girl. I hope you're right." Emma turned and walked away, leaving Dane staring after her. What did Emma mean about losing everything and everyone? Was she talking about her parents? Why was she so afraid?"

Frustrated, Dane turned back to the tree and sank the ax into a branch. She kept swinging the ax as she tried to work through the conflict with Emma. Her thoughts twisted and took her back to another place. The sun was hot on her skin and sweat ran down her spine.

She was running late again. As expected, Michelle was pissed at her. "Just give me five minutes and I'll meet you downstairs at the car," Dane pleaded.

"Why do you always do this? It isn't just your ass on the line, Dane—I need this job. I'm part of this team too."

Dane grabbed Michelle's arm. "I'm sorry, I screwed up, okay. It won't happen again."

Michelle shook her head. "Get your own ride this time. I've got to go."

"Michelle," Dane called as her best friend walked away, pushing through the hotel doors without looking back. She watched Michelle get into the car waiting at the curb. She glanced up at Dane, her eyes full of disappointment, then closed the door. An instant later a red ball of fire exploded in front of Dane. The glass front of the hotel shattered into a million flying shards of shrapnel slicing its way through everything in its path.

Dane hit the floor as glass and shards of metal and mortar rained down on her.

"Dane? Dane, are you okay?"

Dane frowned. Someone kept saying her name. Her head hurt. She reached up and pressed her hand to her forehead.

"Shit, Dane, answer me."

Dane blinked. Emma's blue eyes looked back at her with fear and concern. Dane frowned. "What happened?"

"Thank God. I thought you'd killed yourself," Emma said with a heavy sigh.

"Why would I do that?" Dane was having a hard time figuring this out. One moment she was cutting a tree, the next she was getting blown up.

"You can't just throw an ax around like that. You have to watch what you're doing. You smashed through one of the dead branches and it flew back and hit you in the head." Emma grimaced. "That's one heck of a goose egg you've got there. That's going to hurt for a while."

Dane was mesmerized by Emma's voice and the way she looked at her. She wanted Emma to keep talking so she would stay with her a little longer.

"You have pretty lips," Dane mumbled.

Emma frowned. "What?"

"Tell me another story. I like your stories."

Emma groaned. "Shit. This can't be good." She tugged Dane's arm around her shoulder and helped her to her feet. "I think you have a concussion. We need to get you inside."

Once inside Emma had Dane lie down on the sofa. "Stay here. I'll get some ice."

Dane sluggishly reached for Emma, not wanting her to leave.

"Here, hold this on your head."

"Ouch," Dane complained as the ice pressed into the wound. "It was all my fault. I'm sorry I was late. I should have been with you."

Emma seemed confused. "Who are you talking to, sweetie?"

Dane frowned but wouldn't answer, still having trouble keeping up with what was happening.

"I'm going to call an ambulance. You need to see a doctor."

Dane pushed Emma away. "No. No hospital."

"Dane, you hit your head really hard. You're not making much sense right now. I need to have you looked at. This is serious."

"No hospital," Dane insisted, trying to get up.

Emma pushed Dane back down onto the sofa and sighed. "Okay, let me make a phone call. Just be still for now." She had to get a grip. Panic was making her irrational. Her heart thundered a rapid beat in her ears, and all she wanted to do was hold her hand against Dane's chest to feel the steady beat of her heart, reassuring and strong. Emma was scared. She had seen the limb snap back, hitting Dane in the head. Dane crumpled like a rag doll tossed to the ground. Dane was unconscious when she reached her. She had thought Dane was dead.

Emma reached for the phone, returning to her seat next to Dane the instant she had the cordless in her hand. Fear clutched her like a hand closing around her throat during the few seconds it took to retrieve the phone. Dane was lucky to be alive. Emma pressed her hand to Dane's neck, feeling the strong steady pulse beneath her fingertips. She swallowed hard, feeling her fear loosen its grip. She took a deep relieved breath. She cupped Dane's cheek in her hand, brushing her thumb lightly against Dane's cheek. Dane's skin was silky smooth and warm against her palm.

Emma hung up the phone just as Curtis bounded into the room.

"Dang, Emma, what did you do to Dane?"

Emma glared at him. "I didn't do anything to her. She was cutting a branch off a dead tree and it snapped back and hit her in the head."

Curtis laughed. "Don't worry, Dane, that's happened to me before too. And don't worry about it when she yells at you. She just gets scared."

"I didn't yell at her," Emma protested, her frustration getting the better of her. "You're not helping, Curtis."

Dane was quiet.

"How are you feeling," Emma asked, kneeling on the floor beside her, checking the knot on her head.

Dane moved the ice pack. "I feel like someone hit me in the head with a baseball bat."

Emma was relieved. This sounded more like Dane. "Do you know where you are?"

"I'm in your house."

"Well, you sound better, at least. You were a little confused earlier. Will you go to the hospital now?"

Dane put the ice back on her head. "I don't do hospitals. People tend to die there."

Emma rolled her eyes. "You need to have your head checked."

Dane laughed. "Believe it or not, you're not the first person to tell me that."

Curtis laughed.

"This is serious," Emma protested.

Dane reached for Emma's hand, gripping her fingers in hers. "I know what a concussion feels like, and I'm sure you're right. But I'll be fine. If my headache gets worse or the confusion returns, I'll go to the hospital. But right now, there's no need to waste a day to have a doctor tell me the same thing."

Emma was getting angry. And she didn't want to think of the tingling sensation rippling through her hand where Dane's fingers were laced with hers. "I can see I'm wasting my breath." She turned to Curtis. "Watch her while I go get ready for work. Do not let her go to sleep."

"All right," Curtis agreed.

Dane watched Emma storm out of the room. "What's her problem?"

Curtis shrugged. "She's been a little sensitive about stuff like this since Momma and Daddy died."

Dane considered the information. "I know you said your mother died of a broken heart, but what happened to your father?"

"A bad man shot him."

Dane pushed up onto her elbows. "Who shot him?"

Curtis shrugged. "Nobody knows. Emma didn't live here then. She lived somewhere in the city. She came home to help Momma for a while, but then Momma died too. I was still kind of little. I don't remember much about it."

Holy shit. No wonder Emma didn't trust anyone. Someone murdered her father and ripped her family apart. She'd given her whole life to this place.

Curtis continued talking. "Erin came around for a while, but she didn't like it here much."

"Who's Erin?"

"That was Emma's girlfriend. She stopped coming around after Momma died. Emma got real sad after that. It's just been me and Emma ever since."

Dane had a good idea what had happened. "Wow, I guess I'd be angry too."

❖

Dane spent part of the day going over county records and making phone calls, but her head hurt so bad she couldn't read anymore, and no one would tell her anything over the phone. She was pretty sure she'd found a lead and was eager to check it out. She decided to have Curtis drive her around a while. If he was with her, people were a little more receptive to her questions.

She couldn't stand the thought of just sitting around the house all day. At least driving would help her learn her way around better. She had town mastered, that was no big deal, but the smaller side roads twisted and wound through the mountains like a labyrinth. Just in the time she'd spent with Curtis, she'd realized many of the roads he'd used were not on her map. They were old logging roads or Jeep trails people had cut through the mountains as they cut timber.

Around here it wasn't uncommon to see a family of six go up the road on an ATV on their way to church. They might not own a car, but a four-wheeler or a side-by-side ATV were part of their way of life and gave them access to places that were otherwise inaccessible except on foot. Dane had lucked out when she bought her Jeep. It was the perfect vehicle for what she needed to do here.

Dane went to the house, but Curtis wasn't there. Her next stop was the bar. It was early, so the bar wasn't busy yet. Just a few regulars sat around playing cards and watching a baseball game.

"Hey," Dane said to Emma as she walked up to the bar. "Is Curtis around?"

Emma shook her head. "I thought he was with you. He's supposed to be watching you today. How's your head?"

"It still hurts a little, but it's okay. Curtis didn't want to go to the courthouse with me, so he bailed. I thought he'd be home when I got back, but he wasn't at the house."

"He hasn't been around today. There's no telling what he's up to. What do you need him for anyway?"

"I think I found some information about my family. There's a place I wanted to look at in Smoky Junction, but I don't know if I can find it on my own."

Emma frowned. "Be careful around there. People won't like you poking around. Don't turn around in anyone's driveway or you might be met with a shotgun in your face. The Junction is a tight community. Most of those folks are related to each other and they don't like strangers coming around."

"Ha," Dane laughed. "How is that any different than around here?"

"Trust me. We're friendly compared to those people."

Dane wasn't laughing anymore. She had the feeling Emma was dead serious. "I don't really need to talk to anyone, not yet anyway. There's an old family cemetery up there that may give me some clues. I can't believe it's been so hard to get answers about this. I thought there would be more records at the courthouse."

Emma sighed. "They've been trying to update the records for the past couple of years. Since they built the new justice center, anyway. People complain all the time that things are not right, that things have been lost, or entered wrong. You may do better going through the old archives, if you can get them to let you have access."

Dane bristled. "Those are public records—they have to give me access."

Emma shrugged. "They may not say no, but they may have a good story that keeps you out. Things work a lot different around here, big city, and you're going to have to learn that if you plan on sticking around."

Dane felt her resolve slip. Every turn she made seemed to put her up against a roadblock. Her shoulders slumped. "I need to find them. I need to know about my mother's family. I need to know there's something different for me."

Emma frowned. "What do you mean?"

Dane looked away. "I've been around the world. I've done a lot of things and met a lot of people. But I've never done anything worth remembering. I remember my mother. She was something special. I'd like to think I have something of her in me. I need to know I'm more than a self-centered bastard."

Emma flinched. "That's a bit harsh, isn't it?" She was shocked to hear Dane describe herself this way.

Dane looked Emma in the eye. "No. So far, I think it's a pretty damn good assessment."

Emma opened a beer and slid it across the bar to Dane. She wasn't sure where this was going, but she had the feeling if Dane was up for talking, this was a story she would want to hear. "What are you talking about? What did you ever do to hurt anybody?"

"Thanks," Dane said taking the beer. "I've spent so much time trying to run from my father that I didn't see that I was being just like him. I was never there when it was important. I let people down. I just want to start over."

"Why have you been running from your father?" Emma asked, wanting to keep Dane talking. That hit to her head might have shaken something loose.

Dane clenched and unclenched her teeth, making the muscle in her jaw jump. "He acted like my mother getting sick was something she did to him. It wasn't like he was around most of the time anyway. He was always working, or that's what he had us believe. I don't know why he bothered marrying her if he thought so little of her. After she died, he refused to talk about her. It was as if he wanted to erase every memory of her. I was the constant reminder he couldn't get rid of. He married his second wife only months after my mother died. I don't know which of us was more eager for me to finish school and move out."

The pain in Dane's voice touched something deep inside Emma. "How old were you when your mother died?"

"Fourteen. I had four long years in that house pretending I didn't exist, trying to avoid my father's wife. I wasn't allowed to go to college anywhere but the University of Tennessee. If I'd had my choice, I would have chosen something on the other side of the world. As soon as I graduated, I left. I haven't seen my father in years. We've barely spoken. I get an email from time to time, but he's mostly interested in my job."

"What kind of job?" The more Dane talked, the more Emma found she wanted to know about her. Dane was a mystery. It had been easy to think of her as a troublemaker at first, but the truth was Dane upset her. Dane came from a world that had been stripped from Emma's grasp. Dane was devilishly attractive, and Emma didn't want to fall for her charms. Hearing Dane tell her story made her more relatable. Emma's grip slipped on her resolve not to get close to Dane.

"I'm a photographer. I worked with an overseas news team for the last few years. You know, the stories you read about the real people in different countries, what their lives and cultures are like. Stories that help us see people as human and not as an enemy."

"So you worked hard and made a life for yourself. What's wrong with that?"

Dane grimaced. "Let's just say, I wasn't a very good friend. I used my past as an excuse to do whatever I wanted, no matter who it hurt."

"Who did you hurt?"

Dane shook her head, not ready to tell that story. She never talked about what happened, too afraid she wouldn't be able to control the memory once it escaped. She put the bottle down on the bar with a few bucks to cover the drink. "Thanks for listening, Emma. But that's a story for another time." She slid off the stool. "If you see Curtis, let him know I'm looking for him."

"You aren't going to go up there alone, are you?" Emma asked, her words thick with concern.

"It can't hurt to go for a drive and visit a cemetery. I'll be careful. Promise."

"You could wait till tomorrow or at least until Curtis shows up." Emma bit her lip. "I'll even go with you on Monday if it can wait."

Dane smiled. It meant a lot that Emma would offer to help her. "Thanks. I may take you up on that."

"Dane," Emma called.

Dane turned back to face Emma.

"We all make choices we regret. But regret isn't a fair emotion. It takes away from what we were going through, what we were feeling in the moment. It's like looking through a foggy window. Stories have a way of telling themselves if we give them time. Be patient. You'll either find what you're looking for, or it will find you."

Dane frowned, not sure what Emma meant. She shrugged. "Don't worry. I'll be all right."

She stepped out into the sun, squinting against the blinding light. Her head still hurt. Maybe Emma was right. Maybe she should just take a break today. The dead weren't going anywhere. She'd have more daylight tomorrow and maybe a clearer head.

❖

"Where are we going, Curtis?" Dane asked. They were supposed to be going to the cemetery to look for her family, but Curtis had her off on a wild goose chase. They had been driving through rough Jeep trails for the past hour, and Curtis still wouldn't clue her in on what he was up to.

The road widened and then opened into an expansive circular clearing. There was a large mound of dirt across the clearing with ATV tracks crisscrossing the sides. There was a huge fire pit in the center with evidence of frequent use.

"What is this place?" Dane asked, stopping the Jeep.

"It's just a place where people party. We call it the four-lane."

"Okay. It's the party place. Why are we here?"

Curtis fidgeted with the old silver dollar he wore on a chain around his neck.

Dane was getting a bad feeling about this. Curtis was up to something.

"Look, man, give it up, or I'm turning this Jeep around and going home."

"No. Just wait a minute," Curtis protested. "I'm meeting a friend here. He told me he'd be here."

Dane grabbed Curtis by the arm. "Why here? Why couldn't you meet in town or at the bar? I warned you, Curtis—I don't want anything to do with drugs."

Curtis didn't say anything.

"Curtis?"

"Emma doesn't like me talking to Trevor."

Dane frowned. "Who's Trevor?"

Curtis turned in his seat to face her. "He's my friend. He hangs out with me and doesn't let people pick on me. I do things for him sometimes."

The bad feeling Dane had earlier was getting worse.

The sound of an ATV roared through the trees. Someone was coming. Curtis opened the door and jumped out of the Jeep before Dane could stop him.

"Damn it." This wasn't good.

She waited at the edge of the tree line. She could see Curtis standing next to a side-by-side ATV. The driver was a big man with a bald head and a bushy black beard. Curtis was acting nervous. He kept shifting his feet and moving his hands around in the air. He stepped up to the ATV. His back was to Dane, making it hard for her to see what was happening. Curtis was suddenly very still.

Dane put the Jeep in gear and inched forward.

Curtis stepped away from the ATV. He was laughing. He had one hand in his pocket and waved to the man with the other. The man in the ATV spun the tires, throwing rocks and dirt behind him. He disappeared into the trees as quickly as he had arrived.

"What the hell was that about?" Dane asked the moment Curtis was back at the Jeep. "What are you mixed up with, Curtis?"

"Nothing, I promise."

"Are you buying drugs from this guy?"

"No. He gives me weed sometimes, but that's no big deal."

Dane raised her eyebrows, surprised by the answer. "No big deal, huh? Then I guess it's okay for Emma to know about this."

"No," Curtis said, his eyes wide with fear. "I told you, Emma doesn't like me talking to Trevor. She'll just get mad."

"Is he one of the guys she doesn't want you hanging out with that sometimes get you into trouble?"

Curtis dropped his head, suddenly interested in the strings hanging from a rip in his jeans. "Yeah. You aren't going to tell her, are you?"

Dane wasn't sure what she should do. Curtis was an adult, but not really. And Emma would kill her if anything happened to Curtis and she hadn't said anything about this.

"If you don't want me to tell Emma, you have to promise me you won't meet with this guy anymore. You at least have to promise to tell me and let me go with you."

"Trevor is my friend. I'm not doing anything wrong," Curtis argued. He slumped his shoulders when Dane didn't give in. "Fine. I'll tell you."

Dane sat back in her seat, satisfied this was the most she was going to get from Curtis. She turned the Jeep around. "Let's get out of here. We've already wasted most of the morning with this. I still want to get to the cemetery today. No more stops and no more tricks. Do you understand?"

"Sorry, Dane. Don't be mad."

Dane shook her head, wondering what it would take to get through to the kid. "You can't keep doing this to me, Curtis. I need to know I can trust you."

Curtis sat up suddenly. "You can trust me. I keep secrets all the time. Everyone knows my word is good. You'll see, Dane—I'll take you today, and I'll tell you when I see Trevor again. I always keep a promise."

Dane knew Curtis meant what he said. She just wondered what promises he had made to Trevor.

❖

Curtis led Dane down a narrow dirt path that looked more like a forgotten old driveway than a road. The brush had grown over into the road and scraped the sides of the Jeep as they crawled over the rocks and gullies carved into the path by off-road tires and heavy rains. The road suddenly disappeared into a fast-moving creek. The water didn't look too deep, but she knew she risked sinking into the wet sandy soil if she didn't get this right. She peered across, trying to judge the tracks climbing out of the water on the other side. She eased into the water, not pushing too hard, but making sure to keep the vehicle moving. She bounced and rocked as the Jeep maneuvered over the river rock. The water was getting high, but the old Jeep managed to keep running. Dane drove up the bank, relieved to have solid ground under her. Half a mile later she came to a clearing on a hill.

"This is it," Curtis announced, sounding proud of himself.

Dane climbed out of the Jeep next to a large white oak tree. An old wooden chair leaned against the base of the tree, and a faded American flag hung proudly from a pole attached high up on the trunk. Dane worked her way through the overgrown grass and weeds, carefully reading the names on the stones. Some were so old she could barely make out the words. She was overwhelmed by the number of graves belonging to babies, their ages ranging from one day to only a handful of years. Many of the graves were marked simply with a flat rock turned on its side and driven into the ground. Faint grooves in the sandstone hinted of what had once been etched there. She pulled a pad of paper from her bag and placed it against one of the larger rocks. She rubbed against the paper with the side of a pencil. Slowly the grooves in the stone began to show as empty spaces on the page. Dane could make out a few of the words. "Jacob Wilks 18-something to 1896."

Curtis whistled. "Dang, that's a long time ago."

"Yeah, it was." Dane said moving on to the next grave. The earth had caved in from decay and the stone leaned sideways. A stick snapped under her foot. An eerie rattle sounded from the grave. Dane jumped back. The largest snake she had ever seen reared its head, its tail vibrating a warning for her to back off.

"Watch out, Dane." Curtis pushed Dane back away from the snake. "You gotta be careful. That snake means business. You got too close to its nice comfy bed. I'll take care of it."

Curtis went to the woods and came back with a long stick.

"Hey, don't hurt it. It was here first. He lives here—I'm just visiting."

Curtis grinned. "I won't hurt it. See how big he is? By the number of buttons on his tail, that snake's gotta be at least seven or eight, hell, maybe even ten years old. This old guy has earned his way."

Curtis slid the stick under the snake and gently lifted it out of the hole. The snake was even bigger than Dane thought. It had to be at least four feet long and three inches in diameter in the middle. Curtis carried the snake to the edge of the woods and lowered it to the ground, careful not to get in its path.

Dane grinned when Curtis turned back to her, smiling like he'd just won a ribbon at the fair.

"Thanks, man," Dane said, with praise.

Curtis stuck his hands in his pockets looking sheepish. "What are you lookin' for in these graves, anyway?"

"Answers," Dane said turning back to the headstone. She brushed her hand across the cold gray stone, dislodging years of dirt and bits of moss. A name slowly emerged. Caldwell Stewart. "This is it."

Dane took out her camera and snapped a picture of the stone. This was the first real lead she'd found since she started this journey. She moved on to the next stone. Mary George Stewart. Her heart sped up. Each new stone felt like a step closer to her own truth. Seeing the names made her feel like she had roots somewhere, that there was more to her than the cold distance she'd learned from her father.

She stopped at a large stone at the end of a row. It was newer than the others. The stone was gray granite, and weather and fungus had yet to tarnish the sheen of the polish or fill in the letters engraved on the surface. *Isaak Stewart 1936–1986 and Ida George Stewart 1942–2007. Together in Heaven Forever.* Dane ran her hand across the names as if stroking the weathered face of an elder. Curtis circled the grave, sticking close to Dane. He was unusually quiet.

"Hey, there's writing on this side too," he said excitedly, breaking the silence.

Dane circled the stone. Her heart fluttered. "Oh my God, these people are my grandparents."

"Really?"

"I believe so," Dane said, kneeling before the list of names identifying the couple's children and grandchildren. "See this name here? Pearl Jean Stewart. That was my mother's name."

"That's a nice name," Curtis said, placing his hand on Dane's shoulder.

Dane nodded again, a lump forming in her throat. "I never knew any of her family. I remember vague stories she used to tell me about her mother and sisters, but I don't remember them ever visiting, or even ever talking to them on the phone. I didn't know them at all."

"Sorry, Dane. I can't imagine not having family around. I've got Emma and a bunch of cousins around I can see anytime I want. I would be lonely if I didn't have them."

Dane patted his shoulder. "It's okay, Curtis. I'm okay. I can learn about them now." She took a picture of the stone, front and back. "They haven't been gone that long. Someone has to know something about them, about my mother."

"Like what?" Curtis asked.

"I want to know what she was like as a kid. What her life was like before she met my father. Why she never came back here. Why they were never a part of my life." She turned to Curtis. "Do you know any of the names here?"

Curtis shook his head.

"What about the name George? Do you know anyone with that last name? It doesn't seem too common, even around here."

Curtis shrugged. "I don't remember anybody named George."

Dane wasn't surprised, but she was still disappointed. She had the names she needed, and now she just needed to find someone who knew them, who would talk to her. If she was lucky, some of her family still lived around here.

"What will you do now? Curtis asked.

"I start asking questions, I guess. Who knows, I may get lucky just looking through the phone book."

Curtis nodded. "Don't worry, you'll find them. I'll help you find them."

Dane put her arm around his shoulder. "Thanks, Curtis. You're a good friend."

He beamed. He threw his arm around her shoulder and they walked arm in arm back to the Jeep.

Dane's stomach rumbled. "I don't know about you, but I'm hungry."

"I'm always hungry. I bet Emma will make us a sandwich."

Dane laughed. "I bet she will."

❖

Dane followed Curtis into the bar and settled in her usual spot. The gentle hum of music and conversation surrounded her like the haunting voices of the dead. She was tired from searching for the answers she wanted and running from the memories she couldn't forget.

"What's up, Curtis?" Emma asked, wiping down the bar.

"Just hanging out. We found Dane's grandparents' graves today. Saw a big-ass rattler too. He must have been four feet long."

Emma shook her head, looking to Dane. "Did you find the answers you were looking for?"

"Just a bunch of names for now. The ghosts weren't talking, but maybe someone around here will."

"Give it time," Emma said gently.

Dane looked at the wall behind Emma's head. "How about a shot of Jack and a beer."

Emma glanced back at the bottle of Jack Daniel's. "I don't think you'll find any answers in a bottle of Tennessee Whiskey."

Dane tapped the bar with one finger. "No, but I've got a few things I would like to forget tonight, and my buddy Jack has the cure I'm looking for."

Emma shook her head. "Suit yourself." She poured a shot and set a bottle of beer on the counter in front of Dane.

"What about you, Curtis?"

Curtis grinned. "I'll have a beer and a bologna sandwich with cheese, pickles, and onions."

Emma laughed. "Of course, why did I even have to ask?"

Dane held up two fingers. "How about a double this time?"

Emma sighed and poured the drink.

"What's her problem?" Dane asked as Emma went to the kitchen.

Curtis shrugged.

Dane took another drink, letting the whiskey burn its way down her throat before taking a drink of the ice-cold beer. The familiar burn of the whiskey collided with the cold chill of the beer creating the numbness that she was looking for. She knew it was only temporary. The past would be knocking on her door as soon as she opened her eyes in the morning. But if she was lucky, she wouldn't remember the nightmares that would haunt her through the night.

"I'll catch you later, Dane," Curtis said finishing his beer and pushing his plate aside.

"Where are you going?"

"I got stuff to do."

"Like what?"

Curtis put his hand on Dane's back and leaned close. "I'm going to see a girl," he whispered into her ear.

"Really? Ha, you dog."

Curtis smiled. "Don't tell Emma. I don't want her to lecture me."

Dane slapped Curtis on the back. "All right, man. Good luck."

As Curtis stepped away, a tall man with a thick beard and black cowboy hat took his seat. He nodded to Dane.

"How's it going?" Dane said, tossing back the last of the whiskey.

The big man ordered a beer.

Dane signaled for another double. "Hey, what's your name, man?" She felt a cold shiver run up her spine when the big man turned to her.

"Who wants to know?" His voice was so deep it rumbled when he spoke.

"I'm Dane."

The guy looked at her like she was something he wanted to pick off the bottom of his shoe. He planted his elbows on the bar and leaned forward, blocking Dane with his huge arm.

"Okay. Guess you don't want to talk. That's cool. I was just wondering if you've ever heard of Pearl Jean Stewart?"

The big man's beard bristled as he worked his jaw.

Dane took another drink. "She used to live around here. Ever heard of her?"

He turned up his beer and drained it. "I can't help ya," he grumbled. "Do ya mind? If I wanted to hear a woman yap in my ear all night, I would've stayed home."

"Oh. Yeah. Sure, sorry." Dane pinched her thumb and finger together in front of her mouth and moved her hand from one side to the other. "All zipped up. I won't say another word. Sorry I bothered you."

The big guy turned back to the bar.

Dane looked into her glass, swirling the amber liquid in the glass. She closed one eye and squinted into the liquid. Nope. No answers there either.

Chapter Three

The bar was slammed. It seemed the rain brought everyone out of the woodwork. Emma hadn't had a moment to catch her breath. It was days like this when she wished Curtis would help her out more. It would be nice to have a hand occasionally. Where was that kid, anyway? She hoped he wasn't out in this downpour. Sometimes the kid didn't know his ass from a hole in the ground.

Emma fished six cold beers out of the cooler and arranged them in a tin bucket, then covered them with ice. At least when the orders came in buckets, she got to make fewer trips around the room, but she still couldn't keep up with the food orders. She rubbed her arm across her brow, wiping away the sweat with her sleeve.

She looked up to see Dane walk in through the back door, shaking rain from her hair. Curtis wasn't with her. Dammit. He was never around when there was work to do. She went back to the kitchen to grab the french fries she'd left in the fryer. When she came back, Dane was bussing tables and taking out the trash. Emma was surprised. It wasn't Dane's responsibility, but she was grateful for the help.

Maybe if Dane stayed busy, she wouldn't end up at the end of a bottle by the end of the night. Dane had been drinking more the last few days, and Emma wondered if she was on a course for self-destruction. Dane hadn't caused any trouble, but Emma could tell there was trouble brewing in her eyes.

Emma grabbed the bucket of beer and stepped through the growing crowd. She didn't have time to daydream or fix Dane's problems. She was buried under a heap of her own.

Dane grabbed a handful of napkins and wiped the rain off her face and neck. She tossed her jacket into the small utility closet and grabbed a trash bag. She had learned not to ask Emma if she could help—she just started cleaning up. Emma never broke stride. She went on as if it was normal for Dane to work at the bar.

The hours passed in a blur. Dane wondered how Emma kept up the pace day after day, week after week. Even when she wasn't running the bar, she was doing things on the farm.

By the time the bar closed, Dane was exhausted. She had looked for Curtis all night, but he hadn't shown up. She was getting a little worried. It wasn't like him to miss dinner. Most likely he had seen the crowd and was afraid Emma would make him work if he came inside. She sighed. She hoped he had kept his promise and wasn't off somewhere with Trevor. Emma might be overprotective, but Dane agreed with Emma about Trevor. He was bad news—she could feel it.

Dane cleared empty bottles off the last table as Emma locked the doors. Emma had had a good night, but at a personal price. She looked exhausted.

"Ever thought of taking a day off?" Dane asked as she restocked the cooler with bottles of beer.

"Ha." Emma shook her head. "I'm tempted to take every day off, but someone's got to get things done. I don't know how Daddy did it all those years." She paused. "But I guess Daddy could do anything as long as he had Momma. Together they were an unstoppable force. It's a hard act to follow on my own." Emma opened a beer and handed it to Dane, then opened one for herself. "Thanks for all the help tonight. It would have been rough without you."

It was rare to get thanks from Emma. And it was nice to be on her good side for a change. "You're welcome. I'm glad I showed up when I did. What was with the crowd tonight? I've never seen it like this."

Emma took a long drink from her beer. "It's like that sometimes. Things will be slow for days, and boom, everyone shows up at once." She took another drink. "Someone said the Black Mountain Saloon got shut down a few days ago. We'll probably get a lot of that crowd for a while, at least until the owner can straighten things out, or a new place opens up."

"Why did they get shut down?"

Emma shrugged. "The word is they were smuggling drugs through the bar. There are always a few low-life dealers around trying to move their product through reputable businesses."

Dane frowned. "Have they tried that here?"

"I wish I could say no, but if I had a dollar for every time they've tried, I wouldn't need to run the bar at all. It's a problem. It can be a lot of pressure. But there are some good cops looking out for me. The trick is knowing who's the good guy."

"How do you deal with it?" Dane asked. She had the feeling there was more to the story.

"I say no. I have good insurance, and a good security system."

Dane looked around the bar. "What security system?"

"Samson."

Dane choked on her beer. "Samson? You can't be serious."

"You underestimate his will. He may be old, but he's still got skills."

Dane stared at Emma. She was joking, wasn't she? Dane wasn't sure, but this was the most relaxed she had ever seen Emma.

"Have you ever thought of hiring someone to help out around here?"

"Nope. The minute I turn my back, the dealers will have a hold on the place. As long as I do the work myself, I can sleep at night."

"So how do you have fun?" Dane asked, hoping to crack Emma's hard shell.

Emma didn't answer.

"I have an idea." Dane went to the jukebox and loaded a playlist. A moment later Chris Stapleton's voice filled the room. She took Emma's hand and led her to the center of the floor.

"What are you doing?" Emma asked, grinning up at Dane.

"Dancing."

"I don't dance," Emma said in protest, allowing herself to be guided around the room.

Dane took Emma into her arms, swaying gently to the melody of the song. "You're good at this," she said playfully.

"You're a bad liar," Emma countered.

Dane spun Emma around. "I would never lie to you."

Emma tilted her head back and peered up at Dane, a sly grin curving the corners of her lips.

Time slowed. Emma's hair fell across her shoulders, her eyes sparkled in the dim light, and the skin of her neck presented itself like an invitation. Dane desperately wanted to press her lips to Emma's neck and taste her.

Emma leaned closer into Dane letting herself be swept up in the moment. The air grew thin. It had been a long time since she had been this close to a woman. Too long.

Dane wrapped her arm around Emma's waist. Emma watched Dane's lips, only inches away from hers.

"This is nice," Dane said her thighs brushing against Emma's.

Emma drew in a shallow breath. Her heart raced, and her hands were clammy with sweat. It felt good to be held. Dane's lips were only inches from hers now. Dane was going to kiss her. She wanted Dane to kiss her. Butterflies danced in her stomach in anticipation. Emma leaned closer.

The phone rang, making Emma jump. She blinked, breaking the spell. The phone continued to ring but Dane didn't let go. "I should get that." Emma pulled away, letting her hands slide down Dane's arms, not ready to give up her touch.

Dane went back to the bar and opened another beer. She watched Emma as she talked. As if sensing something was wrong, Dane moved closer to her.

"I won't be able to do anything tonight. I'll have to wait till tomorrow morning when the courthouse opens." Emma pinched the bridge of her nose. The sigh that escaped her carried the weight of her hurt and disappointment. "I don't want to hear any excuses right now, Curtis. You got yourself there, and you can sleep on it tonight."

Emma slammed the phone back onto the receiver.

"What is it?" Dane asked.

"Curtis is in jail."

Dane flinched. "What the hell? What did he do?"

"He said he's been charged with possession with intent to sell."

Dane swallowed hard. "Oh shit."

"Oh shit is right. I've told him a million times to stay away from those guys."

"What did he say?"

Emma glared at her. She took Dane's beer out of her hand. She turned up the bottle and drained the contents in one drink. She took a moment before answering.

"It's the same old story every time. He always has an excuse. How many times does this have to happen before he realizes those guys are not his friends?"

"What will happen to him?"

Emma got them both another beer and sat down at the bar. Her shoulders slumped in defeat. "If they don't plea it down, it could mean jail time. Right now, I'm just hoping it isn't a felony charge. If we can get it down to a misdemeanor, he'll be okay. Probation would probably do him good." Emma raked her hand through her hair. "I don't know what to do with him sometimes."

Dane nodded. She knew what she meant. Curtis did what he wanted. He didn't seem to get that there were consequences.

"There's nothing I can do until morning. He'll be arraigned tomorrow, and we'll see what the charges are and what the judge has to say. He'll be assigned a public defender. The Lord knows I can't afford to hire a lawyer every time he does something stupid."

"It sounds like you've been through this before. You know the ropes pretty well."

"He's been in jail for driving without a license, breaking and entering, trespassing, vandalism, and simple possession. Every time he's been in trouble, it's been because of his so-called friends putting him up to no good. I can't babysit him twenty-four seven. At least in jail, I know where he is."

Dane was surprised Emma was so calm. She expected her to throw a fit, get angry, even storm down to the police station and demand to see her brother. But Emma seemed resolved, even a little relieved.

"Will you bail him out?"

Emma tossed her empty bottle in the trash. "Yeah. I can't leave him there long. I can be mad as hell, but he's still my little brother. I'll make him pay for it though."

"How?"

Emma smiled. "His chore list just grew by a mile, and this bar just got a busboy."

"Why doesn't he work here already? You could use the help. He should do his part."

Emma shook her head. "You'll see. He's a total disaster. After a few days, he'll drive me so crazy I'll be ready to pay him to leave me alone."

Emma's kidding was quickly replaced by a more pensive mood.

"What?" Dane asked, reading the change as if a light had just turned on.

Emma looked at her. "I have to wonder what he'll get into next. I'm afraid he's going to do something one of these days that I won't be able to get him out of."

Dane thought of the meeting with Trevor, wondered if he had anything to do with this. "Who are these guys you were talking about that get Curtis into trouble?"

"Mark and Johnny are the two he's around the most. They used to think it was funny to get Curtis to do things when he was a kid. They almost got him killed with a couple of their stunts. Curtis never knew better. They were assholes then and they're assholes now. Both have been in and out of jail for various drug crimes, domestic violence, child neglect..." Emma rubbed her eyes. "You get the picture."

"What about Trevor?" Dane asked.

Emma's eyes shot open. She glared at Dane. "How do you know Trevor?"

Dane felt the hair on the back of her neck stand on end. The electricity vibrating off Emma at the mention of Trevor's name was enough to scorch hair.

Dane shook her head. "Curtis met him in the woods a few days back. I didn't like the guy and asked Curtis not to go around him without me anymore. Curtis said he was a friend, but he didn't want you to know he was talking to him. He said you didn't like Trevor."

"He's dead right about that. Trevor is bad news. He's been trying to get me to move drugs through the bar for years. If he's got my brother selling drugs for him, I'll kill him."

"Whoa," Dane said, putting her hand on Emma's. "Let's just slow down a little. We don't know he got Curtis to do anything. I just thought you should know he's been around. Now that I know who he is, I can keep a better watch on Curtis. He promised he wouldn't go around Trevor without me."

Emma shook her head. "I wish I could believe that. Curtis likes to make promises. But he'll also make up a lot of excuses to get around those promises."

Dane's gut twisted. She wished she had said something to Emma before. Maybe they could have stopped this from happening.

Emma seemed to read Dane's thoughts. "Don't worry about it. You didn't know. But for the record, you can't trust Curtis." Emma pulled her hand away. "You'll tell me if he goes around Trevor again, right?"

"Of course."

Emma sighed. "Let's get out of here. I have a long day tomorrow."

Dane climbed into her Jeep and waited for Emma to start her truck. As she turned out of the lot, her headlights bounced off a black truck parked at the end of the road. Someone was watching them. Dane stopped, peering into the night, trying to see who was there. She took out her phone and snapped a picture, but it was too dark to make out anything.

Someone started the truck and turned on the lights, blinding her. She blinked and covered her eyes as the truck pulled out and turned down the road. There was a dark cover over the license plate obscuring the number. She had a bad feeling about this. She was tempted to follow the truck, but what would she do when they stopped? She sat in the lot for a while, waiting to see if the truck came back. Nothing happened.

She didn't know what this meant, but it gave her a bad feeling. Were they watching Emma or the bar? Dane turned the Jeep and headed to the farm. Maybe this had something to do with Curtis, or maybe they were just a couple of people hanging out after the bar closed. She shrugged it off. She was probably just jumpy after what happened with Curtis.

❖

Court was an experience Dane would never forget. Curtis and six other men and three women were led into the courtroom in bright orange jumpsuits, white socks, and slip-on sandals. Their hands and feet were shackled and chained. But it wasn't the inmates that made the biggest impression—it was the people in the gallery.

Most of the men wore blue jeans, or camouflage pants and jackets, with work or hunting boots. More than half had a plug of tobacco in a bulging cheek and regularly spit into plastic soda bottles. Most of the women looked like they hadn't bothered to change out of their pajamas, and some obviously hadn't brushed their hair in days. Dane had been to war-torn countries, and she had never experienced this kind of culture shock.

People talked to each other like this was a family reunion, laughing and making jokes about the police and the judge. No one seemed worried about what would happen. Court seemed more like an inconvenience than a serious situation.

Emma had been right about it being a long day. They sat through child abuse cases up for review, civil suits, traffic violations, and domestic violence cases, before the judge got to Curtis.

The judge looked over the bench at Curtis and shook his head. "Mr. Reynolds, we meet again."

Curtis stood at the podium looking like a child. He glanced back at Emma, who waved him off.

"Pay attention," she mouthed.

"Mr. Reynolds, I thought you and I had an agreement. I recall you promised not to come back to my court."

Curtis grinned. "Yes, sir."

"Do you have an attorney, Curtis?"

Curtis shook his head.

"Speak into the mic, please," the judge ordered.

Curtis jumped as if he'd been pinched. "No, sir."

The judge looked around the courtroom. "I see your sister is here today. Ms. Reynolds, will you please come up?"

Emma stood and went to the podium as requested.

"Ms. Reynolds, I am aware this is not the first time Curtis has put you through this. Are you willing to take your brother back in?"

"Yes, Your Honor," Emma answered.

The judge nodded and shuffled through some papers. "The court will appoint Mr. Zack Long with the public defender's office to represent Mr. Reynolds. The court will hear this case next Wednesday. Mr. Long, does that work for you?"

An attorney stood at the end of a long table facing the judge. "Yes, Your Honor."

The judge nodded. He looked back to Emma and Curtis. "Mr. Reynolds, normally I would be inclined to let you go under your sister's supervision with bail, but in this case, I feel that would be a waste of her money and my time. These are serious charges against you, Mr. Reynolds, and this is not your first rodeo. Your sister works hard to keep you up, young man, and I think it is unfair to continue to punish her generosity by asking her to be responsible for you when you clearly lack personal responsibility for yourself. I am going to hold you in jail pending your hearing. That will give you ample time to meet with your attorney and to think about what you have done."

Emma went white. Curtis looked at her wide-eyed. This clearly wasn't what they expected. Emma was visibly shaking. She watched as Curtis was led out of the courtroom, back to jail. Once Curtis was out of sight, Emma turned and walked out of the courtroom.

Dane grabbed her jacket and followed Emma. "Are you okay?" Dane asked catching up to her.

Emma didn't answer until they were inside the truck. She slammed her palm against the steering wheel until her frustration burned out. She laid her head against her hands. She didn't cry. She didn't seem to know what to do.

"How can I help?" Dane asked.

Emma shook her head. "There's nothing you can do. I'll come back and visit him tomorrow. I'll put money on his commissary and bring him socks and long underwear."

Dane frowned. "What's the long underwear for?"

"They keep the jail cold to keep the germs down."

Dane frowned. "Good to know." She learned something new every day.

"I'll talk to his attorney and see what we can do. But he probably won't know anything right away."

Dane wanted to make things better. It was hard to see Emma so upset. "It sounds like they're just trying to teach him a lesson."

"He is. The judge isn't a bad man, and he's been more than lenient with Curtis in the past. It's just that Curtis is burning his bridges. Even I'm tired of his excuses." She stared blankly out the window. "I don't know what to do with him or what is going to happen to him."

Dane got out and walked around the truck, opening Emma's door. "Move over. I'll drive us home."

Emma sighed and slid across the long bench seat. "Thank you for being here. You didn't have to."

Dane brushed a strand of hair off Emma's cheek, tucking it behind her ear. "I wanted to be here. I want to help. Everything will be okay."

Emma turned to peer out the side window. Dane knew she didn't believe her. She wasn't sure she believed it herself.

"What's the plan for the day? Are you still going to open the bar?"

"I think I just want to go home."

Dane started the truck. "Okay. How about something to eat? My treat."

Emma looked at her with a faint smile. "That sounds good. It will be nice to have someone serve me for a change."

❖

Emma couldn't remember the last time she had gone out to dinner with anyone other than Curtis. Even when she wasn't working, she didn't see the point in going out. Most of the time she just wanted to put her feet up or soak in a hot bath. She was still too mad at Curtis to be worried. She didn't want to let him spoil this for her.

"It's nice of you to do this," Emma said as Dane pulled into the parking lot at the Crab Bucket.

"I'm happy to do it. It'll be a treat for both of us." Dane opened the door for Emma and followed her inside.

Wooden tables were scattered around the patio in a random pattern, allowing people to gather in small groups without feeling crowded. They were a little early for dinner, so they had the patio to themselves.

Emma ordered a Crown and Coke.

Dane raised her eyebrows, as if surprised by her choice of drinks this early in the day.

"What?" Emma asked, daring Dane to say anything.

"Nothing. Sounds good to me." She looked to the waitress. "I'll have the same."

Emma sipped her drink. Dane was calm and relaxed as usual. Nothing seemed to faze her. Emma stirred her drink, unsure what to say. She realized she and Dane didn't talk about anything besides Curtis, and she really did not want to talk about him. She wanted to enjoy this time with Dane. A thrill of excitement made her skin tingle. This felt nice. It was almost like a date. She smiled to herself. She took a sip of her drink, sneaking glances at Dane. She felt bad that she hadn't asked Dane how her search for her family had been going.

"Any luck finding your family?"

Dane quickly met Emma's gaze, her eyes steady, but holding the faintest hint of disappointment.

"I've had some leads, but I keep hitting these roadblocks. Most of the roads around here are not on my map, and when I do find something, no one seems to know anything, or they aren't willing to talk to me."

"What do you know about your mother's family?"

Dane shrugged. "Honestly, when I was young I was too self-absorbed to listen or think to ask questions. When she got sick, all I could think about was making her better. Later I tried to ask my father, but he refused to talk about it. I always thought he was just a jerk who didn't like her family. But since I've had so much trouble finding answers, I get the feeling there were things they didn't want me to know."

"What kind of things?"

Dane sighed. "I have no idea. Maybe I'm just getting paranoid."

"Or they're really out to get you."

Dane laughed. "What do you have to do to get people to talk to you around here? You'd think I was asking for the key to the safe or their firstborn child."

Emma felt sorry for Dane. She could tell this was important to her. "Well, you are an outsider, and it doesn't help that you look like a cop."

Dane frowned. "Who's the one being paranoid?"

Emma leaned forward and placed her hand on Dane's. "I know it's frustrating, but this region has a long history of mistrust of the authorities. For generations this county survived on bootlegging moonshine. People learned to only trust family. The wrong name was often all it took to start a family feud that lasted generations. Even today I bet half of the police department wouldn't turn over information about a family member to the Feds. People here feel like their business is their business."

Dane pulled her hand away abruptly and threw her leg over the bench to face Emma. "I have to get past that. I just want to know something about my mother. I feel like I never knew her at all."

Dane was intense. Emma could feel the emotions vibrate through her skin like tremors of an earthquake.

"I might be able to help you."

"Really?"

Emma pressed her hand against Dane's thigh. "I can talk to some of my family. Maybe someone knew your mother, or at least some of your relatives. They may be willing to talk to you if I do the asking."

Dane grabbed Emma's face between her hands and kissed her abruptly. "Yes. Please. That would be wonderful."

Emma blinked, shocked by the kiss. Although the kiss was brief, she could still feel the tingle where Dane's lips had met hers. Butterflies fluttered in her stomach.

"Thank you," Dane continued, her voice full of hope. "That's the best news I've had since I arrived here."

Emma raised her hand palm out. "Slow down. I haven't done anything yet, and I can't make any promises."

Dane nodded. "Yeah, I get it. But thank you. It means a lot to me that you would try."

Emma picked up a menu, pretending to be interested in the food. Dane was glowing with excitement, and all Emma could think about was the warmth of Dane's lips.

The change of focus seemed to calm Dane down, and she turned back around in her seat next to Emma. "What would you like to eat?"

Emma bit her tongue as images of tasting Dane's lips flooded her mind. "The peel-and-eat shrimp are really good. I think I'll have that."

Dane smiled. "I like a woman who knows how to use her hands."

Emma felt the heat flame beneath her cheeks. "Does everything have to be a come-on with you?"

Dane laughed. "And a dirty mind doesn't hurt either. You may be the woman of my dreams."

Emma smacked Dane on the thigh. "*In* your dreams is more like it." Emma picked up her drink and sipped the cold liquor, hoping the alcohol could settle her nerves. She was certain her dreams were going to be hotter than usual tonight as well. Dane was flirting, and for whatever reason she was allowing herself to be tempted, even if Dane was only kidding around.

Dane broke the silence that had settled between them. "So why isn't there a woman of your dreams around?"

Emma almost choked on her drink. "Excuse me?"

Dane shrugged. "Don't you get lonely?"

"Of course. But if you haven't noticed, I'm a little busy."

"Too busy for—"

"Yes," Emma interrupted. "You've seen what my life is like. No one is interested in putting up with that all the time."

Dane heard the hurt in Emma's voice. "Is that why your girlfriend left?"

Emma pierced Dane with a deadly stare. "What did you say?"

"I'm sorry. I didn't mean to upset you." Dane shook her head and put her hands up. "I'm sorry, Curtis said you had a girlfriend for a while, and that she went away." Dane knew she was walking on thin ice, but she had to break through that ice if Emma was going to open up.

"Curtis needs to learn to keep his mouth shut," Emma said through gritted teeth.

"He worries about you."

Emma sighed and her shoulders relaxed a little.

Dane placed her hand over Emma's. "It must be hard to do all of this alone."

"Erin wasn't ready to leave the city. This wasn't her dream. It wasn't her life. She shouldn't have to give up her dreams for me."

Dane watched Emma. "What about your dreams?"

"That's all they were, dreams. Reality showed me that family and loyalty were more important to me. Can't you understand that?"

Dane shook her head. "I can't say I've ever felt that way about my family."

Emma frowned. "What about you?"

"What do you mean?" Dane pretended not to know what Emma meant. Emma was turning the tables on her.

"Why are you alone? Is there someone out there missing you right now?"

"No."

"I hear you yell out sometimes in your sleep. Who is it that keeps you up at night?"

Dane ground her teeth. She'd started this conversation. Turnabout was fair play, but Michelle was someone she wasn't ready to share.

"It wasn't like that. Something bad happened. I lost my best friend. I made a mistake and I can never take it back. She's the one who paid for it."

"What happened?"

Dane shook her head. "I think we need a new topic."

"You started it."

Dane attempted a smile. "Agreed. But I need to keep a little of my mysterious charm. I wouldn't want you learning all of my secrets and deciding I'm boring."

"I doubt I would ever find you boring."

Dane grinned. "So you do like me."

Emma scoffed. "That's not what I meant."

Dane laughed. "It's okay. You can play hard to get if you like. I enjoy a good chase."

Emma rolled her eyes. "That's funny. I had you pegged for a runner."

Dane let her smile slip. "What does that mean?"

Emma leaned closer. She was so close Dane wanted to lean in and taste her lips. "Whether you know it or not, you're running from something."

Dane opened her mouth to protest but Emma stopped her.

"I know you're looking for answers about your mother, but you're running from something, or someone. Something lit the fire that brought you here—otherwise you would have come looking for your family a long time ago."

Dane thought about what Emma said. Of course, she was right. Michelle's death had ripped her off her foundation. She had been exposed for the shallow, self-centered ass she had been.

"You're right. I thought I had life all figured out. I never needed anyone. I chased the job, and money was my mistress, although I had plenty of those along the way too. I thought I had everything anyone could ever want. I had a nice apartment in New York City, fast cars, adventure, women—you name it, it was mine. I was a jerk to everyone, especially those who cared about me." Dane clenched her teeth, fighting the memory.

Emma sat frozen in her seat waiting for Dane to finish the story. Her heart broke for the anguish she heard in Dane's voice.

Dane continued. "That stupid thinking cost me my best friend, my job, everything. I knew I had to change. I had to find answers because I have to believe there's more to me than selfishness and greed. So yes, I guess I am running. I'm running from myself."

Emma reached for Dane, closing her fingers over Dane's hand. "Who we are isn't found in our DNA, Dane. It's in our choices. If you want to be different, all you have to do is choose another way."

Dane nodded. "Maybe. Or maybe that's just an act. I need to know I'm grounded in something real."

Emma squeezed Dane's hand. "What if you don't like what you find?"

"I don't know. I hadn't considered that. I guess I can't afford to think that."

Emma smiled. "For the record, I hope you find what you're looking for. I think you have more good in you than you know."

Dane stared at her fingers laced through Emma's. "I hope you're right."

CHAPTER FOUR

Dane stared at her computer. She had made a breakthrough. She had managed to find a lot more information about her mother's family online than she was able to dig up in the local records. She had discovered a genealogy site that listed most of her family origins. She learned her great-great-grandfather had been in the logging business and settled in the area when the forests here had been rich with virgin timber. He had met and married her great-great-grandmother, who was a schoolteacher. Together they had eight children, although four had died as infants, and two had not lived to be adults. They had a son, Tobias, and a daughter, Ruth. Ruth had been her great-grandmother. Ruth had six children, including her grandmother Ida. Ida had one child who died at birth, another had died in a house fire at age five, and one uncle had died in his early teens in a car accident.

Dane studied the list of names she had compiled in her search. She still had one aunt and one uncle to find. She hoped they still lived in the area. A few more searches and she learned that her aunt Ester Wilson and her uncle Thomas Stewart appeared to be local. She peered at the name and address scrawled on the piece of paper. Why hadn't her mother talked about them? Why had her mother walked away from her family? Did her father have anything to do with it? Dane sighed. Her mother's whole life was a mystery to her. She didn't know her own family. She picked up her phone and considered calling her father to ask him, but the thought of his condescending tone set her teeth on edge. He had never answered her questions before. Why would things be any different now?

Dane checked her watch. It was still early. If she was going to get answers, she wanted them firsthand, not the twisted version her father might give her. She grabbed her keys. Her heart raced with excitement. With a little luck she was about to meet her uncle for the first time. It was the closest she had felt to her mother since her death. She had so many questions. What was her mother like as a child? Where had they grown up? Why did she leave? Why hadn't they kept in touch? Maybe she was finally going to get some answers.

Dane slowed the Jeep as she neared the address listed for her uncle. The house was small and was in dire need of repair. The paint was chipped and faded. The grass looked as if it hadn't been cut in a year, and a dead tree had fallen, taking out the corner of the front porch roof. It didn't look like anyone had lived here for a while.

Dane's hopes were crushed. She had been sure this was the lead she needed. She pulled into the drive. The closer she got to the place, the worse it looked. She stepped out to look around. Beer cans littered the front porch. Someone had nailed a board over the door, and a handwritten sign hung from a nail on the porch railing: *Keep out or get shot.*

Dane took a step back. Emma had warned her about going to places on her own. The last thing she wanted was to be on the receiving end of someone's shotgun. She would have to try again. She snapped a few photos of the house. As she pulled out of the drive, she noticed a woman walking up to a mailbox just down the road. She pulled to a stop just across the street from the woman.

"Excuse me," Dane called to get the woman's attention.

The woman peered at Dane over reading glasses. A gold chain dangled from each arm of the glasses as she scrutinized Dane.

"I don't mean to bother you, but can you tell me anything about the man who lives in the house just across the way?" Dane pointed in the direction of the derelict house. "I'm trying to find Thomas Stewart or Ester Wilson."

The woman frowned. "Well, Ester's dead, honey. Left the house to that no-good brother of hers. But you won't find Thomas around here for at least another six years or so. He went to prison a few years back. He got into some kind of argument with his girlfriend and another man. He shot the guy and almost beat the girl to death before the police could get here." The woman pulled off her glasses, letting them hang from the chain around her neck. "What do you want with Thomas, anyhow?"

Dane shrugged. "I just wanted to ask him a few questions. We are talking about Thomas Stewart, right? Do you know if he has any family around?"

The woman peered at her and hesitated before asking, "Are you with the police?"

Dane shook her head. "No, ma'am. It's nothing like that."

The woman bit her lip, as if she was trying to decide something. "Well, yeah, his last name was Stewart, and I think there was a boy if I remember, but I'm not sure if he belonged to Thomas or his girlfriend. I haven't seen anyone around here since he got sent off."

Dane hadn't seen anything in the records about Thomas having any children. "Do you remember the boy's name?"

The woman shook her head. "Can't recall. He was just a young fella, last I saw him. He wasn't around here much."

Dane smiled. "Well, thank you for your help." She knew she'd gotten all the information the old woman was willing to share.

"Uh-huh." The woman smiled and waved as Dane pulled away.

This wasn't anything like what she had expected. Her uncle didn't sound like the kind of guy she really wanted to get to know, but he still had the answers about her mother she needed. For now, it was back to the drawing board.

❖

Emma glanced through the kitchen window to see Dane running up the drive. Her dark hair was wet with sweat and her T-shirt clung to her body like a second layer of skin. Dane's body was a mixture of strength and beauty. Emma wiped a bead of sweat from her brow, suddenly aware of the rising heat in the room. Dane was up earlier than usual. Emma licked her lips, remembering the dreams that had kept her stirred up most of the night. She might be able to keep Dane at a distance during the day, but she wasn't able to keep her out of her dreams at night.

She had heard Dane cry out in her sleep a couple of times that night after staying late drinking at the bar. Dane had been drinking even more than usual. Emma wanted to go to her. She wanted to comfort her. But this was a battle only Dane could settle. And Emma couldn't afford to get involved.

She jumped as the screen door slammed against its frame and Dane's steps thundered up the stairs. A few minutes later Emma heard the shower running. Time seemed to stand still as she waited for Dane to come down for her coffee. Emma dried her hands on a dish towel as Dane entered the kitchen.

"Good morning," Emma said casually, trying to hide the concern in her voice.

Dane didn't look at her. "Good morning."

"I just made a fresh pot of coffee. Would you like breakfast?"

Dane pulled a mug from the cupboard and poured her coffee. "No, thanks, this will do."

Emma was disappointed. Dane didn't seem in the mood to talk, and she wasn't sure how she should approach the subject. She wasn't much for tiptoeing around things, but she was nervous about this.

"You seem upset about something. Is everything all right?"

Dane slumped into her chair. She ran her hand through her damp hair. "Just frustrated. I thought I had a really good lead on my uncle, but it didn't pan out. If I want answers from him, I'll have to arrange a visit at Pikeville Prison." She looked up at Emma. "Do you know anything about Thomas Stewart? You might have heard a story of him shooting a man and almost beating a woman to death sometime back."

Emma took a seat at the table across from Dane. "Most people around here have heard about that, but I thought the guy's name was

Tom Sikes. He was always a troublemaker, but a few years ago he almost killed a couple of people and got sent off to prison."

Dane nodded. "Yeah, sounds like the same guy."

Emma studied Dane over the rim of her cup, her breath sending wisps of steam billowing from the hot coffee. "Are you sure your uncle and Sikes are the same guy?"

"I have no idea. Maybe along the way he started using a different name."

Emma's eyes widened. "Could be."

"It's okay. I know it isn't good news. So far it doesn't look like my answers are going to be good ones. Maybe there's a good reason my mother left here and never looked back."

Emma swallowed her judgment and replaced it with sympathy. "I'm sorry. Tom is just one person in your family. I'm sure there's more to this story. There should be something in the old newspaper articles about it."

"Yeah. The woman I talked to mentioned a boy, but she wasn't sure if he belonged to Tom or the girlfriend. Do you know if Tom had any kids?"

"I don't know." Emma took Dane's hand. "I'm sorry this isn't what you wanted to hear. Maybe this is why your mother didn't talk about her family. Maybe she was trying to have a better life."

"Maybe."

"Are you sure you want to know more?"

"Yeah. I need to know the truth."

Emma nodded her understanding. Dane's need to find her family had become an obsession over the past few days. She was worried about Dane. She wasn't sleeping, she barely ate, and her drinking was getting heavier. "Are you coming to the bar tonight?"

"Sure. Why?"

Emma shrugged. "I think it will be a busy night. I could use some help."

Dane raised an eyebrow.

"Don't get the big head just because I asked you for help," Emma growled.

"You've got it, boss. What time do I start?"

Emma was relieved. "The crowd will start rolling in around six. Don't be late."

"Yes, ma'am."

Emma smiled. She hoped that keeping Dane busy would curb her drinking. The questions she was looking into were eating through her like acid, and she wasn't sure how long Dane could go on like this. She hated to admit it, but she had grown to like Dane. She wasn't the troublemaker she'd thought she would be, but she was troubled.

With Curtis in jail, Emma was lonely. She was used to having someone to look after, and Dane seemed to need looking after. Emma studied the dark circles that were growing under Dane's eyes. She was hurting. She studied the scars on Dane's hand. Did they have something to do with the nightmares Dane suffered? What had happened to Dane's friend to cause such self-hatred and guilt?

Emma filled Dane's coffee cup and topped off her own, hoping she wasn't making a big mistake.

❖

Dane showed up at the bar early, but the place was already picking up and Emma had her hands full. She went straight to work, clearing beer bottles and food baskets off tables. This crowd was close to being on their way out, but the next round would be the all-nighters. The band had set up in the corner and was starting off with some Charlie Daniels. Dane sang along with the tune, letting the song lift her spirits. Wrestling was playing on the television over the bar, and Dane reached for the remote to mute the volume.

Emma nodded to her as she carried a bucket of beer to a table in the back. She knew Emma had things covered, but she already looked tired, and a band night was always a crazy night. She was glad Emma had asked for her help.

She saw Emma look up from the cooler she was stocking as Trevor walked through the door. He took a seat at a booth with his back to the wall, giving him a clear view of the room.

Dane kept her eye on Emma as she went to the table for his order. She had an uneasy feeling about him being there. Was he there to pressure her to sell his drugs again?

Dane grasped Emma's arm as she passed behind the bar. "Are you okay with him being here?" A muscle jumped at the side of Emma's jaw and her eyes were wary. "I don't like this."

Emma met Dane's gaze, her eyes hard as cold stone. "As long as he behaves, he has just as much right to be here as anyone else."

"Do you want me to wait on him?"

Emma pulled her arm away. "I've got it." She softened her tone, not wanting to take her feelings out on Dane. "Thanks."

"Just let me know what you need me to do."

Emma didn't speak but the softness she saw in Dane's eyes settled her nerves. She was on edge. It was like all the hair on her body was standing on end. Every time she went to Trevor's table, she felt like she was facing a snake. Dane was keeping a close eye on her, and it made her feel better knowing she wasn't alone.

"What else can I get you?" Emma asked coldly, as she stared into Trevor's eyes, refusing to flinch away.

"I heard Curtis got himself in a bit of trouble. How long till he gets out?"

Emma bit the side of her cheek, trying not to swear. "You probably know more about it than I do."

The corners of Trevor's mouth lifted in a grin. "Tell Curtis I need to see him when he gets out. He has something of mine and I need it back." He tossed a twenty on the table. "Who's the new girl?" He nodded toward Dane. "I understand she's been asking a lot of questions around town. People aren't liking that."

"She's not bothering anyone and it's none of your business."

Trevor stood. "We'll see about that. Good seeing you, Emma." Emma stared after Trevor until the door closed behind him.

"What was that about?" Dane asked as Emma dumped the waste into the trash and put the cash in the register.

"He was asking about Curtis. He said Curtis owed him something and wanted to know when he would be getting out of jail to pay up."

Dane glanced at the door Trevor had just left through. "That doesn't sound good. What would Curtis owe him?"

Emma shook her head. "I don't know. But if Trevor had anything to do with the drugs Curtis was carrying, this could mean trouble."

A weight began to build in Dane's chest. What if Trevor decided to take what he thought was his?

"There was something else," Emma added. Dane snapped to attention. "He was asking about you. He wanted to know who you were and why you've been asking so many questions around town."

Dane was confused. "What's it to him?"

Emma met Dane's gaze. "Who knows? But I warned you about asking questions around here. If he has something to hide, you might be making him nervous. You've been spending a lot of time with Curtis. He may think you know more than you should. Be careful, Dane. Trevor is bad news."

Dane glanced around the room. Her nerves were stretched and edgy. She'd never felt more out of place here. "I don't know anything. No one has talked to me except one old woman, and she told me the same story you did about Thomas. As for Curtis, he hasn't said anything about Trevor, except to try to convince me he was his friend." Dane stilled, and her blood went cold. She had almost forgotten the drug deal Curtis brought her to at the trailer. "Oh shit."

"What?" Emma's voice edged with anger.

"Curtis took me to a guy's house once. I think his name was Mark. Curtis sold him marijuana. The guy was real paranoid about me being there."

Emma grabbed Dane's arm and pulled her into the kitchen. "You saw my brother sell drugs and you didn't say anything to me?"

Dane tried to recover. Now she'd made Emma mad at her. "I'm sorry. It was one time right after we met. He thought the guy would know something about my family and took me along. He swore it wasn't something he was into. He said it was a favor for someone and wasn't a big deal. I made him promise he wouldn't do it again, and I just put it out of my mind. I wasn't thinking. I didn't think he was doing it on a regular basis. I'm sorry."

Emma was fuming mad. "What else haven't you told me?"

"Nothing. It's not like I was hiding anything from you. I just hadn't thought about it. I was still trying to figure you guys out and looking for my own answers." Dane felt her own anger rise. She knew Emma was scared, but she was tired of being on the receiving end of Emma's ire. "It's not like I was his babysitter, and you weren't exactly open to talking to me anyway. What do you expect?"

Emma's face blazed red. "You're right. I know better than to expect anything." She stormed off.

"Damn it. That's not what I meant," Dane said to the now empty room. She kept her distance the rest of the evening. She guessed it was a good sign Emma hadn't told her to get out. She pulled the garbage can to the back door and closed the bag. She already had three bags stacked outside, and she needed to carry them to the dumpster across the parking lot. The fresh air would do her good.

As she lifted the first bag over her head and tossed it into the bin, something slammed against the back of her head. Dane fell against the metal dumpster and hit the ground hard. Someone grabbed her by the belt, yanking her upward as they dragged her into the dark. She was thrown to the ground and kicked in the back. Another blow landed against her cheek. She rolled into a ball, putting her arms up around her head.

"Fucking Fed. When are you going to learn to stay out of here? We don't answer to you." He kicked her again. "This is our land, our people. What we do here ain't none of your business." A rough hand yanked her wallet from her back pocket. "Dane Foster. New York."

"I'm not a Fed," Dane groaned. She licked her lips and spit out a pool of blood that had gathered in her mouth.

"You sure got a lot of questions for someone claiming not to be a Fed."

Dane clutched her side and squinted up at the dark figure looming over her. It was too dark to make out any features other than general size. A grizzly bear came to mind.

He leaned down and closed his hand around her throat. "What are you lookin' for if you ain't no Fed?"

"My family," Dane croaked. "I'm looking for my family."

The big man laughed. "Right, and I shit pink Easter eggs." He leaned close, turning Dane's face away so he spoke directly into her ear. "Mind your own business, Fed bitch. We have to talk again, I'll be putting you in there with the rest of the trash." He pushed Dane's face into the dirt as he stood. He gave her another kick to the back of her thigh. He laughed as he walked away.

Dane lay on the ground waiting for the pain to recede enough for her to move. Little by little she managed to sit up and brace herself against the bin. The lot was almost empty. She pulled herself up and staggered back to the bar. She had to get inside before Emma closed up, or she'd be out there all night. She held tight to the doorframe and pulled herself inside. She stumbled and fell to the floor. The band was packing up and the last customers were on their way out. The room fell silent as everyone looked at her.

Emma ran to Dane as she tried to push herself up. "What the hell happened to you?"

Dane peered through the swollen flesh closing around her eye. "I received a personal message out by the dumpster. Someone around here thinks I'm a Fed."

"Damn it, Dane. If you keep this up, you're going to get yourself killed."

Dane grimaced. "That was the message."

Emma looked around at the crowd of people watching. "Call the police, Alton." She pulled Dane into a chair. "That's it tonight, folks—we're closed." She didn't have to say it twice. The room was empty except for them and the band in seconds. No one wanted to be there when the police showed up.

Emma placed an ice pack over Dane's eye and handed her a cold beer.

"How about a bottle of whiskey instead?" Dane said, holding the ice to one cheek and the beer to the other.

Emma brushed a smudge of dirt off Dane's forehead and picked leaves and dirt out of her hair. "Not tonight, slugger." She handed Dane two Ibuprofen.

Dane laughed. "You think that will help?"

Emma shrugged. "Can't hurt."

Dane nodded. She tossed the pills into her mouth and chased it with the beer.

"Are you okay?" Emma asked.

Dane heard the worry in Emma's voice. At least she wasn't mad at her anymore.

"Yeah. I'm okay. I don't think I'll be running for a couple of days, but I'll live."

Emma caressed Dane's cheek in her palm. She took Dane's hand and lifted the ice pack back to Dane's eye. "Keep that on there for a while. You need it."

The police arrived and took her statement, but without identification or at least a description of the guy, there wasn't much they could do.

Emma left Dane to answer the officer's questions. "I have to get back to work. Let me know if you need anything."

Dane talked to the officer as she watched Emma work. This had to be hard on Emma. It had to bring back memories of her father's murder. Dane wondered what it had been like for Emma, not knowing who had taken her father's life. How was Emma staying here, knowing that her father's killer could be sitting in her bar, drinking her beer, and eating the food she prepared?

Dane sighed. How had her life gone so crazy?

Emma paced the floor of her room. Trevor had made it clear that Curtis was in some trouble, and that meant she was in trouble. Dane was lucky not to have broken bones after her encounter. She couldn't prove it, but she knew Trevor was behind what happened to Dane. Emma rubbed her hands up and down her arms, trying to rub away the chill of fear that had settled into her bones. She felt the walls closing in on her. A storm was coming, and she had no idea what she could do about it.

She needed to talk to Curtis, but there was no way she could do that while he was in jail. Not without the jailers using the information against him. His attorney was pretty sure he would get out at the next hearing, but there were no promises. The judge was trying to get through to Curtis, just like she was trying to get through to him. But if she didn't get some answers soon, she was afraid she would be the one paying for the mistakes Curtis had made. Emma sighed. Maybe it was better if Curtis didn't get out of jail. He was safe on the inside, at least for now. How long would it be before Trevor got to him there? It sure seemed that Curtis had bitten off more than he could chew this time. A visit from Trevor was as good as a call from the devil.

Emma turned to the photo of her parents hanging on the wall. It had been there as long as she could remember. It was a photo of her mother and father on the day they opened the bar, only one week after getting married. Her father had said he had to choose between the good book and the banknote. He opened the bar to support his family and pay for the farm. Jellico was already a dying town and he knew alcohol was the one thing people would spend their money on.

She'd grown up in the business. She knew everything she needed to know to run the place by the time she turned sixteen. But she never understood the sacrifice Daddy made until it was her turn to make the bar her own.

She touched her fingers to his face, letting them rest against the cool glass. He had always been an honest man. He always stood for what was right. But it had gotten him killed. She had asked herself a thousand times if she should close the bar. It would have been easier to leave it all behind if it hadn't been for Curtis. He wouldn't do well anywhere else. This was his home. It was all he knew. Tears stung her eyes as she stared at her father's picture. Part of her had always hoped his killer would come back. She had dreamed of confronting the coward who had killed him. Like most things in a small town, it was just a matter of time before the secret was revealed.

Emma heard a muffled cry upstairs followed by the gentle creek of the floorboards. She wiped her face with her hands and brushed her hair back. She took a deep breath, filing her feelings away in the deepest recesses of her heart. She slipped down the hall and climbed the stairs to Dane's room.

She knocked gently on the door and waited. A moment later the door opened. Emma was shocked at the sight of Dane's swollen face. Her eyes were red and a sheen of sweat coated her skin. Her T-shirt had a line of sweat that ran from her chest around the curve of her breasts. She wore a pair of running shorts and her feet were bare. The smell of alcohol was thick in the room.

"I heard you pacing. Are you okay?" Emma took a step toward Dane, placing her hand against her chest. Dane's muscles were tense, and a slight tremor shook her body.

"I don't feel so well," Dane answered.

Emma spotted the half empty bottle of whiskey on the floor next to the bed. She lifted her hand to Dane's forehead, feeling for a fever with the back of her hand. "You're all clammy, but I don't think you have a fever. What's wrong?"

"Bad dreams. I don't think I can get through this," Dane said, her voice barely more than a whisper.

Emma frowned. She'd seen Dane drink before, but she'd never seen her like this. She wasn't sure what to do. She took Dane's hand and pulled her back into the room, leading her to the bed. "Sit down."

She held Dane's hand as she sat on the edge of the bed. She could tell Dane was hurting, but this was more than the beating she'd taken. She'd seen this look before in the faces at the bar, men and women trying to chase away memories too painful to forget. "Do you want to tell me about it?"

Dane dropped her head and stared at the floor. "She's there every time I close my eyes."

"Who?"

"Michelle."

Emma swallowed the prick of jealousy at the mention of another woman filling Dane's dreams. She was surprised by her reaction. She hadn't wanted to admit she was attracted to Dane, let alone had any feelings for her. She didn't want to have her heart broken again. It was only a matter of time before Dane would leave to go back to her life. She took a deep breath, pushing her feelings aside.

Dane looked at Emma, her gaze blazing with guilt and regret. "Have you ever done something that hurt someone else and no matter what you do you can't ever make it right?"

Emma didn't know where this was going. "No. I don't think so."

"Well, I did. I let my best friend down, and I can never make it right."

Emma remembered the story Dane had told her over drinks and dinner. "Why not?"

"Because I got her killed."

Emma flinched. Had she heard right? "I don't understand."

Dane rubbed her temples. "We had an early shoot scheduled. It was a tight deadline and we needed to get in and out of a war-stricken area in Iraq. I was late for our meeting, as usual. But this shoot meant a lot to Michelle. She'd become obsessed with how the women and children were suffering. The guide insisted we leave. Michelle refused to wait for me. I said I was sorry, but she wouldn't wait." Dane buried her face in her hands, rocking back and forth as if her body wanted to escape her mental pain.

Emma waited for Dane to continue. It was clear something bad had happened to Michelle.

"Michelle was awesome. I'll never know why she put up with my shit as long as she did. She had the most amazing blue eyes I've ever seen. You know, the kind of blue that makes you feel like they can see inside you." Dane shook her head and gripped her hair in her fists. "I can't stop seeing those eyes. She begs me to help her. She screams my name. No matter what I do I can't save her."

Emma's heart raced. She could feel the danger building. "What happened to her, Dane?"

Dane continued to rock back and forth. "She left. I stood in the hotel lobby and watched her get into her car with one last look back at me. I saw the hurt and disappointment in her eyes. The next second a car across the street exploded. Glass shattered all around me. Pieces of cars, buildings, and people were everywhere. When I managed to get up, her car was on fire and she was pinned inside. I couldn't get her out. Blood streamed from her ears. She was burning and begging for help. Those desperate blue eyes were burning into my soul, and I couldn't get her out. People converged and pried the shards of metal away and did their best to control the fire. She never took her eyes off mine all the way to the hospital. I held on to her with everything I had in me. I begged, I demanded that she not give up. But I saw it. I saw the moment the light in her eyes went out."

Tears welled in Emma's eyes as she imagined the horrific scene as Dane described the death of her friend. "Oh, Dane. I'm so sorry."

Dane shook her head. "If I'd been there when I was supposed to be, she would be alive. My carelessness killed her."

Emma gripped Dane's hand. "There's no way you could have known."

Dane's skin burned with the depth of her grief. Emma couldn't imagine what it would be like to see someone she loved die in such a horrific way. She understood Dane's guilt. She knew what it was like to believe things could be different—if only.

"You were there, Dane. You didn't let go. In the end she had you with her. She was with someone she loved."

"It should have been me."

Emma put her arm around Dane, pulling Dane's head to rest against her shoulder. "You fought for her. She knew that."

"It doesn't matter though, does it?"

Emma sighed as she brushed her fingers through Dane's hair. "I believe it does."

Dane fell silent. She let go of some of the tension ravaging her body. Emma didn't move. She held Dane until she heard Dane's breathing change. She had managed to break free of the nightmare.

Dane sat up. "I'm sorry to put all that on you. Thank you for listening, for being here."

"I'm glad I could be here. That's something you shouldn't hold in. It sounds like Michelle loved you, and I can't imagine she would want you to blame yourself for what happened."

Dane looked across the room at a spot on the wall, avoiding Emma's gaze. "I just can't get the image out of my mind."

Emma looked at Dane. The side of her face was swollen and bruised. Her shoulders were slumped, and her heart was broken.

"Tell me about her. How did you meet? What made you friends?"

Dane smiled at the memory. "We met on a blind date." She shook her head. "It was a complete disaster. We spent the whole evening debating every topic we could think of. We were opposites in almost every way. She had a way of telling me I was an idiot without completely picking a fight. The friends who set us up were right to introduce us, but not for the reasons they thought. We were a horrible match as a romantic couple. We knew instantly that would never work. There was no attraction between us. But we were fast friends. We were pretty much inseparable after that night."

Dane talked most of the night, sharing stories about Michelle. She made herself sound like she was a selfish scoundrel, but the stories of their friendship said differently.

Emma got the impression that Dane was a kind soul, even if she could be a bit reckless. Her heart was wounded, and she had lost faith in herself. The space Michelle left in Dane's life had left her ungrounded. Dane had come here looking for her family because she needed to feel connected to someone. She needed a place to belong. She needed to be loved.

Dane curled up on her side, gripping the pillow in her arms. Emma sat with her back against the wall and watched Dane drift off to sleep. She was glad Dane was there. She was glad she was able to offer her a respite for a little while. She knew the nightmares would return, but for now, at least, Dane could rest.

Chapter Five

Emma paced the lobby floor, waiting for Curtis. She was anxious to have him home, but afraid of what he might do next. She would set some strict rules but knew there was no way she could stop Curtis from doing anything. If he wouldn't listen to her, maybe his probation officer could get through to him.

She stopped pacing as the door opened and an officer escorted Curtis from holding to the lobby. Curtis looked sheepish, pushing his hands into his pockets and looking at his feet.

Emma smiled. Curtis had only been in jail for a few days, but it had taken a toll. It was good to see him in the open, not behind a glass partition and locked doors.

Curtis stopped in front of her, looking like a puppy that knew he was in trouble. "Hey, Emma."

Emma pulled Curtis into a hug. "Hey, sweetie."

Curtis wrapped his arms around her and hugged her back. "Are you still mad?"

"Yep. But I still love you too."

Curtis pulled away and looked at her. "I'm sorry."

"I know," she answered. "We have a lot to talk about."

Curtis groaned. "I was afraid you'd say that."

Emma brushed her fingers through his hair. "We'll get to all of that later. Come on, let's get you home."

They pushed through the doors into the open air. Curtis blinked against the bright sun, his eyes unaccustomed to the light. An engine revved. Emma looked up to see a black Dodge truck with dark tinted windows pass in front of them. She watched as it circled the parking lot and stopped at the end of the row facing them. Emma had the feeling they were watching her and Curtis.

"Do you know them?"

"No. I don't think so. I can't see inside."

"Let's go." Emma took Curtis by the arm, turning toward her truck. She stopped dead in her tracks as Trevor stepped around the truck parked next to hers.

"Hey, Trevor," Curtis said cheerfully.

"Get in the truck, Curtis."

"But—"

"You heard me. Get in the truck."

Curtis did as he was told.

Trevor crossed his arms over his broad chest and leaned against the truck, blocking Emma's way.

Emma stepped in front of Trevor. "What do you want?"

"I told you. Curtis has something that belongs to me."

"I doubt he has anything that belongs to anyone at the moment," Emma countered, "unless you're interested in the pair of tube socks I brought him and dirty underwear."

Trevor smiled. "I wanted to remind Curtis that he owes me. I'll give you a few days to work it out, but I'll be back for what's mine. If he doesn't have what I need by then, you and I will have to talk about other arrangements."

Emma ground her teeth together, holding back her anger. "There will be no arrangement between you and me. I told you before—my bar is off-limits. If you bring any of your filth around there, I'll call the police."

Trevor pushed away from the truck, using his six-three frame to intimidate her. She refused to back down.

"We'll see." Trevor rapped his knuckles across the window of her truck and pointed his finger at Curtis. He turned back to her, taking another step closer. "Talk to your brother."

Emma refused to back down. "Stay away from us."

Trevor leaned to the side and spit on the ground next to Emma's boot. "Talk to your brother. I'll see you in a few days."

Emma seethed as she watched Trevor walk away. She hated everything about him. Whatever Curtis was into was bad.

She sighed, opening the truck door. She slid onto the leather seat and slammed the door. She wanted to get away from this place and Trevor.

"What's up with Trevor?" Curtis asked.

"That's what I want to talk to you about. Trevor says you have something that belongs to him. What's he talking about?"

Curtis looked nervous. "I don't know. Maybe I should go talk to him."

"No," Emma said, her tone stern. "Listen to me, Curtis. I know Trevor had something to do with the drugs you had on you when you were arrested."

"But I don't have those anymore," Curtis insisted. "The police took those."

Emma closed her eyes and tried to rein in her growing anger. "Is there more? Do you have more drugs somewhere?"

"No," he said in the familiar tone he used when he wasn't telling the truth.

"Curtis, this is serious. I need you to be honest with me. Trevor means business. You have to tell me everything."

"Can't we just go home? I'm hungry."

Emma sighed. "You aren't leaving the house until I know what happened. And I mean everything. Plus, you'll be working at the bar with me. No running around on your own. I expect you up in the morning to take care of the animals too."

"Aw, Emma, that's not fair."

"Really? You don't think that's fair. You will pay me back every penny you owe, and you'll be paying your own probation fees and all your fines. I can't trust you not to get out and get yourself in trouble, so you can work it off. You have a year of probation—get used to it."

Curtis slumped down in his seat. He wouldn't look at her and didn't say another word during the drive home.

He jumped out of the truck the moment it came to a stop in front of the house and ran to the porch. He stopped, looking around from side to side. He turned to Emma as she climbed the steps.

"Where's Samson?"

Emma heard the worry in his voice. "He's fine. Dane has been taking him with her when she's out. He likes riding in her Jeep."

Curtis shrugged and pushed through the door, heading straight for the kitchen.

"Oh no, you don't. You go get a shower and put on some clean clothes. I'll have lunch ready for you when you come down."

Curtis rolled his eyes. "Maybe I should have stayed in jail."

"Maybe you should have," Emma countered as Curtis bounded up the stairs.

Dane parked the Jeep next to Emma's truck. She had hoped to be there when Curtis got home but had some trouble finding some of the old addresses she'd been researching. Samson turned out to be a great guard dog. She wasn't convinced he was really deaf. That or he had a sixth sense about trouble. He would seem sound asleep or oblivious to things around him until the moment someone approached her or her Jeep. Samson would growl and show his teeth if anyone came near the Jeep, and he would stand between her and any person who approached her. She'd never been afraid to be out on her own before, but after the beating she took at the bar, she was happy he had her back.

Samson jumped out of the Jeep and ambled onto the porch. He circled his usual spot by the door and lay down with a groan. Dane patted his head. "Thanks, buddy. Have a good nap."

The smell of fried squash filled the house, making Dane's mouth water. She stepped through the door to the kitchen to find Emma sitting at the table. She looked worried.

"Hey, you okay? Where's Curtis?"

Emma unlaced her fingers and pushed back in her chair. "He's taking a shower."

Dane could tell something was eating at Emma. "What's wrong?"

"Trevor was waiting for us outside the jail. Whatever Curtis has gotten into must be bad."

Dane frowned. "What did Curtis say about it?"

"He says the police took the drugs he had. He says he doesn't have anything else."

"What's the story?"

Emma sighed. "I don't know yet. That's what I'm waiting for him to tell me."

Dane was unsure what to do next. "Do you want me to stick around? Maybe he'll talk to me."

"Let me see how far I can get. Maybe he'll open up to you more later if he doesn't think we're ganging up on him."

They heard footsteps on the stairs. Dane nodded. "Is that lunch I smell cooking?"

"Yes. It will be done in a few minutes if you're hungry."

Dane turned as she heard Curtis behind her.

"Dang, Dane. What happened to you?"

The bruises to her face were just beginning to heal, and she still looked like she'd gone a few rounds in the ring.

Emma spoke before Dane could answer. "Someone beat her up outside the bar the other night."

"Why?" Curtis asked, still staring at the bruise on Dane's face.

"Someone thinks I'm a Fed, and they don't like me asking questions about my family."

Curtis whistled. "Man, that's bad. Is that why you took Samson with you today?"

Dane nodded.

Curtis took a seat at the table across from Emma. "Who did it?"

"We don't know," Emma answered.

Curtis jerked as if he'd been hit, his eyes wide with surprise. "It's like before, when Daddy died?"

Emma nodded. "Dane didn't get a look at the guy's face. He jumped her when she took out the trash. When you come to work tonight, I don't want you going out by yourself. One of us needs to be with you at all times."

Curtis looked a little green.

"There's a lot going on right now, Curtis. That's why it's important for you to tell me what happened with Trevor. He's been coming around trying to make me push his drugs through the bar. I won't have drugs around here. You know that. Whatever you've been into, you've brought *me* into it now. You have to tell me the truth."

"I just took some stuff to one of Trevor's friends, one of the regular guys. It was no big deal. But the police showed up and the next thing I know, the guy was cussing me out, saying I was a narc. I tried to tell him I wasn't, but he kept yelling at me. Then the police arrested us and took me to jail."

Dane studied Curtis. "What happened to the other guy? Did he give you a hard time in jail?"

Curtis shook his head. "They kept me in solitary for a couple of days. When they took me to the pod, he wasn't there."

Dane frowned. She looked at Emma. "Sounds like a setup. It's possible this guy is working with the cops and rolled on Curtis. It's easier to take out the little guy than go after the big guy."

"Do you really think Trevor is mad at me?" Curtis asked.

"This is so much worse than Trevor being mad at you," Emma snapped.

Dane cleared her throat, signaling Emma to calm down.

"But Trevor is my friend."

"This doesn't have anything to do with whether or not Trevor likes you, Curtis. Drugs are his business. If you lost his drugs, he lost money."

Curtis nodded.

"What else do I need to know, Curtis?" Emma asked not ready to let this go.

Curtis hesitated. "Nothin'." He glanced back at Dane. "I promise I won't do it again. I didn't mean to cause trouble."

Dane took the hint that Curtis didn't want to say any more with her there. "I've got some pictures I need to go through. I'll let you guys talk. Let me know when lunch is ready?"

Emma nodded.

As she made her way up the stairs, Dane could hear Emma's muffled voice pushing Curtis to say more. She was grateful not to be the one on the receiving end of Emma's anger for once.

Emma tossed Curtis a bar towel. "I need you to clean that table at the end, then bring out more Bud Light."

"Got it."

Emma was relieved that Curtis had kept his head down and worked hard the first two nights at the bar. She knew he felt bad about the trouble he had brought on, but she worried he was more hurt by Trevor than afraid of what might happen next. He had been even more quiet since his meeting with his probation officer. She wondered how long his compliance would last. By this time, he would usually be driving her crazy.

Curtis carried out two cases of beer and started stocking the cooler.

"You've been a big help tonight. Thanks."

Curtis nodded.

Emma's heart ached a little. She worried she'd been too hard on him. His spirit seemed broken. His usual happy-go-lucky attitude had been replaced by quiet brooding. She was exhausted, and Dane was still nursing her bruises. They could all use a break.

"I was thinking maybe we would get some of the family together tomorrow and do a bonfire. What do you think?"

Curtis looked up, a glint of excitement in his eye. "Really?"

"Why not? It's been a while since we all got together and just had a good time."

"That'd be great. Paul could bring his guitar and James his banjo. You could even play your fiddle."

Emma smiled at his enthusiasm. "It's been a while, but I guess I could dust off the old bow."

"Can Dane come?"

Emma shrugged. "If she wants to." She realized she'd just assumed Dane would be there. Dane had become a part of their daily lives. Emma hadn't realized how much she'd accepted Dane until this moment. The thought made her uneasy. She wasn't used to relying on anyone. Dane had earned some trust, but that didn't mean Emma would let her guard down. She knew Curtis was attached to Dane and she didn't want to think of what it would do to him when Dane decided to move on. Emma knew that pain. She never wanted to feel that emptiness again.

"Emma?"

Emma jumped at the sound of Curtis's voice. She'd been lost in her thoughts and lost track of what she was supposed to be doing. "Yeah."

"You okay?"

"Yeah. I'm okay. You just caught me napping." She glanced over at Dane, sitting at the end of the bar nursing a whiskey. "When you finish, I'd like you to clean up in the back. Then you can take a break. I'll bring you and Dane some dinner."

"Fried bologna and cheese for me."

Emma laughed. "You got it."

When Curtis was out of sight, Emma went to check on Dane. "Something wrong with my whiskey?"

Dane glanced up at her and shrugged. "Just trying to slow things down a bit."

"Your eye is looking better. How are the ribs?"

Dane took a sip of her whiskey. "Not bad. Doesn't hurt much anymore, just looks ugly."

"Listen, we're going to have a bonfire tomorrow. It won't be anything big, just some family. We get together and tell stories, play some music, dance, and have a few drinks. Want to come?" As soon as the words were out of her mouth, it was as if a kaleidoscope of butterflies had swarmed in her stomach. Why was it so important to her that Dane be there? *Please say yes.*

Dane's eyes widened and her brows lifted in surprise. "Sure. Sounds like fun."

Emma clutched the bar towel, trying to hide her relief. She wondered when it had become so important to her that Dane be a part of things. "Okay then. We'll meet at the house around seven tomorrow."

"Hey, Emma," Dane said as Emma turned away.

Emma turned back to Dane. "Yeah."

"Thanks."

Emma smiled. "Sure. There will be a few folks there that may know something about your mom. I hope you make it."

Dane brightened. "I'll be there."

Emma felt warmth spread across her skin at the sight of hope in Dane's eyes. Curtis wasn't the only one feeling down. They could all use a break.

CHAPTER SIX

Dane spent the day helping Curtis gather wood for the fire. The hay had been cut and stacked in rows along the tree line, leaving the field open. Stones circled an area marked by chunks of charred wood, making the perfect place to gather around a fire.

Curtis tossed the branches from the old pine tree onto the pile as Dane set her load aside. He plopped down onto one of the stones and wiped his brow with the back of his hand. "This is too much work."

Dane laughed. "I thought you were excited about tonight."

"I was. But I think this was just Emma's way of getting me to carry this tree out of the yard." He tossed another branch onto the pile. "Haven't you noticed everything always turns into work?"

Dane laughed again. "It isn't that bad. It's good to help. She can't do everything alone, you know."

"I know. But I don't like all this stuff."

Dane kept her voice smooth as she tried to help Curtis understand. "I know, Curtis. But I can't imagine Emma likes it very much either. She's tired. She needs your help."

Curtis kicked a rock with his shoe. "She's really mad at me."

"She's really worried about you," Dane countered.

"She's always telling me what to do."

Dane clapped her hand on Curtis's shoulder. "She's trying to protect you."

Curtis scuffed his shoe across the ground again. "I don't need protection from my friends. She never likes any of my friends."

"Why do you think that is?"

Curtis shrugged.

"How did you and Trevor become friends?" Dane asked.

"Trevor wouldn't let the other kids pick on me at school. He wasn't afraid to fight anybody, and I was his little buddy. He didn't have much, so I would bring extra food to school so he had lunch. We looked out for each other."

"What kind of trouble did you get into? Emma said you almost got killed a couple of times."

Curtis frowned. "We went to his old man's place one night after a football game to pick up some of his stuff so we could go camping over the weekend. His dad was drunk and mad about somethin' and started hitting Trevor's mom. Trevor tried to make him stop. His dad got real mad and got his gun. We ran. He shot at us out the back door. The neighbors called the police, and Trevor's dad told the police that we were stealing from him."

"Didn't his mom tell the police what happened?"

Curtis shook his head. "No. She was too scared of him."

"How did you start selling marijuana?" Curtis was in a talkative mood, so she might as well get as much of the story as she could.

Curtis grinned. "When we got a little older, Trevor's dad gave us a little if we would take some to his friends. After Trevor's mom left and his dad got sent off, Trevor did it to make money. I just helped him out when I could. He didn't have anybody, and I didn't either. He's always been my friend."

Dane understood Curtis for the first time. "I get it. I can see why he's so important to you. Friends take care of each other. But I don't think they do things to get friends put in jail or get them hurt."

Curtis frowned. "You sound like Emma."

"I'm just trying to be a good friend too, Curtis. Sometimes friends have to tell us when we are screwing up."

"Friends don't tell on each other," Curtis countered.

"I know you want to protect Trevor. But you have to ask yourself—why would your friend threaten your sister?"

Curtis bristled. "Trevor wouldn't hurt Emma."

"Then why would he say it? Why scare her like that?"

Curtis stared at his feet.

"What's Trevor so upset about?"

Curtis shook his head.

"Look, I know you sell weed for him. What else is going on?"

"I don't know. Emma won't let me talk to him to work it out." Curtis shrugged. "The cops took the weed and the money I had. He knows I can't do anything about that."

"Just remember—I'm your friend too. You can talk to me."

Curtis nodded.

Dane wasn't getting very far with Curtis. She wasn't sure if he would ever tell what was really going on. "I think this should be enough wood for tonight. Let's go back to the house and get cleaned up."

Curtis stood. "Good, I'm hungry."

Emma tossed another log on the fire, scattering sparks and embers into the air. It was good to see her family. She should have everyone get together more often. It made her feel less alone. She tossed the last of the food trash into a bag and loaded it into the bed of her truck. She plucked a beer from the cooler on her way back.

Her cousin Paul had started to strum his guitar and his wife Sue was humming along to the tune. It was time to get down to business. Sue started to sing. Her angelic voice started soft and slow as she told a story of a soldier going to war, leaving his family to scrape by and work the land alone. A chill ran down Emma's arms as she listened to the haunting tune.

Emma sat next to Dane, swaying and humming along with the song. Dane looked mesmerized as she snapped photos of the group. She was glad Dane had joined them. She seemed to be enjoying herself.

"Are you having a good time?" Emma asked.

"Yes. This is wonderful," Dane said, smiling up at Emma. "Thanks for sharing it with me."

"Just wait. We're just getting started."

The song changed, and Emma's cousin James plucked his banjo and Mary picked up the vocals. This was one of Emma's favorites from when she was a girl. She remembered her mother and grandmother singing along to Loretta Lynn together when the Grand Ole Opry came on TV.

Emma lifted her violin and tucked it under her chin. The slow pull of the bow added a mournful tone to the simple tune.

Emma let her heartache pour out through the violin. Music was the one thing that she felt explained her when words failed. She could put all her feelings into the notes and let the music carry them away. She looked across the fire at Curtis. His broad childlike smile warmed her heart. Her aunt Lily wrapped her arms around Curtis and planted a kiss on his cheek, making him blush. Emma laughed.

It was getting late. The stars blanketed the sky like a map of the heavens. A half-moon hung above, giving the field an ethereal glow. The wood popped and crackled, adding its own notes to the songs they played.

"Come on, Emma. It's your turn," James said. Her niece Emily joined in with her mandolin.

Emma rested her violin on her knee and kept time with each tap of her foot against the ground. She could feel Dane's gaze on her. She steadied her breath as she tried to remember the words to the old song. Emmylou Harris had always been one of her favorites, but this time the song held more meaning to her.

Emma nodded to James, closed her eyes, and they began to sing.

❖

Dane put down her camera and stared at Emma. She was sure she had never heard a voice more beautiful than Emma's. The subtle lines around her eyes and mouth softened, and her body relaxed into the words of the song. She was transformed.

Dane snapped a few photos capturing Emma. She wanted to preserve the moment and the feeling forever.

As the song ended, the group transitioned into the next. They picked up the tempo with Lynyrd Skynyrd's "The Ballad of Curtis Loew." Emma looked at Dane and smiled. Dane's heart skipped a beat.

"That was beautiful," Dane said, awe edging her voice.

"Thanks," Emma said, a smile curving the corners of her lips.

Dane held Emma's gaze. "Does everyone in your family play or sing?"

Emma nodded. "It's a family tradition."

"What about Curtis?"

Emma smiled. "Oh yeah. Him too."

"Really?" Dane said, surprised.

Emma's eyes sparked. "Just wait."

Dane was shocked when Curtis pulled out a harmonica and began to play. The kid was good, really good. She shook her head. "Wow."

Emma nudged her shoulder against Dane's. "What about you? Do you play?"

Dane shook her head. "No, but I wish I did. This is fun." Dane looked around at the group. The night was winding down, and she could see that Emma's aunt Lily was getting tired.

"All right, guys," Emma said. "I think it's time we took this back to the house."

The group packed up their instruments, and Dane helped Curtis load the coolers into the back of the truck while Emma helped her aunt Lily to her feet and steadied her as she made her way to the truck.

Emma held the door for Lily. "You're staying at the house tonight, right?" Emma asked.

Lily smiled. "If you don't mind. I know it isn't far, but I don't see well at night and I may have had a little too much whiskey."

"I had hoped you would. It's been a long time since we had a good talk."

Paul and Sue gave everyone big hugs. "Thanks for having us out. It's been too long," Paul said.

"We'll do it again soon," Emma promised.

Dane hoped Emma would stick to her word. She had a good family. She was guilty of letting work get in the way of her life. This had been good for all of them.

James and Mary were next in line.

"Aren't you staying at the house?" Emma asked.

James shook his head. "Better not. It was sure fun, Emma, but we both have to work tomorrow, and I know if we go up to the house, you'll have us up all night playing and talking."

"All right then. I'll let you off the hook this time."

Dane was having a good time, but she was eager to get back to the house and talk to Lily. This was her best shot at finding out something about her mother.

Dane poured whiskey into two glasses and handed one to Lily. Emma settled for another beer.

"So, what is it you wanted to talk to me about," Lily said, placing her hand on Emma's knee.

"We were hoping maybe you knew Dane's mother."

Lily looked at Dane. "Well, I don't know. What's her name?"

"Pearl Jean Stewart," Dane answered. "She grew up around here. Her parents were Isaak and Ida."

Lily frowned. "Well, yes. But I knew her as Jenny. She grew up a few miles down the road from us. That poor family sure had a hard time."

Dane sat forward, resting her elbows on her knees. Her heart thundered as her excitement grew. This was the first time she'd met anyone who actually knew her mother. "What do you mean?"

"Well, it was just awful when her little brother died in that fire. He was a little rascal even back then. The best they could figure was that he was playing with matches in the house. Jenny had a terrible time with it. Her family split up and stayed with friends and relatives until they could rebuild. I don't think her parents ever got over his death. I don't remember Isaak talking much after that."

"What was Jenny like?" Dane asked.

Lily tilted her head to the side and studied Dane. "Has something happened to Jenny?"

"She died when I was fourteen. Breast cancer."

"Oh, that poor girl." She shook her head. "I always hoped she had a happy life after she left with David."

"You knew my father too?"

Lily smiled. "Sure, I met him a couple of times. Jenny used to talk about him. He was her knight in shining armor. They had a lot of fun together. He was never made for this town. His father was transferred here to run the plant. But David was a college man. He planned on making his mark in the city, and Jenny was more than willing to go with him. Her cousin Thomas didn't like the idea of Jenny being with an outsider. He thought Jenny's place was here." She took a sip of her drink. "Thomas and David never got along. David hated Jenny's family for how they treated her and for letting Thomas control her. Thomas said David thought he was better than him. The two were like fire and gasoline. They couldn't be in the same place together without a blowup."

Lily fell silent for a while as if thinking about what she wanted to say next.

"Jenny showed up at our house one night. I know something bad happened, but she wouldn't tell us. She just said Thomas beat her up and went after David. Said he was going to kill him. Poor Jenny was terrified."

"What happened?" Dane asked, her concern turning to fear. What had her mother gone through?

"Thomas didn't find David. He had already left town. But what Thomas didn't know was that Jenny and David had made plans. A few days later David came back for her. When Jenny left, no one ever heard from her again."

Dane frowned. "Why? There must be more to this story. My mother barely mentioned her family to me. What could be so terrible that she would want to leave like that and cut them out of her life?"

Lily pursed her lips and sighed. She shook her head. "I don't know, sweetie. I just know your momma was a kind, sweet woman. Her family was the rough sort. They had their own way of doing things. Your momma was smart and outgoing and had plans of her own that they didn't understand. She had to make a choice between freedom and family. Personally, I think she did the right thing. That cousin of hers was always trouble. He never would have let her have a life here."

Dane couldn't wrap her head around this story. It answered some of her questions but opened the door for so many more.

"Is there anyone else I can talk to about my mother? Someone she was close to, or any family left?"

Lily frowned. "Thomas would be the only one left. He went off to prison for a few years for assaulting a woman, and robbery, I think. He started getting into all kinds of trouble not long after Jenny left. When he came back, he changed his name. Went by Tom Sikes. Of course, he's back in prison now."

Dane nodded. "Yeah, I did hear about that."

"Is David all right?" Lily asked.

Dane looked up at her, surprised by the question. "Yeah. He's fine."

"Well, I'd ask him if I were you."

Dane shook her head. "He won't talk about it. He won't talk about her."

Lily frowned. "I don't know what all happened back then, sweetie. But David loved Jenny. I can't imagine there was anything he wouldn't do for her."

Dane frowned. That didn't sound like her father at all. "Thank you, Lily. I appreciate you talking to me."

Lily smiled. "You have her eyes."

The statement made Dane smile. "Thanks."

Lily turned to Emma. "Now, tell me what's going on with our boy. I hear he's gotten himself into more trouble."

Emma sighed.

Dane gathered the glasses. "I think I'll let you two visit. Thanks again, Lily. I'll see you in the morning."

Dane shut the door to her room and lay on the bed, her arms folded behind her head. She stared up at the ceiling, trying to read between the lines of the story she'd just heard about her parents. What changed with them? Lily talked about them like they were lovestruck soul mates. That wasn't what she remembered at all. What had her mother gone through? What was so terrible that she would just disappear and leave her family behind?

CHAPTER SEVEN

Emma was worried about Dane. It had been two days since their talk with Lily, and Dane hadn't been down for meals and had not been to the bar. Emma put on the coffee and looked out the window. Dane's Jeep was gone. She frowned. Curtis hadn't been down either. Did he go with her?

She went to the bottom of the stairs and called out, "Curtis?" There was no answer. She went to his room and knocked on the door. When he didn't answer, she opened the door and looked inside. Curtis wasn't there. What were those two up to?

She had her coffee and set about the morning routine. A missing Curtis meant none of the chores had been done. She had to admit it was nice having the morning to herself for a change. She didn't have to cook breakfast, so there was no mess to clean up. Once the animals were taken care of, there wasn't much left she had to do right away. Everything would keep for another day.

She decided to take a walk along the property like she used to do with her father. It was what she did now when she needed to clear her head, and it made her feel a little closer to him. Sometimes she was amazed by how much she missed her parents. It was times like this that not knowing who killed her father haunted her. Most of the time she stayed too busy to think about anything more than the next thing that needed to be done. But there were other times when she would be at the bar and every hair on her body would stand on end, and her heart would ache. Those moments were the hardest. She would always search the faces of the people around her and wonder if her father's killer was right there in the room.

She imagined this was something like what Dane must be feeling after learning about how her mother was treated. The more she learned, the more she needed to know. Emma was sad for Dane. She was searching for a place to belong, proof she could change. Emma wasn't certain the answers Dane would find would lead to the revelations she had been searching for.

Emma walked along the creek and stopped to run her fingers through the cold water. She had always been drawn to water. She smiled, remembering her father teaching her how to swim. He had built her confidence in the shallow wading water and taught her how to hold her breath and dunk her head under. Then one day when they came to the creek to play, he picked her up and threw her in the deeper water. She had squealed as she flew. The instant she hit the surface, she knew what to do. From that moment on she had been his little minnow, spending every moment she could in the water.

Emma stripped off her clothes and waded into the crisp, cool water. It was invigorating to feel the cold against her naked flesh. She dipped her head under allowing the silence to engulf her. She raked her hands through the pebbles at the bottom, feeling the sand and stone slip through her hands like time through an hourglass. She pushed to the surface, her face breaking the water to be kissed by the warm rays of the sun.

A branch snapped nearby. Emma spun around to see the source of the sound.

Dane stepped out into the light. "I hope I didn't scare you."

Emma glanced to her clothes draped across a tree limb.

Dane followed her gaze, a wry smile spreading across her face. "This must be my lucky day. It isn't often I stumble across a beautiful woman swimming naked in the woods."

"What are you doing here?" Emma snapped, sinking deeper into the water to hide herself.

"You weren't at the house. I came looking for you."

"What do you want?"

Dane's smile widened. "I can see I've caught you off guard. This isn't fair." Dane began to remove her clothes.

Emma stared in disbelief. "What are you doing?"

"Joining you."

"No, you are not."

"Looks that way to me." Dane kicked off her shoes and draped her jeans and her shirt over a bush. She grasped her sports bra and pulled it over her head, exposing her breasts.

Emma froze, unable to look away. The scars on Dane's arm seemed benign compared to the jagged scars adorning her side and upper thigh. The lean muscles in Dane's legs and stomach flexed as she moved. Dane slid her hands to her briefs. Emma was sure she would stop breathing.

Dane stood exposed to her, allowing Emma to study her before she walked, tenderfooted, into the water.

Emma felt heat flood her face as Dane's nipples hardened from the chill of the water.

"This feels amazing," Dane said as she leaned back, dipping her head into the water, her bare breasts mounds of refuge tempting Emma. Emma followed the stretch of muscles along Dane's neck to her shoulders. This was so unfair. Her pulse raced, and her mouth watered at the thought of taking Dane's breast into her mouth.

"Why are you doing this?"

"What?" Dane said, grinning at Emma.

"You know what."

"Would you prefer I stayed on the bank and watched you?"

"I would prefer that you had left me in peace. I thought I was alone, or I wouldn't have done this."

"But here we are." Dane disappeared beneath the surface.

Emma peered into the water, trying to see where Dane had gone. She turned around and around, panicked.

Dane surfaced across the creek. She crawled along the rock ledge, her buttocks breaching the surface of the water.

Emma swallowed. She eyed Dane, unsure what she would do next. Emma began to move toward her clothes. She was torn. If she stayed, she would have to face her growing desire, and if she left, she would have to bare her naked body. Either way she would expose herself.

"What are you so afraid of?" Dane asked. "We're only swimming."

"Right," Emma said in disbelief.

Dane slipped beneath the water again, this time surfacing only inches from Emma. "See, this isn't so bad."

It was Emma's turn to disappear beneath the water. Two could play this game. She surfaced in the center of the pool. Rivulets of water cascaded down her face as she brushed her hands across her hair, pushing it away from her face. She drew in a deep breath, relieved by the distance between them. Dane turned toward her. Emma slipped back under the water.

Emma repeated this move each time Dane tried to come near her.

"What are you afraid of, Emma? I'm not going to hurt you. Just have a little fun."

Emma considered the question. Dane wasn't trying to hurt her, but that was exactly what would happen if she let this go too far. Dane would leave, and she would hurt.

Dane circled her arms in the water. Emma gazed at the strength in Dane's shoulders, the pale lines of skin left untanned, protected by her clothing on her long runs. Dane swam for a while, keeping her distance. Emma was tempted to reach for Dane. She wanted to feel the silky smoothness of her skin, slick against her body.

Dane seemed to read her thoughts. With each turn of her arms, Dane slowly closed the distance between them. Her expression was playful. Emma liked the way Dane's eyes sparkled when she looked at her.

Dane took a deliberate step toward Emma. Once again, Emma sank into the water. When she surfaced, Dane was gone. Emma turned, unable to see anything. Her heart raced with anticipation. She squealed when Dane's hand brushed against her side. Dane pulled her against her, Dane's body gliding against Emma's as she surfaced in front of her.

Emma was shocked by the sudden contact. Her head swooned, and she caught her breath as she clasped her arm around Dane's shoulder. She didn't have time to think or react. Dane's lips were on hers. The tender brush of Dane's lips and the heat of her body took her breath away.

Emma wrapped her arms around Dane, giving in to the kiss.

Dane stroked her back. She kicked her legs, propelling them upward. Emma's foot brushed against the soft, pebbled bottom. They were moving into more shallow water. Dane never relinquished her hold, deepening the kiss with each stroke of her tongue.

In the shallow water Dane lay back, pulling Emma on top of her, their bodies gliding against one another.

Emma was lost. Dane was strong yet tender. She was persistent but not demanding. Emma felt something change between them. She wanted this. She wanted Dane. But she couldn't let this happen. She couldn't.

"Stop," Emma said breaking the kiss. "I have to stop this."

Dane peered up at her. Emma could see the desire and confusion mingling in her eyes. "Why should we stop? I've wanted to kiss you for ages." Dane placed her palm against Emma's cheek. "I know you want this too."

Emma shook her head. "Please. I just can't." Emma pulled away. Her heart ached as she slid out of Dane's arms. She walked out of the water and gathered her clothes, dressing quickly.

"Don't go. You don't have to go," Dane pleaded. "We can just talk. At least stay and talk to me."

Emma pulled her shirt over her head and sighed. Her heart stopped. Dane was propped up on her elbow on the rock ledge, submerged to her breasts in the water. Her skin glistened in the sunlight. It was all Emma could do not to go to her.

"I'm sorry, Dane. I have to go."

Dane followed Emma out of the creek. She reached for her clothes, but it was too late, Emma was already leaving.

"Just wait, okay." Dane hadn't meant for things to go this far. She'd wanted to tease Emma. Help her loosen up a little. She hadn't planned to seduce her. "I crossed a line. I'm sorry."

Emma didn't stop. Dane pulled on her jeans and T-shirt. She stuffed her underwear into her shoes and ran barefoot after Emma.

Emma had already reached the porch before Dane caught up with her. She dropped her shoes and grabbed Emma's arm, spinning her around to face her. "Stop it. Just talk to me. Why are you running away from me?"

Emma let out a sharp breath as she met Dane's gaze with a piercing stare. "Because you're just going to leave anyway," she blurted.

Dane flinched as if she had been slapped.

"Just forget this ever happened," Emma said, her voice softening.

"What if I don't want to forget?"

The sound of tires on gravel interrupted them. Emma looked up to see Curtis coming up the drive. She shook her head. "Don't do this, Dane. Not now."

Dane let go of Emma's arm. Emma stared into her eyes. Her heart ached for what Dane offered and what she knew she couldn't have.

Emma went into the house, leaving Dane staring after her. She could feel Dane's eyes on her as she walked to her room, silently closing the door, shutting Dane out.

Dane drove the back roads with no real destination in mind. She wasn't sure what was happening between her and Emma, but she couldn't get the whole encounter out of her head. The wind whipped through her hair as she sped along the narrow curving roads. Memories of touching Emma whirled through her mind like a storm kicking up dust. Emma had turned her away, but there was more—Emma had looked stricken. Emma was right, she was just passing through here. This wasn't her home. It wasn't fair to Emma to start something she wouldn't finish.

It was late when she returned. The bar was dark. Emma had already closed for the night. Dane drove to the house. A single light glowed through the kitchen window. Emma was up.

She leaned against the kitchen doorframe. Emma had fallen asleep sitting at the kitchen table, her head resting on her arms. Dane kneeled beside her and touched her hand gently to Emma's thigh.

"Emma."

Emma jolted awake.

"It's okay. It's just me."

Emma looked at her, wild-eyed and confused.

"What are you doing in here? You should go to bed."

Emma shook her head. "I was waiting."

Dane's heart sped up. Had Emma been looking for her?

"Waiting?"

"Curtis hasn't been home. He didn't come to the bar. I hoped he was with you."

Dane swallowed her disappointment and quickly replaced it with worry. "He wasn't with me."

Emma buried her face in her hands.

Dane frowned. She expected Emma to be worried or even angry, but this was more than that. "What's happened?"

"The sheriff stopped by earlier looking for Curtis. Several people died today after smoking some kind of new drug, some kind of new marijuana. They think it was the same stuff Curtis had on him when he was arrested."

"Shit."

"They need to find him. They need to know where he got the stuff, so they can prevent more of it ending up on the street."

Dane's blood ran cold. "That means the police are not the only ones looking for him."

Tears flooded Emma's eyes. She nodded her head again.

Dane reached for Emma, pulling her into her arms. Emma twisted her fists into Dane's shirt and pressed her face into Dane's neck. "What if he uses that stuff? What if they get to him first?"

"Shh. I'm sure he's okay."

"I told the police that Trevor has been looking for Curtis too. I told them he threatened me."

"What did he say?"

Emma faced Dane. "They are pretty desperate to stop this. He asked me if I would be willing to set Trevor up. I could agree to run the drugs to save Curtis. If the police can catch Trevor in the act and they can trace this drug back to him, he could face murder charges."

Dane shook her head. "There has to be another way."

"I don't know. I don't know what to do."

Dane cupped Emma's face in her hand, brushing aside a tear with her thumb. "Give him a little time. Curtis will turn up."

Emma nodded.

"Come on," Dane said, getting to her feet. "You need some rest. I'm sure Curtis will show up tomorrow asking for one of your famous bologna sandwiches."

Emma stood, still holding on to Dane's hand. "If you see him, promise me you'll tell me."

"I will. I'll drag him in by his ear if I have to."

Emma smiled. She pressed her fingers to Dane's lips. Her gaze lingered on her hand touching Dane's mouth. She looked up into Dane's eyes.

Dane had the overwhelming desire to kiss Emma. She wanted to wrap her arms around Emma and hold her. But she didn't move. She didn't want Emma to run from her again.

Emma's chest swelled as she took a deep breath. She stepped back, putting distance between them. Dane still didn't move.

Emma pulled her fingers from Dane's lips and walked out of the room.

Dane thought her heart would burst. She shuddered trying to break the spell. She looked around the room at the tired wallpaper and the worn Formica table.

Emma was right—she was a visitor here. She had come here looking for answers. If she was ever going to have anything to offer anyone, she had to get to the roots of who she was. Emma didn't need her adding to her problems. She had lost enough.

The sun was already high above the trees by the time Emma finished the morning chores. There was still no sign of Curtis.

Emma climbed the narrow wooden stairs to the hayloft, hoping to find Curtis dozing among the hay bales. The loft was full of square bales of hay harvested earlier from the surrounding fields. Curtis wasn't there. She hadn't really expected to find him. She just wanted to be close to him, and this was his favorite place. She drew in a deep breath, pulling in the smell of drying straw and the history of her family. Her heart was heavy with fear and worry. Something bad was coming. She could feel it.

Dane had left early, and Emma never knew from one day to the next if she would be back. The farm was quiet without Curtis and Dane. The chickens clucked and there was the occasional bleat from a goat, but the life of the farm seemed to be dwindling. Fall was in the air and everything was changing. She was tired of being scared. She had chosen to stay here for Curtis, but in truth she stayed to hold on to her past, her parents' dream, her family. Aunt Lily had offered to take Curtis in when her momma died, but Emma felt guilty that she had been away so long pursuing her own dreams.

Maybe it was time to do something different.

Emma looked up at the sound of tires on the drive. She went to the loft door and peered out over the farm. She gasped. Curtis was driving up to the house. Emma turned and ran down the stairs to meet him.

Curtis stepped out of the truck just as Emma reached him. She threw her arms around him and squeezed with all her strength.

"Hey, Emma," Curtis said. "You're gonna squeeze me to death," he grunted.

Emma let him go. She punched him on the arm. "Where the hell have you been? I thought you were dead."

Curtis shook his head. "Naw, just had some stuff to do."

Emma took a closer look at him. His clothes were dirty, there was mud in his hair, and blood was crusted in his nose.

"What happened to you?"

"Nothin'. I just fell down a bank down by the river."

Emma narrowed her eyes at Curtis. "What were you doing down by the river?"

"I just needed to get away for a while."

"Listen, Curtis, I think you're in some real trouble. The sheriff was here."

Curtis flinched. "Why? I ain't done nothin'."

"Did you hear about the people who died this week after smoking some of that stuff you were arrested for?"

Curtis looked confused. "Who died? What are you talking about? That's just crazy."

"I'm serious, Curtis. People are dead."

He stared at her as if the words didn't make sense.

"You have to go to the police. You have to tell them what you know. If they don't get these drugs off the street, more people could die."

Curtis shook his head. "No. I don't believe you."

"All right then, come inside and look at the newspaper—you can see for yourself."

Curtis followed Emma inside. He stared at the newspaper as if it were written in a foreign language.

"Whatever it is you've gotten into, you have to go to the police," Emma said, placing her hand on his arm.

"I just gave them a little weed. Weed won't hurt nobody."

Emma shook her head. "It wasn't just marijuana. The stuff the police took from you was some kind of new marijuana, something they called K2, and it had some other drug in it."

Curtis frowned.

"You haven't smoked any of this stuff, have you?" Emma asked.

"I haven't smoked in a while. I gave the last of what I had to Mark weeks ago. I had just picked up the other stuff when the police got me. I didn't smoke any after that because of the drug tests for probation. I knew you'd kill me if I failed one of those."

Emma felt the sting of tears in her eyes. "Thank goodness for that."

"I didn't hurt nobody, Emma. I promise. It wasn't me. The cops took my stuff."

"Okay, sweetie. I believe you. But do you understand how important it is that they know where you got the drugs? Someone else has the same stuff, and they're selling it to your friends."

Curtis shook his head. "I'll talk to my PO. I have a drug test today. Sam will tell me what to do."

Emma sighed. "Okay. But don't go anywhere else. If you are involved in this, whoever you got those drugs from will be getting pretty edgy. Don't talk to anyone except Sam or the police. Okay?"

Curtis nodded. "Okay, Emma. I promise." He looked back at the paper he'd crumpled in his hand. "I think I'll go take a shower." He tossed the paper on the table.

Emma watched her brother walk up the stairs. She knew the information had rocked him. He had some hard choices to make. She just hoped the police got to Trevor before Trevor found him.

CHAPTER EIGHT

D ane pulled into the visitor lot at the Pikeville Prison. The grounds were surrounded by fields of vegetable gardens. Inmates in gray-and-black striped jumpsuits dotted the fields, harvesting the crops.

She took a steadying breath and willed herself out of the Jeep. This was the last place she had ever expected to find a connection with her mother's family. But she had unearthed too much to turn back now. She needed to know what had happened to her mother.

The entrance looked like the waiting room at a doctor's office. A guard came to the glass window. "Can I help you?"

Dane stepped closer to the glass. "My name is Dane Foster. I'm here to see an inmate by the name of Thomas Stewart. I called yesterday."

The guard checked the visitor log. "ID, please."

Dane handed over her driver's license.

"Have you been here before?"

"No, ma'am."

"You should leave any personal items outside in your vehicle."

Dane patted her pockets. "All I have is my wallet."

The guard nodded. "We'll bring you into the corridor where you will be searched. From there you will go to the visitors' room. You are not allowed personal contact with the inmate. A glass divider will be between you and the inmate at all times."

Dane nodded.

"Step up to the metal doors," the guard said, pointing to the left.

The farther Dane went into the bowels of the prison, the colder it became. She wondered if that was the temperature or the chill in her veins.

Once she was seated on a small round stool bolted to the floor, she waited. A few moments later Thomas Stewart was led into the room. He was taller than her, his hair more gray than black, his eyes the same ocean blue as her mother's, the same as hers.

He sat down in front of her, looking at her curiously. "Who the hell are you?"

Dane swallowed. "My name is Dane. I'm Pearl Jean's daughter."

"Ha. Is that so? What does little Jenny want from me after all these years? I thought she was too good for us."

Dane took a deep breath. "She didn't send me. I wanted to meet you. I wanted to see what you could tell me about her. Why she left."

He laughed. It was an eerie sound that vibrated in his chest. His voice was coarse, and his teeth were yellow from years of tobacco use. "What do you want to know? What did Jenny tell you?"

"Not much. That's why I'm here. I never got the chance to know anyone on her side of the family. She never said much about you or her life before she married my father."

Thomas frowned. His body tensed. He leaned forward. "How is that prick, anyway? Still got a stick up his ass?"

"I take it you two didn't get along."

He glared at her. "David was a spoiled rich kid who put ideas in Jenny's head. He made her think she was better than me. Our ways weren't good enough for David."

"What ways?"

Thomas shook his head and looked Dane up and down. "A woman has her place. Jenny was always getting out of line. Sometimes she needed a little reminder of where she belonged. I looked after Jenny. David wanted to take her from me."

"So you didn't want her to go to college or move away."

"It wasn't like she couldn't take classes or get a job. But those city boys had no right to come into town and take our women."

Dane frowned. "Your women?"

He shook his head. "Doesn't matter. David thought he was better than me. He thought he could take Jenny from me. But he could never have what I took from him."

Chills ran down Dane's arms. She felt sick.

He turned his head from side to side, studying her. He started to laugh.

Dane stared at him, afraid to ask the next question.

"How old are you? If I had to guess I'd say you're about forty. Am I right?"

Dane swallowed the bile rising in her throat. She ground her teeth, fighting the rage boiling in her veins. "What did you do to my mother?"

He laughed. "You should ask her."

"She's dead."

He grinned. "Ah, that explains it." He sat up and stretched as if he was bored with the conversation.

Dane wanted to slap the stupid smile off his face. She gripped the edge of the table until her knuckles were white. "Tell me what you did to her."

"I told you. I put her in her place. I showed her what a real man could do."

Dane shook her head. Her face burned with rage. "You son of a bitch, you raped her."

He smiled. "I wanted to tell David myself, but the coward left town. I thought I was rid of him. But then Jenny ran off." His lips stretched across his teeth in a sneer. He looked like he'd just bitten into something sour.

"You hated my father so much you raped your own cousin? What kind of sick fuck are you?" Dane was reeling. She didn't want to believe him. She didn't want to believe this was possible. "You were right about one thing. She was better than you. She was better than all of you."

He leaned close to the glass, glaring into Dane's eyes. "Maybe she was. But it looks like I got the last laugh after all."

Dane frowned. "What do you mean?"

"Who's your daddy, girl? Who's your daddy?"

Dane pushed back against the table so hard she fell off the stool. She scrambled to her feet, glaring at him. "That's not possible. That's not true," she yelled.

Thomas laughed uncontrollably. He slapped his hand on the table and pointed at her, mocking her.

Dane called for the guard. "Let me out of here. I'm done."

She could still hear laughter as the door closed behind her. She was trembling. She needed air. She needed to get away. Thoughts of what that monster had done to her mother slashed through her mind like razors tearing through everything she had ever believed.

She ran to her Jeep. It couldn't be true. He couldn't be her father.

Emma put the ticket on the table in front of Trevor.

"I've been patient, Emma, but I have a business to run. You have one week. If Curtis doesn't come through, you better get on board."

Emma crossed her arms over her chest to hide her fear. Her stomach was twisting in knots. "What is it that you think Curtis owes you? I can't help you if I don't know what he's done."

Trevor stood. "Tell him he has one week." He tossed two twenties on the table. "Keep the change." He brushed Emma's shoulder as he passed.

Emma had barely caught her breath when Dane entered the bar. Dane looked sick. Sweat clung to her skin, and her head was bowed as if she wore a badge of shame. Something was wrong. How could this day get any worse?

"Where have you been all day?" Emma asked as Dane sat down. "You don't look so good."

"Whiskey and a beer. Keep them coming."

Emma hesitated. Dane's hands were trembling, and her eyes were red as if she'd been crying. Emma reached for the bottle of Jack Daniel's. She set the bottle and a glass on the bar in front of Dane and opened a beer.

"I'll tell you about my day if you tell me about yours. What happened?"

Dane shook her head. "Be careful what questions you ask. You might not like the answers."

"About your mom?"

Dane nodded. Emma poured the whiskey into the glass and handed it to Dane.

"Give me a minute," Emma said. "I have to fill this order. I'll be right back."

Emma had no idea what was going on, but it was bad. She'd never seen Dane like this. She looked around at the few customers left in the room and was tempted to tell everyone to leave. At least it was a slow night.

Dane was still nursing her drink when Emma returned. At least she was pacing herself tonight. Emma braced her arms against the bar in front of Dane and waited.

Dane looked at Emma over the glass as she drank. "Looks like you were right."

"I usually am. What was I right about this time?"

"You said I might not like what I find. You said I was trouble."

Emma frowned. "Whatever you found doesn't make you trouble, Dane. Our families aren't perfect, but we get to make our own choices about how we want to live."

Dane pursed her lips in thought. She slowly nodded her head.

Emma placed her hand over Dane's. "I don't know what happened today. But I know you're not trouble. I can close up in a few minutes and we can talk. Okay?"

Dane stared blankly at the whiskey swirling in the bottom of her glass. "Yeah. Sure."

Emma was able to get the coolers stocked and the tables cleaned before she even locked the doors. She said good night to the last couple on their way out. She was happy the night was over, but she had a feeling more bad news was on the way. Dane hadn't moved from her spot at the bar. She had pushed the whiskey aside and had stuck with beer.

Emma sighed. At least she wouldn't have to carry Dane home.

She opened a beer and sat on the stool next to Dane. Dane's shoulders were slumped, and she didn't look at Emma when she sat down.

"Feel like talking?" Emma asked.

Dane turned her head, meeting Emma's gaze.

Emma's heart sank. Dane's eyes were glassy pools of despair. "Is it that bad?"

"He raped her."

Emma flinched. "Oh God. How do you know?"

"I went to see him today at the prison. He bragged about it. Said he was putting her in her place. It was his way of hurting my father."

"Jesus. That's terrible."

"Yeah," Dane agreed. "But there's more."

Emma braced herself this time. She couldn't imagine what could be worse than knowing your mother was raped. "What?"

"He insinuated he might be my father."

Emma gasped. "Oh, Dane." She didn't know what to say. What could she say? Everything Dane thought she knew about her family just blew up in her face. Dane was already in some kind of identity crisis, and this was the last thing she needed.

"This could explain everything. No wonder my father doesn't want anything to do with me. Maybe I was destined to be a screwup."

"No, that's not true. You can't let this monster determine that for you. You're better than that."

Dane laughed.

Emma was confused. "What?"

"He kept saying my mother thought she was better than he was. She just wanted a life of her own. He wanted to control her. He did everything he could to destroy her."

Emma wrapped her arm across Dane's back. "I'm sorry."

Dane leaned her head on Emma's shoulder, surprising Emma. She froze for a moment, but then gave in to Dane's hurt. She leaned her head against Dane's, a small act of comfort. "What are you going to do now?"

"I don't know. I don't know where to go from here."

Emma stilled. "There's no rush. You can stay."

Dane didn't answer.

Emma closed her eyes. Wasn't this what she had expected? Dane was only a visitor here. This was not her home. Dane had never intended to stay. She swallowed her disappointment. It didn't matter what she knew—she cared about Dane. She didn't want to see her go.

"What did you plan to do with your life before your dad died?" Dane asked.

Emma was surprised by the question. "Why does it matter?"

"I just want to know. I want to talk about something else. Anything but what that monster did to my mother."

Emma nodded. "I wanted to be a biologist."

Dane sat up and looked at her. "Really?"

"Don't sound so surprised."

"It's just not what I pictured, that's all."

"What did you think then?"

Dane narrowed her eyes and studied her.

Emma grinned. "Stop it, just tell me."

"Okay then, I thought you would have been a social worker or in business. Someone out there trying to help the less fortunate get back on their feet or starting your own business somewhere."

"Really?" Emma laughed. "To be honest I've always liked animals more than people. I don't think I would have made a good social worker. The business thing was just part of the package. I learned a lot from my dad."

Dane nodded. "Isn't it weird how things work out? I never wanted to be anything like my father, but I ended up a lot like him anyway." She cringed. "At least he's better than the alternative." Dane was thoughtful. "Everyone says he loved my mother. What if having me destroyed that?"

Emma brushed her thumb across Dane's cheek. "No, sweetie. No matter who your father is, you didn't have a choice. You were the child. You didn't ask for any of those things to happen. And from what you've told me, you were your mother's joy. She must have been a very strong woman to have overcome everything that happened to her and build a whole new life. She made sure you never had to know the things she'd known."

Dane nodded.

Emma finished her beer and tossed the bottle into the trash. "It's been a long day. Let's get back to the house. Are you ready?"

"Sure."

Emma took Dane's hand, lacing their fingers together, hoping the connection would help Dane feel a little less lost. If she was honest, she needed the connection too. Dane was the first person she'd allowed close since losing her parents. She wanted to hold on to the tenuous connection between them as long as she could. But it was just a matter of time before Dane would leave like everyone else.

❖

Dane knew something was wrong the moment her headlights beamed across the lawn. Samson stood next to something piled on the grass. He barked ferociously as they pulled up.

Emma jumped out of her truck and ran toward Samson. Dane slid to a stop and jumped out to run after her. Samson was limping, and blood dripped from a cut across his snout.

"Curtis!" Emma screamed. She fell to her knees. Curtis lay in a heap on the ground. He groaned and rolled onto his back.

"Curtis, are you okay? What happened to you?" Emma asked as Curtis pressed his hands to his head.

"Nothin'. I'm okay."

"Don't give me that shit. Someone beat the crap out of you, and by the looks of it they went a round with Samson as well. Now tell me what happened, or so help me, I'll finish what they started."

Dane looked up at Emma, surprised by the threat but certain Emma would follow up on what she said.

"Dang, Emma, give me a minute," Curtis groaned.

"Who was it?" Emma demanded.

Curtis sat up. "I don't know. I didn't know him. He was a big fella, kind of looked like a bear. He was in a black truck."

Emma looked at Dane. "Sounds like the same guy that jumped you outside the bar."

Dane nodded. "What did he say, Curtis?"

"He told me to keep my mouth shut. Said he'd be watching me."

Emma pinched Curtis's face in her hand, looking over the cuts and bruises.

"Ow," Curtis said, trying to pull away.

"Be still. Is anything broken?"

Curtis pushed her hand away. "No. Stop it. I said I'm okay."

Emma turned to Samson. "Come here, boy."

Samson whined as Emma held his face gently in her hands and inspected his snout and then his leg. "I don't think anything's broken, but we need to clean this cut."

Dane was amused by how gentle Emma was with Samson after her handling of Curtis. She turned her attention to Curtis. "Come on. Let me help you to the house. We'll be able to see better once we're inside."

Curtis groaned as Dane threw her arm around him and lifted him to his feet. She steadied him a moment. "Are you good?"

"Yeah, I'll be fine as long as you don't let Emma get me again. I think I'd rather fight the bear."

Dane laughed. "You'll live."

Once inside, Dane took Curtis to the kitchen. She wet a towel and began to clean his wounds. Emma did the same for Samson.

"What was this about, Curtis? What are you not telling us?" Emma demanded.

"I don't know. I went to see my PO, and when I got back, this guy shows up. I went out to see who it was. He got out and just clocked me. He got in a few punches and kicks before Samson got to him. Samson got a good bite of his arm. He knocked Samson off and got back in his truck. He told me I better learn to keep my mouth shut. He said if we had to talk again, he'd shut me up for good. Then he just left."

Emma finished with Samson and came back for another look at Curtis. "It's about those damn drugs of course, or is there another mess you've gotten yourself into that I don't know about."

Curtis turned. "I said I was sorry. What else do you want me to do?"

"I want you to stop acting like this is no big deal. This isn't a game."

Curtis pushed back his chair. "Forget this. Just leave me alone. I can take care of myself." Curtis stormed out of the room and stomped up the stairs. A minute later they heard his door slam shut.

"You were a little hard on him, don't you think?" Dane said, as she rinsed the towel in the sink.

Emma glared. She closed her eyes and sighed, releasing some of her frustration. "Yeah, maybe. He just scares me to death sometimes, and it pisses me off."

Dane laughed. "Noted."

Emma shook her head. "I don't know what to do. I don't even want to call the police about this. I'm afraid the guy will just come back if we do."

"I think I've seen that truck outside the bar a couple of times, but I never get a look at who it is."

Emma considered this. "I'm pretty sure it's the same one that was outside the justice center when Curtis was released from jail."

"Someone is watching you guys pretty close. Whatever Curtis knows must be pretty big."

Emma put her elbows on the table and held her head in her hands. "What if Curtis doesn't know he knows? It's possible he doesn't understand. He may not be able to tell us because he hasn't put the pieces together."

"He knows where he got the drugs."

Emma nodded. "But what if there was more going on and Curtis didn't realize it?"

"It's possible. That doesn't help us much, though."

"I know. Trevor has to be behind this. He was in the bar earlier handing out his usual warning. He said Curtis had one week to get him what he's owed, but he wouldn't say what."

"So it definitely wasn't Trevor who did this."

Emma shook her head. "Not personally, but that doesn't mean he didn't send the messenger."

"Trevor was at the bar the night I was beaten too."

Emma nodded.

"It sounds like Trevor has a fixer. That's a convenient way to cover up what he's doing. He just made you his alibi for this."

Emma put her head down on the table and groaned. "I hate this. I hate all of this. I hate what it's doing to us, and I hate not knowing what to do about it."

Dane placed a hand on Emma's shoulder. "He knows you love him."

"Yeah," Emma agreed. She was grateful Dane was there. She wasn't sure she could hold herself together if she had to face this alone.

Chapter Nine

The rooster crowed, signaling the start of another long day. Emma rolled over in bed wishing for a miracle to take away all her worry. The smell of coffee drifted into her consciousness, luring her from the sanctuary of her bed. Her eyes felt heavy and her lids were swollen from crying herself to sleep the night before. She wouldn't be winning any beauty awards today.

She slid her feet into the worn slippers waiting at the side of the bed. She thanked God for Mondays. At least she didn't have to rush around to get things done today. Maybe she would go to town and talk to the sheriff again. Maybe they could figure a way out of this mess Curtis had made.

She stretched, her muscles sore and stiff. This was nothing new. Every year she felt the grip of time robbing her of her youth. She glanced to the picture of her parents dutifully standing guard at the door as always. They had shared a love greater than time. She wondered what it would be like to have someone in her life, someone she could love and be loved by in return. She thought of Dane. She shook her head. No. Not Dane.

She pulled on her father's tattered old robe and made her way down the hall. Music emanated from the kitchen like a beacon calling a lost ship to safe harbor. She slowed, enjoying the melody of the notes as they drifted through the house like a breath of fresh air.

Dane stood at the stove, her hips swaying to the tune. Emma stared, enjoying the sight of Dane's long lean legs, her tight buttocks strained against the fabric of her shorts, the broad shoulders tapering down her back to a narrow waist and hips.

Emma grinned, forgetting her resolve to keep her distance from Dane. She stepped up behind Dane, placing her hand on her waist.

Dane jumped at the touch. "Ow. Shit."

Emma blanched. "I'm sorry. I didn't mean to startle you."

Dane turned holding her wrist. An angry burn scorched the flesh of her arm just above her palm.

Emma took Dane's hand and led her to the sink, then turned on the cold water. "Here, hold it under the water for a few minutes. Is it bad?"

Dane shook her head. "No. I've had worse. I think it scared me more than it hurt."

Emma grimaced, thinking of the scars that snaked up Dane's arm. "I am sorry."

"I'm not." Dane lifted her good hand to Emma's face, brushing a strand of hair from her cheek. She slid her thumb beneath Emma's eye.

Emma glanced away, knowing her eyes were red and puffy, her hair carelessly brushed.

"Did you get any rest at all?" Dane asked, her tone soft, her touch gentle.

Emma pulled a towel from a drawer and patted Dane's arm dry. "Not much." She focused on the feel of Dane's hand in hers as she pressed the towel to her arm. The warmth of Dane's skin felt good against her hands, making her ache to touch more of her. Emma stilled, afraid to move. She wouldn't look at Dane, afraid of what she might see in her eyes.

The smell of burning bacon filled the room, saving Emma from the desire raging through her body, making her knees weak. She pulled away, then turned to the stove to rescue Dane's breakfast.

Dane placed her hand over Emma's, pulling her away from the stove. She removed the skillet from the flame and turned off the burner. She pressed her body against Emma's back, molding their bodies together as she moved.

Emma placed a hand over Dane's arm crossing her chest. "I need to finish this."

Dane turned Emma to face her. "Yes, you do. What were you going to do when you first came in here and touched me?"

Emma looked away. "I don't know," she whispered, embarrassed.

Dane took Emma into her arms, gently guiding her across the floor with small steps as their bodies swayed together in rhythm with the music. Dane led Emma in the dance, sliding her hands along Emma's back. "Yes, you do," she said, her voice deeper than usual.

"I was just being playful. I saw you dancing, and it just felt good."

"Does this feel good?" Dane asked as she leaned down and kissed Emma's lips.

Emma felt dizzy, as if the air had grown too thin. She threaded her fingers through Dane's hair and opened to her.

Dane's lips were hot, firm, but tantalizingly gentle. She explored Dane's mouth with her tongue, answering the demands of Dane's lips on her own. Dane pulled Emma against her, her kiss eager and hungry as she wrapped her arms around her.

Emma moaned. She raked her fingernails down the length of Dane's back, feeling her stiffen in her arms. "Yes," Emma hissed.

"Yes what?"

"Yes, you feel good." Emma pulled away, feeling the last of her breath escape in one exasperated sigh. "Too good."

Dane didn't let go. She held her in her arms, falling back into the slow rhythm of the dance. "Then just give me this moment. Just dance with me."

Emma laid her head against Dane's chest, listening to the steady beat of her heart. The burn of Dane's kiss lingered on her lips, and she swelled with want for her. She closed her eyes, trying to shut out the desire that threatened to overwhelm her resolve. She couldn't deny her attraction to Dane. She knew if she touched Dane the way she longed to touch her, allowed Dane into her bed, she wouldn't be able to stand the loss of her when the time came for Dane to leave. But what good did it do to push Dane away? She knew the answer as clear as if it were written on the wall. She could deny Dane her body, but she wasn't so sure about her heart.

❖

Dane pressed her cheek against Emma's head, drawing in a deep breath, inhaling the scent of lavender and vanilla. The burn on her wrist was nothing compared to the burning need she felt as her clitoris swelled and throbbed. She struggled to remain calm and just hold Emma, when all she wanted to do was to claim her mouth and explore every inch of her body with her hands, her tongue, her own flesh. The thought sent a shiver through her.

"Are you okay?" Emma asked, pulling away to look up at her.

Dane smiled at her. "I'm fine. I guess I was just enjoying this a little too much."

Emma blushed. Dane brushed the back of her hand across Emma's cheek and leaned in to kiss her again, but just as their lips were about to touch, Emma pulled away.

"What?" Dane asked.

Emma took another step back, allowing her hands to slip away from Dane, breaking the embrace. "I don't think this is a good idea."

Dane knew when not to push her luck. She didn't want Emma to run from her again. "Okay."

Emma helped herself to a cup of coffee and took a seat at the table. Dane noticed the slight rosy tinge to her cheeks that hadn't been there before. She smiled. Emma was feeling this too. Not wanting to let the moment fall apart completely, she quickly thought of a plan.

"What are you doing today?"

Emma shook her head and seemed about to answer when she was interrupted by the phone.

Dane waited, turning back to the ruined breakfast.

Emma went to the edge of the stairs and called up to Curtis. There was no answer. She heard Emma's steps pound up the stairs. A moment later her steps were hurried as she rushed back down the stairs and ran to the front door.

Dane turned and looked out the window. The beat-up little truck was gone. Curtis wasn't there. She frowned. When had he left? She hadn't heard him get up in the night and he hadn't come down for breakfast. It wasn't even like him to be up this early in the morning. Dane had a sinking feeling in her gut.

She heard Emma's voice, still talking on the phone. "He isn't here. I don't know where he is." There was a pause as Emma must have been listening to the phone. "I'll let him know when I see him." She came back into the kitchen looking bereft. Dane braced herself for more bad news.

"Curtis is gone again. Did he say anything to you before he left?"

Dane shook her head. "I didn't realize he was gone until just now. I didn't hear him leave."

Emma closed her eyes and sank back into her chair. "I shouldn't have yelled at him. I know how easily he gets his feeling hurt. What have I done?"

"You didn't do anything. Curtis has a mind of his own. He has a lot to sort out right now. Give him a little time—he'll come around." The look of fear and regret in Emma's eyes broke Dane's heart. She was doing her best to take care of Curtis and keep their family together, but this time Curtis had crossed a line Emma might not be able to save him from.

"I have to find him." She looked up at Dane. "Will you help me?"

"Of course." Dane had been trying to figure out a way to get Emma to spend the day with her, but this wasn't what she had in mind.

Dane eased the Jeep down the old dirt road. The vehicle rocked back and forth as it lumbered through deep gullies cut into the earth by countless off-road vehicles over the years. Emma had been quiet on the drive, her jaw set, and her brow furrowed with worry.

"Where are we going?" Dane asked.

Emma nodded her head upward toward the road in front of them. "Our dad kept an old hunting cabin out here. Curtis likes to come here when he wants to get away. I'm hoping that's where he's been running off to."

Dane focused on the road ahead. "I doubt that little truck of his could make it back here."

"No, but Curtis grew up in these woods. He would leave the truck someplace and hike in." Emma pointed to a path up ahead. "There, take that road."

The road turned out to be little more than a path. It didn't look like anyone had been there in a long while, and small trees and wild grass were beginning to take over the path. At last Dane eased the Jeep into a small clearing in front of a run-down structure that looked more like a woodshed than a cabin.

Emma stepped out of the Jeep, peering at the dilapidated old building. She shook her head. "I can't believe it's changed so much. I haven't been here in years, but I wasn't expecting it to be so forlorn."

Samson jumped out of the Jeep and sniffed around the grounds, peeing on as many trees as he could.

"Curtis, you in there, man?" Dane called as she walked up to the door.

There was no answer.

Dane pushed the door open and peered inside. Beer cans littered the floor and she spotted more than one used condom in the refuse. She stepped back outside. "He's not here. It doesn't look like anyone has been here in a while, but the place is a mess."

Emma turned, placing her hands on her hips as she studied the area around her. "Where could he be?" She shook her head as Dane stepped beside her. "I spent a lot of time here as a kid. We would come here and spend days at a time as Daddy hunted. It was like going camping in some exotic place. I loved it because they weren't working, and we all got to spend time together playing games, talking, playing music, and telling stories. I was almost fourteen when Momma had Curtis. They thought she couldn't have any more children and it was a risky pregnancy. Momma struggled with her blood pressure. She went into labor early and there was a problem. It was winter and there was heavy snow on the ground, so the midwife had trouble getting to the house. There was a problem with the umbilical cord that restricted the oxygen getting to the baby. Momma cried and begged God to save him. When they handed Curtis to her, the love in her eyes was like nothing I'd ever seen. He was just a tiny wrinkled mess, but she loved him with all her heart. At the time no one knew how the lack of oxygen would affect him. He grew like any other baby, and it was quite some time before the deficits really became clear. Of course, he was only four, almost five, when I moved away to college. It took me longer than most to get through school because I had to work so much to pay for my classes. I wasn't around much. My parents helped me when they could, but they didn't have much to spare. I was in my final year when Daddy was murdered, and Momma got sick. Curtis was nine. I promised Momma I would take care of him."

Dane placed her hand on Emma's shoulder. "You have. You kept your promise. Anyone with half a brain can see how much you love him, and he loves you. Whatever is going on with him now isn't because of anything you did or didn't do. It may be hard to remember sometimes, but Curtis is a grown man now. He has a mind of his own and he has to make his own mistakes."

Emma sighed. "This is so much more than just a mistake."

"I know," Dane agreed. "Can you think of anywhere else he might go?"

Emma looked up at Dane and shook her head. "I'm not sure. He could be anywhere."

"We'll keep looking. He'll show up sooner or later. He always does."

"Okay," Emma agreed.

"Come on, Samson, let's go, boy," Dane called. She waited at the Jeep, watching Emma looking back upon the memories of her family. Wherever Curtis was, she hoped for Emma's sake he was okay.

Dane chose to cross the mountain instead of going out the way they came. She wanted to check out some of the places Curtis had taken her when they were out together. It was a long shot, but it wouldn't hurt to look, and it meant she would have more time with Emma.

She stopped the Jeep at the edge of a wide puddle of muddy water. She looked from side to side, but there wasn't any way to go around the rank muddy soup. Samson sniffed the air as if gauging the risk by the foulness of the smell.

"What do you think?" she asked Emma.

"It's hard to tell. It could be nothing, but it could be a pit."

Dane pointed to the right side of the road. "Looks better on that side. Maybe if I hug the bank over there, we can make it through."

"Agreed."

"Okay, here goes nothing."

Dane got a slight run at the puddle. When the tires hit, a spray of mud and stagnant water gushed outward, stirring the rank smell of rot and filth. The Jeep climbed out the other side, the tires slipping on the slick bank. The tires spun, throwing mud and muck into the air. Emma cried out as a wave of the rancid water washed over her.

Dane stopped the Jeep as soon as they were safely planted on firm ground. She laughed at Emma, who was covered in a brown muddy film. She reached out her hand and touched Emma's face, then pulled a slimy glob of frog eggs out of her hair.

"Yuck," Emma yelled. She cringed in disgust. She climbed out of the Jeep, desperately trying to brush the gelatinous substance out of her hair and back into the muck from which it came. She was horrified at the nasty smell covering her and appalled that they had damaged the eggs.

Samson sniffed around the water and snorted his disapproval of the whole mess.

Dane was still laughing as she attempted to help pick the slime out of Emma's hair.

"It's not funny," Emma said, throwing a handful of frog eggs into the water.

"Yes, it is." Dane laughed.

Emma scraped a glob of mud off her arm and smeared it across Dane's face.

"Ooh, you are going to pay for that." Dane scooped up a handful of black mud and threw it at Emma, hitting her shoulder, bits of the nasty mixture splattering Emma's neck and face.

Emma spit and sputtered, trying to expel the bit of filth that had hit her in the mouth. She scowled at Dane. "You are dead."

Dane laughed again but faltered when she saw the murderous look on Emma's face. She took a step back to put more distance between herself and Emma's wrath. She lost her footing and slipped on the slick muddy bank, and her boot was swallowed as she sank into the mud. She tried to right herself but was unable to regain her balance. She grasped helplessly in the air for imaginary holds that could save her, but there was nothing she could do to recover. Dane landed with a splash and felt the sucking force of the mud grab hold of her hands and arms as she sank farther into the sludge.

Emma laughed hysterically as she watched Dane try to extract herself from the clutches of the bog. Each time Dane pulled one hand out she would sink deeper with the other. Her clothes were soaked through with the rancid water and black sludge.

Samson barked and grabbed hold of Dane's sleeve, trying to pull her out of the mud, but he only made it more difficult for Dane to get her balance.

Despite Samson's intervention, Dane finally managed to pull herself back onto the bank. She was laughing so hard she could hardly catch her breath. She lay back on the rough ground, laughing and gasping. Emma was doubled over holding her side, pointing at Dane as she laughed.

Dane smiled. "I guess I deserved that."

Emma laughed even harder, lying back on the ground. Her side hurt from laughing so hard. Dane was a mess. Emma couldn't remember a time when she'd laughed this hard. They lay on the ground until the laughter died away and their breathing returned to normal. Emma peered up through the branches of the trees, still heavy with leaves. The laughter had cleansed some of the weight of fear and dread that clouded her thoughts. She felt lighter, happier than she had felt in ages.

Dane sat up, unbuttoning her shirt. She peeled the soggy cotton away from her skin and let it fall with a sodden thud to the ground. Her T-shirt beneath was wet too, but at least it didn't have the layer of mud clinging to it. Her jeans were wrecked.

Emma was amused by the mess they had made of themselves. She thought of the day at the creek when Dane had stripped off her clothes and followed her into the water. The image of Dane's bare nipples hardening under her gaze stirred her desire as she trailed her eyes along Dane's body, remembering every detail of smooth skin and hard muscle.

Dane tilted her head slightly to the side when she caught Emma staring. "What are you thinking?"

Emma shrugged. "Nothing." She pushed herself up and stood. "We should get going." She was embarrassed that Dane had caught her thinking about her naked and hoped Dane couldn't see the flush of arousal she felt creeping up her neck.

Dane could feel the wave of disappointment radiating from Emma as they pulled up to the house. Curtis's truck wasn't in the drive. She reached out and took Emma's hand, giving it a reassuring squeeze.

Emma tightened her fingers around Dane's.

"He's okay. Try not to worry."

Emma nodded.

Dane could see tears gleaming in Emma's eyes as she turned away. She wished there was something she could do, but she had no idea where Curtis was or what he was into. She was helpless to do anything about Curtis, but she wouldn't give up on Emma.

She lumbered out of the Jeep and made her way to the house.

Emma stopped her, placing a firm hand against Dane's chest. "Wait. Come around here."

"What?"

Emma grinned at Dane. "There is no way you are tracking all that mud into my house."

Dane frowned and looked down at the dried mud caked to her boots and jeans. She sniffed. She stank of stagnant water and rancid mud.

Emma pulled out a hose and turned on the water. She bent over at the waist and rinsed the remains of frog eggs and mud out of her hair, then rinsed her arms and kicked off her boots.

"Your turn," she said, turning to Dane. With a wicked grin Emma turned the hose on her.

Dane ducked and turned, trying to avoid the cold jet of water, but at the same time letting Emma spray the filth from her clothes and her body. The water was cold and gooseflesh pimpled her skin.

Emma laughed. "What's wrong? I thought you were a tough girl."

Dane kicked off her boots and tugged down her sodden jeans, exposing her bare legs. She pulled her T-shirt over her head and faced Emma.

Emma wasn't laughing now. Her look was hungry and focused, her gaze locked on Dane's near naked body.

Dane felt her nipples harden under Emma's gaze, her flesh hot despite the cold spray of water washing over her. She stepped closer to Emma, placing her hand on Emma's neck, sliding her fingers through her hair to caress the back of her head. She dropped her head, her lips barely out of reach. Dane slid her other hand around Emma's waist, pulling her closer.

Emma froze, her gaze locked on Dane's lips. Dane could feel her breath against her skin. In a sudden rush of urgency, she took Emma's mouth, claiming her with her kiss. Emma answered with the same intensity, the same ravenous desire, wrapping her arms around Dane's neck as she dug her fingers into Dane's shoulders. Dane pressed her body against Emma's, no longer able to control her need. She took the hem of Emma's T-shirt in her hand and pulled it up over her head. Emma dropped the water hose, the nozzle hitting the ground and spraying water into the air around them. A rainbow arched overhead as sun hit the mist.

Dane cupped Emma's breasts in her hands, rubbing the firm nipples beneath her thumbs as her tongue swept deep into Emma's mouth. Emma shuddered. Dane closed the distance between them until her thigh was pressed firmly against Emma's sex. She pressed one hand against Emma's back, holding her as she continued to knead Emma's breast with the other.

Emma gasped, and she closed her eyes. Dane pressed her lips to Emma's neck, grazed her teeth along the soft pulse just beneath her flesh. She kissed Emma hungrily, feeling her melt into the kiss. Emma slid her hand into Dane's hair, pulling her against her, deepening the kiss.

Emma's mouth was hot, her tongue firm and demanding as she met each thrust and pull of Dane's mouth. Emma's skin was like sun-warmed silk sliding beneath her fingers. She wanted Emma. She needed her. Her desire swelled, and her clitoris throbbed until the ache for Emma became painful. She pressed harder against Emma, giving in to her need.

"God, Emma, please let me touch you. I want to feel you, taste you."

Emma gasped, her breathing fast and shallow. She had fought to deny her attraction to Dane, but she was beyond reason now. Now that her desire had been set to flame, there was no turning back. She wanted Dane. She wanted to lose herself in the soft contours and strong planes of Dane's body. She wanted to put aside all the fear, all the hurt from the past. She just wanted to feel Dane in her arms.

Emma slid her hands down Dane's back, slowly caressing the tense muscles as she made her way down to cup Dane's butt. She was done running. She was done hiding. No matter what happened afterward, she wanted Dane, needed her. She was drunk with the feel of Dane's skin against her. The air was thin, and she struggled to think as her body burned with the craving for Dane's mouth on her. Her legs threatened to give as Dane's tongue filled her mouth, her hand cupping and working her breast. Her eyes rolled back as Dane pushed her thigh against her aching swollen clitoris. Her heart pounded, resonating in the thundering pulse of her sex.

Emma raked her fingers down Dane's back, feeling her shudder in response to her touch. "Inside," Emma gasped. "Shower."

Dane relinquished her hold on Emma's breast, then took her hand, lacing their fingers together. Emma pulled, and she followed.

Samson had taken up his spot on the porch, hardly acknowledging them as they passed. They left wet footprints across the floor as they walked, still dripping with water from the hose.

Emma turned on the water in the shower and steam quickly filled the room. She skirted her gaze across Dane's naked breasts, her strong lean body. Emma shivered as her clitoris pulsed. She unbuttoned her shorts and pushed them to the floor. Dane watched her undress, her expression dark, hungry, her eyes half closed, her lips slightly parted. Emma moved forward and brushed a kiss against Dane's hard nipple before lifting her lips to Dane's mouth.

She shivered as Dane cupped her breast in her hand and squeezed before sliding her fingers beneath the thin fabric, pushing the bra up, releasing her breast. Emma discarded the last barrier between them and stepped into the shower, reaching out her hand to Dane. Dane followed.

Emma filled Dane's hand with liquid soap before filling her own. She rubbed her hands through Dane's hair, down her neck, across her shoulders, before finding Dane's breast.

Dane's hands explored her body as if tracing a map, following the curves and contours of her flesh.

Emma took Dane's nipple into her mouth and sucked. Dane's hands were in her hair caressing her head, holding her as she sucked and worked her tongue, feeling the nipple harden in her mouth.

Dane's head was spinning. Emma's mouth on her breast pulled at her clitoris with each suck as if a thread were tied between the two. Her hips pumped, seeking a connection with Emma. She rubbed her hands through Emma's hair, down her back and up her thighs, feeling the suds slick against wet skin.

Emma released her breast, throwing her head back into the spray of the water. Soap trailed down her body, filling the room with the familiar scent of lavender and vanilla. Emma turned in her arms, bracing her hand against the wall as the spray cleansed her face. Dane pressed against Emma's back, finding her breast with one hand. She kissed Emma's neck as she traced eager fingers along her stomach to the short curls shielding her wet folds. Dane slid two fingers between Emma's legs, parting her, exposing her swollen clitoris, hard and ready. Emma's skin was like silk, delicate and warm as Dane stroked her fingers along the length of her sex, gently teasing the opening before returning to brush light circles against her clitoris.

Emma was everything she had imagined. She worked Emma's clitoris in long sweeping strokes of her fingers, intermittently circling the swollen clitoris with the tip of her finger. Emma's hips rocked against her making her own clitoris pulse and swell. Dane dipped her finger into Emma, deeper and deeper with each thrust. Emma pressed against Dane, her arms rigid, braced against the wall, keeping her upright as her legs shook with the early tremors of her release.

Dane held Emma's breast cupped in her hand as she filled her. Emma tensed.

"Oh, please, don't stop." Emma threw her head back against Dane's shoulder, her hips pumping in short burst as her orgasm erupted with wave after wave of sweet release. Emma relaxed, her body limp after the last surge of her orgasm released her. She clasped her hand over Dane's as she slumped in her arms. Dane kissed her neck, her ear, her cheek, holding her firmly in her arms.

"You are so beautiful," Dane whispered. "You take my breath away."

Emma opened her eyes. Steam filled the room, blocking out everything except the sight of Dane, strong and beautiful, gazing down at her. Emma turned in Dane's arms, brushing her hands across Dane's chest. The muscles beneath the tender skin were tense from Dane's need. Emma smiled up at Dane before brushing tender needy kisses against her skin. She sucked Dane's breasts one at a time before trailing her lips down Dane's body. Dane's hands were in her hair, not guiding but holding her, silently encouraging her onward.

Emma kneeled on the floor, pressing her hands against Dane's thighs, encouraging her to open her legs. Dane obeyed.

Emma spread Dane's folds with her thumbs as she brushed her lips against Dane's sex. Dane's hips jerked. Emma smiled. She was going to enjoy this. She took Dane's clitoris into her mouth, sucking the engorged flesh until Dane's hips rocked against her face. Dane's fingers pressed against her head, asking for more.

"Emma..." Dane's voice was hoarse, the word barely more than a whisper.

Emma flattened her tongue and stroked up and down Dane's clitoris.

"Please. Now, Emma. Now."

Emma sucked hard on Dane's clitoris as she pushed two fingers inside. Dane's hand slapped against the wall, her legs stiffened, her body rigid with the power of her orgasm.

Dane groaned. Her hips bucked. Pleasure bloomed everywhere Emma's mouth touched. She looked down at the beautiful woman filling her with warm sweet strokes of her tongue. A shudder ran through her, flooding her nerve endings with pure pleasure. Her muscles tensed. Her body strained to contain the building force of energy gathering beneath the tender strokes of Emma's tongue. She pressed her hand to the back of Emma's head, silently asking for more.

"Emma—" The name barely slipped from her lips before her orgasm crested and she was rocked by wave after wave. She pulled Emma away and fell to her knees in front of her. She pushed her hands into Emma's hair and kissed her hard, her mouth pressing against Emma's lips, her tongue filling her with urgent strokes. She pulled Emma against her, relishing the feel of Emma's body against hers. She slowed the kiss as the last ripples of her orgasm subsided and she slowly regained control.

Dane held Emma's face in her hands and brushed gentle kisses against her lips. "You are amazing."

Emma smiled shyly, turning her head away. Dane stopped her. "Don't. Don't run from this. Just let it be perfect."

Dane kissed Emma again before standing and guiding Emma to her feet. "I think we might need another shower now."

Emma smiled. "I think I better let you have this one alone."

"Where's the fun in that? After what you just did to me, I won't ever want to shower alone again."

Emma smiled. "Don't worry. There's more where that came from." Emma handed Dane the soap and kissed her tenderly. "I'll start dinner."

Dane watched Emma step out of the shower and wrap herself in a towel. Dane pressed her hand against the cold tile, bracing herself so she wouldn't pull Emma back. She hoped Emma wouldn't close herself off again the moment she stepped through the bathroom door.

❖

Emma looked out the kitchen window out of habit, half expecting Curtis to be rambling about the yard. She frowned. His truck wasn't there. There was no sign he had been home. She went to the fridge and pulled out some chicken and began to peel potatoes. Samson's thundering bark made her jump, the knife slicing through her thumb. "Shit." She grabbed a towel and peered out the window to see what had triggered the alarm. Samson stood on the edge of the porch, his hackles raised as he peered down the drive.

Emma wrapped her thumb in the towel and stepped onto the porch in her shorts and bare feet, her hair still damp from the shower. She called Samson to her as she watched a maroon Chevy Tahoe pull in front of the house. Her aunt Lily threw the door open and called out to Emma.

"Well, don't just stand there, come and help me out of this thing."

Emma patted Samson on the head and jogged out to the car.

"What are you doing? You shouldn't be driving, Aunt Lily."

"Oh, hush now, it wasn't that far. Besides I need to practice now and then. You never know when something will come up. I need to know I can still manage on my own. I'm not that old—I just need to get up the nerve for that hip replacement. Maybe then I could show you kids a thing or two."

Emma smiled and leaned in to kiss her aunt on the cheek. "Why didn't you just have one of the boys drive you?"

Lily grasped Emma's shoulder and hauled herself off the seat. She held on to the door and motioned to Emma to get the walker out of the back seat. "I like to never got that damn thing in there. I thought about throwing it in the ditch, but then I remembered I needed a way back into the house later."

Emma retrieved the walker. Once Lily was situated, they ambled back to the house.

"Are you going to tell me what's brought you all the way out here? You could have called, and I would have come to you."

"Oh, shush your dithering, child. I may be old, but I can still do what I please."

Emma tamped down a smile. Lily had always had a mind of her own. Something obviously had her feathers ruffled. She would just have to wait until the old woman got around to telling her what it was.

"I was just starting dinner. Would you like some sweet tea?"

Lily scuttled into the kitchen and plopped down into one of the chairs as if she'd just run a marathon. "Don't you have any whiskey around?"

Emma laughed. "Of course." She opened a cupboard and pulled out the half-empty bottle of Jack Daniel's. She filled the glass with ice and poured the amber liquor.

"You might want to make one for yourself too."

Emma paused, looking at her aunt, an uneasy feeling washing over her. She poured another drink and sat at the table across from Lily.

"What is it, Lily? Tell me."

Lily sipped her drink. "What is going on with you and Curtis? He came to my house early this morning. Said you two had a fight. His face was a mess. He wasn't making much sense."

Emma flinched. "What? I never—"

Lily put her hand up. "Now I don't think for one minute that you hit that boy. I've known you your whole life, and I know that's not in you, even when there have been times when he could use a good skinning. But something happened. He was in a terrible mood. I tried to get him to stay with me for a while, but he said he had to go somewhere. He was awfully upset."

Emma shook her head. "Someone came to the house yesterday while I was at work and beat Curtis up. He's in trouble, and he won't tell me what he's done. I was scared, so I yelled at him. He was gone when I got up this morning."

Lily peered at Emma the way she used to when she was a little girl and wasn't telling the whole story. Lily could always tell when Emma was keeping something from her.

"What kind of trouble?"

It was Emma's turn to take a drink. "You know he got arrested a few weeks back for having some drugs on him. Well, it looks like more of the same drugs have been linked to the deaths that have been in the paper. Some people he hangs out with are involved and have been coming around threatening us. I tried to get him to tell me what this is about, but he doesn't get it. I'm not sure he even knows what's going on."

Lily sat back in her chair, her head bobbing slightly in a nod. "I see." She took a drink. "Who is this person who threatened you?"

"Trevor."

Lily narrowed her eyes. "That little snot that Curtis used to follow around at school that put him up to breaking in to that house?"

Emma nodded. "That's him."

"You sure this is about Curtis?"

Emma was confused. What else could it be? "Trevor told me Curtis owed him something. He warned me that Curtis had one week to make things right. Why? What did you think this was about?"

Lily pursed her lips in thought. "Those questions your friend Dane has been asking, you know how people are when it comes to family secrets."

Emma shook her head. "No. It isn't Dane. She went to the prison to see Thomas. It didn't go very well. I'm afraid it was even worse than we thought."

"That girl needs to leave things be. Some secrets need to stay buried."

"Do you know more about Dane's family than you told us? Is there something you don't want her to know?"

Lily waved Emma off. "Of course not. I just know that family. No good can come from nosing around that bunch."

Emma frowned. She had the feeling Lily knew more than she was letting on. "Aunt Lily, did Curtis say where he was going or when he was coming home?"

"No. He just said he had to go somewhere. Said he had stuff to do. I tried to call, but you didn't answer your phone. I got worried something was wrong with you, so I came to see for myself."

Emma placed a hand over Lily's. She rubbed her fingers over the brown age spots and purple bruises coloring the frail thin skin. "I'm sorry. I was out looking for Curtis. I didn't mean to worry you. I should have called."

Lily's eyes softened. "Don't you worry. Things are going to be all right."

Something settled in Emma's heart. Her aunt was the one person who could always soothe her when she felt lost and out of sorts.

Lily pulled her hand away, then reached for her glass. "How about another drink, and where is that handsome girl you have staying with you, anyway?"

Emma felt the heat rise in her cheeks. "Um. She's upstairs, I think."

Lily peered at Emma, making her squirm. She was sure her aunt could read her like a book.

"I see." Lily smiled. "Hmm. Yes, I think another drink would be good."

❖

Dane heard Emma talking to someone in the kitchen as she padded down the hall. She wasn't sure if Emma was on the phone or if someone had stopped by, so she ducked up the stairs to her room for some fresh clothes. She doubted Emma would want to explain what a naked woman was doing coming out of her shower.

She dressed and combed her hair, taking her time to allow Emma privacy in her conversation. Dane was disappointed their evening had been interrupted. Now that she had a taste of Emma, she wanted more. She wasn't ready for the real world to come crashing down on them.

A soft knock at her door made her jump.

"Yes."

The door opened, and Emma stood smiling sheepishly at her. "You going to hide up here all night?"

Dane smiled. "I thought you might need some privacy."

Emma stepped into the room and placed her hands on Dane's chest. "I do need privacy, but it doesn't look like I'm going to get it. My aunt Lily is downstairs, and she wants to see you."

"Really?"

"Yes, really. I think she has a crush on you."

Dane laughed. "I can work with that, but she isn't the girl I was hoping would notice me."

Emma kissed Dane lightly, pulling back to run her tongue along her lips. "I notice." She pulled away. "Now come downstairs before she starts asking questions."

Lily was in the sitting room, her elbow propped on the end of the sofa, a glass of whiskey aloft in her hand. The bottle of Jack sat on the table in front of her. Dane crossed the room and planted a quick kiss on the old woman's cheek.

"Hello, Lily."

Lily narrowed her eyes studying Dane and then Emma. The corner of her mouth lifted in a wry smile. "I'm glad to see you're still with us. You're good for Emma."

Dane made sure not to look at Emma, who she knew would be turning scarlet. "Thank you," she said as Emma slipped out of the room.

Lily held up her glass as Emma came back into the room with a fresh glass for Dane.

Emma placed her hand lightly on Dane's back as she came to her side. Dane took the glass, letting her fingers graze across Emma's hand. Emma reached for the bottle filling first Dane's glass, then Lily's, before filling hers.

Lily's gaze was like a hot branding iron burning into Dane's flesh. She felt exposed. It was like the time when she was in middle school and had been caught kissing Faith Litton in the girls' bathroom.

Dane cleared her throat. "Emma said you wanted to see me. What did you want to talk to me about?"

"Yes. I thought a lot about your mother after our last talk." She leaned over and rifled through a large leather purse that looked like it could hold a bowling ball. After a moment searching, she pulled out a small stack of photographs.

"I went looking through our old albums and came across these. Your mother was always at our house for one thing or another and more times than not ended up in the family photos. I thought you might like these."

Dane set down her glass and reached for the pictures. She stared, shocked by the image of her mother as a young girl, her arm slung loosely across the shoulder of another girl about the same age.

"Dane, that's your mother Jenny, and this is my sister Ann. Thick as thieves those two. I used to tease Ann that she loved your mother more than she did me."

Emma gasped. "Our mothers were best friends?"

Lily nodded. "Jenny and your mother were inseparable when they were younger, until the house fire and Jenny going to live with her uncle Tobias and his family. But even though Jenny couldn't come around as often, they were still close. Ann tried to look after Jenny when she could. I hadn't thought about her in years. I was older and didn't pay much attention, so it took me a while to remember these."

Dane turned to the next photograph. It was her mother and Ann again. They wore plaid skirts and white shirts. Each had a ribbon tied in her hair. They could have been sisters. They were wearing roller skates and were holding hands. The photo captured the moment they were looking at each other, a beaming smile on Ann's face, Jenny's head tilted slightly back in laughter.

"She looks so happy." Tears stung Dane's eyes. Had she ever seen her mother this happy?

"She was always like that. I remember our dad used to call her Smiley."

The next picture showed changes in her mother. She was a teenager, her hair long and shiny, draped across her shoulders, one side tucked behind her ear. She was seated at a booth at a diner. Dane recognized her father sitting next to her mother, his arm cast casually around the back of the booth behind her mother, his gaze riveted on her as she smiled at the camera. Ann sat across from Jenny next to a boy Dane guessed was Emma's father.

"Is that your dad?" she asked leaning forward, so Emma could see the photo.

"Yeah."

Lily reached for the bottle of whiskey. "That was just before I married and moved out. And not long before Jenny and David left. I wish Ann was here to tell you about her. She knew Jenny better than anybody."

Dane nodded. "Thank you for this. I can't tell you how much this means to me."

"It's no trouble. I'm glad I thought of it."

Emma frowned. "I don't know much about the time when mom and dad were dating. Dad always said Momma was the prettiest girl in town, and he fell in love with her the moment he laid eyes on her. But they didn't talk about things they did or much about any of their friends."

Lily sighed. "Well, by the time you came along, Jenny had gone. As far as I know not even Ann knew where Jenny and David had ended up. Back then things were different. It was a lot harder to find someone that didn't want to be found, and most folks around here don't bother looking for anything outside the county lines. You'd think the world just drops off into nothing once you pass the sign at the edge of town."

Dane leaned close to Emma so she could see the photo. Emma had scooted her chair next to Dane's and leaned close so that their shoulders touched. The heat of Emma's skin was a comfort. She had come here looking for her mother and she had found her at last. She smiled down at her mother's smiling face, so much like the woman she had known, but different. She couldn't help but think that this was what her mother had wanted her to remember about her.

Emma shifted, sliding her arm around Dane's shoulders. "You do have your mother's eyes."

"You think so?"

Emma nodded. "Yeah, they even crinkle at the sides like yours do when you smile."

Dane looked back at the photo. She was thankful for this connection to her mother. She wanted to believe she was like her. There was still so much she didn't know, but her mother's smile looking back at her from the photograph gave her hope. She could almost feel her mother's arms around her. Her gaze shifted to her father. She couldn't remember him ever looking at her mother with that much love. Had she been the wound that separated them? Was he ashamed of her?

Dane swallowed the lump forming in her throat. She imagined how their lives could have been different if that terrible thing hadn't happened to her mother.

Emma must have sensed the change in her mood. She tightened her arm around Dane's shoulders and ran her hand up and down her back. "I think there are some answers you can only get from him."

Dane shook her head. "That will never happen. I don't know that man. He isn't like that anymore. Not with me."

Emma stroked her back. "Things change."

Dane looked up to see Lily watching her, a faint smile lifting the corner of her mouth.

Lily nodded. "Yes, they do."

CHAPTER TEN

Emma poured drinks and waited on tables while Dane ran the kitchen and kept the trash emptied. It was one of those nights when Emma thought she needed a bigger place and the staff to run it. Maybe—anywhere else but here. She would never be able to trust anyone with her bar. She glanced at Dane as she ducked out the back door, dragging two giant trash bags behind her. Emma took time to go to the back to watch Dane. She couldn't stand a repeat of the night Dane had been beaten up outside. She had installed floodlights around the bar to illuminate the parking lot and the trash bins and had discreetly placed hunting cameras around the property, so she would have evidence if anything like that ever happened again.

Dane smiled as she stepped through the door, her arm brushing lightly against Emma's breast. "Nothing better to do than ogle the staff?"

Emma laughed. "Nope. Nothing at all."

"Just wait, I have a few things I'd like to show you later."

Emma shook her head. "Just help me get through this night, and you can have anything you want."

"Oh, I can't wait to show you what I'm thinking right now." Dane waggled her eyebrows.

Emma shook her head. "Get back to work before I forget myself."

Dane winked at Emma as she turned back toward the kitchen.

Emma stopped in her tracks as she looked up to see Trevor walk through the door. "Oh no. Now what?"

"What?" Dane asked, following Emma's gaze. She clenched her jaw when she saw Trevor. "This can't be good. Let me handle him this time."

"No. I'll do it." Every time Trevor made an appearance, something bad happened. She braced herself for the next wave of shit he'd send their way. She felt Dane's watchful eyes on her as she went to the table Trevor had chosen in the back.

Emma cleared her throat. "What can I get you," she asked, stepping up to Trevor's table.

He folded his large hands on the table, looking up at her. "You know why I'm here."

"Curtis isn't here."

"I'll wait. For now, I'll have a Coors and a shot of Jack."

Emma's blood boiled as she went to the bar. What did he mean by he'd wait? Wait for what? Why did he insist on coming here to torment her? She would never let him peddle his death drugs in her bar. Her only hope was to get him to say something on tape that would prove he was dealing drugs and behind the recent overdose deaths.

The glass clinked on the table as she sat the beer and the shot down sharply. "Anything else?"

"I want to talk to Dane."

Emma flinched. "Dane?" What could he possibly want with Dane?

"You heard me. I know she's here."

Emma hardened her gaze and her voice took on a warning tone. "She's working."

Trevor shrugged. "Fine, I'll find her after work then, but I will talk to her."

Emma shook her head and stormed off. She went to the kitchen and pulled Dane aside.

"He wants to talk to you."

"What?"

Emma searched Dane's face for any sign that there was something going on that she needed to know, but Dane appeared as shocked as she was.

"What do you two have to discuss?"

Dane shook her head. "Your guess is as good as mine."

"Shit."

Dane placed her hand on Emma's arm. "I guess there's only one way to find out." She didn't like this any more than Emma, but she wouldn't back down from this bully. Besides, she was curious about what he was up to.

Trevor watched her as she approached, his gaze moving up and down her body, sizing her up.

"You asked for me," Dane said, stopping a couple of feet away from Trevor.

He studied her a moment longer before motioning for her to sit.

Dane slid into the booth. "What's this about?" She didn't like the way he was looking at her. What was he up to?

"I wanted to meet you. You've been asking a lot of questions lately."

"What's it to you?"

He smiled. "I understand you went to see Thomas Stewart at the prison the other day. I wanted to see for myself what the fuss was all about."

Dane tried to put the pieces together, but she wasn't sure what he was getting at. How did he know about her visit to the prison, and why did he care? "Well, here I am. Like I said, what's it to you?"

Trevor laughed. "He said you were a dumbass."

Dane wasn't about to let her emotions show. "Look, if you have something to say to me, just say it. I have work to do."

"Yeah, it looks like you've gotten pretty cozy with Emma. Maybe you can help her out. That brother of hers owes me something. Maybe you and I can work something out together."

"Fuck you."

Trevor leaned forward. "Now, is that any way to talk to your brother?"

Dane flinched. She squinted at Trevor. "What the hell are you talking about?"

He grinned. "Thomas Stewart is my father. I never thought about having a sister, but now that you're here, I thought we could do a little brother-sister bonding." He tilted his head to the side, appraising her.

"You are not my brother."

He shrugged. "That's not how I heard it."

She slapped her hand down on the table. "I don't care what you heard. That sick fucker is not my father and you are not my brother."

Trevor held her gaze, a stupid smile on his face saying he'd gotten the reaction he had been looking for. "Suit yourself. But one way or another I'm going to collect what's owed me. If you decide you want to save Emma a little heartache, give me a call and we'll see what we can work out." He slid a piece of paper across the table to her with a number. "It's the least I can do for family."

Emma stepped up to the table, looking down at the paper Trevor handed Dane. "Is everything all right?"

Dane slid out of the booth. "Yeah, we're done here."

Emma watched Dane storm off before she turned back to Trevor.

"Was it something I said?" He laughed.

Emma wanted to smack the smirk off his face. "What, no threats tonight? Found another way to sell your poison?"

Trevor shook his head. "I have no idea what you're talking about. I just came in for a drink. I'm meeting an old friend."

Emma frowned. This wasn't the answer she'd been looking for. "Really? I wasn't aware you had any friends."

"Now, Emma, is that any way to treat a customer?"

Emma held his gaze. "That doesn't even scratch the surface of what I'd like to say to you."

Trevor smiled and lifted his glass to her. "Cheers. I'll have another."

Emma ground her teeth together and marched off. She grabbed the bottle of whiskey from the shelf and poured two fingers. She seethed with anger. She hated having to serve Trevor but didn't want to cause a scene in the bar. She had no idea what he'd said to Dane, but she was clearly upset.

Emma turned. She dropped the drink on the floor, the glass shattering at her feet. "Curtis?" She gaped as Curtis slid into the booth across from Trevor. "Where have you been?" Emma demanded.

Curtis looked up at her. His eye was mottled black and green, but the swelling had gone down. "Hey, sis."

"Curtis, you need to go home."

Curtis shook his head. "No. I have to talk to Trevor. I have to make things right."

Emma glanced at Trevor. "Haven't you caused enough trouble? Get out."

Trevor smiled, leaning forward. "Easy. Think about what you're saying, Emma. Curtis doesn't look so good. Do you want me to meet with little brother here where you can keep an eye on him, or would you prefer we go somewhere a little more private?"

Emma blanched. "Curtis, please."

"I'll see you at home later," Curtis said dismissively.

Emma glared across the room, trying to read lips as Curtis talked with Trevor. She couldn't imagine what Trevor was putting Curtis up to this time. What would it take for Curtis to learn that Trevor was no good?

She struggled to focus on orders. Her heart was pounding and sweat trickled down her back. Trevor had Curtis in his clutches, and he was flaunting it in her face.

She straightened when Curtis stood and walked toward her. "I'm sorry, Emma," he said as he stepped up to her, his head bowed.

"What is all this about, Curtis?"

He shook his head. "I gotta go. I'll see you later."

Emma grabbed his arm as he turned to leave. "Curtis, wait. You have to tell me what's going on. Let me help you."

"Everything's fine. I told you I just needed to talk to Trevor. Everything's fine. I'll see you later, Em."

Emma stared after Curtis as he walked out the door. Curtis clearly didn't understand.

Trevor stood, tossing a few bills on the table. He tipped his hat to her on his way out, his smile telling her this was far from over.

Emma wanted to run after Curtis, but the bar was full, and Dane had disappeared after her chat with Trevor. What the hell was going on?

❖

Emma was relieved to see Dane's Jeep sitting in the yard when she pulled up. The light was on in Dane's room, but there was no sign of Curtis.

Emma patted Samson's head before going inside. She made her way up the stairs, stopping at Dane's door, listening for signs that she was awake. She heard the faint clink of glass. She raised her hand and knocked on the door. "Dane?"

"It's open."

Emma slowly opened the door. Dane sat on the bed with her back to the wall. A bottle of Tennessee Whiskey sat open on the floor. Dane held a glass of the amber liquid in her hand.

"Can I come in?"

"Suit yourself. Want a drink?" Dane said raising her glass.

Emma shook her head. "Are you okay?"

"I don't think I'll ever be okay."

"What happened? What did he say to you?"

Dane sipped the drink. "It doesn't matter."

Emma could see Dane wasn't going to share. "You can talk to me."

"Not this time, Emma. I'd rather let this one die."

"Okay." She sat on the edge of the bed, pulling one leg up so she could face Dane. "Have you seen Curtis?"

"Nope. He hasn't been here."

Emma sighed. "He came into the bar right after you left. He talked to Trevor for a while and left."

Dane looked at her, her eyes sharp. "What did he say?"

"Nothing really. He just said everything was fine and he'd see me later. Trevor was his usual smug self. He didn't say anything, but I could tell this was bad for Curtis. I hoped he would be here when I got home."

Dane reached for Emma's hand.

Emma leaned over until she was lying on the bed next to Dane. She wrapped her arm around Dane's waist and rested her head on Dane's thigh. She was tired and worried sick. She was used to being in control. This thing with Curtis was out of hand and she was terrified.

Dane placed her hand on Emma's shoulder and squeezed. "Give him time."

"I just don't know how much time he has left. I have a bad feeling about all of this." Emma's voice shook when she spoke.

Dane combed her fingers through Emma's hair, wishing there was something she could do to ease her mind. Trevor was an evil son of a bitch. Had he really thought she would work with him after learning what his father had done to her mother? Screw DNA, he was not her brother.

She gazed down at Emma. "You should get some rest. I doubt Curtis will be back tonight."

"No, I don't think so. He said he'd be here, but I know Curtis and his promises are usually meant to get him out of something uncomfortable instead of a real commitment to something. I should have known. He's always been that way. When he was little, he would run off down by the creek or wander off into the woods. It didn't matter how many times he was grounded or scolded—he would always promise not to do it again, and the next day he'd be right back out there. As he grew older, those decisions grew more dangerous. He would fall for the pranks the boys pulled, often getting hurt in the process. He jumped off a bridge once because Trevor promised to take him to the movies. He got a broken leg instead. Mom and Dad tried everything. Curtis would promise not to play with those kids anymore, and of course the first time one of them pretended to be nice to him he would fall for the trick again. I can't help but wonder what kind of lie Trevor has told him this time to get him to follow him. What will be the cost?"

"Curtis isn't a little kid anymore. He'll be okay."

"I wish I could believe that."

Emma took Dane's hand in hers, pulling Dane's arm around her. She ran her fingers over the hard ridges of scars along Dane's hand. She traced the damaged skin up Dane's forearm as if following lines on a map that led to Dane's past.

"Do they hurt?"

Dane swallowed the last of the whiskey in her glass. "Not anymore. It took a long time for the nerve endings to settle down, and the skin was thin and tight for a long time."

"How long?"

Dane was silent for a moment. "It's been eighteen months."

Emma rubbed her finger over a deeper scar that ran along Dane's wrist. "This one is different." She hesitated. "Did you…?"

Dane understood the question. She didn't blame Emma for asking. She had been witness to her emotional scars too. "No. I thought about it a million times, but I never wanted to end my life. That was from the fall during the bombing. A piece of glass or metal or something cut me. I don't really know exactly how it happened. I didn't even notice the cut until we were at the hospital and one of the nurses grabbed me."

Emma stared at the wound. "That's when you were burned?"

Dane nodded. "There was fire everywhere, but most of these were from trying to get Michelle out of the car."

Emma closed her eyes against the image and the pain she felt for Dane. "I don't understand why people hurt other people. What gives one person the right to take so much and cause so much pain?"

Dane tightened her hold on Emma. "I don't know. Greed, maybe. Hate. It's hard to say what drives people to do these things."

"Revenge," Emma added.

Dane waited.

"I used to dream of getting my hands on the person who killed my father. Hate and anger ate away at me for years. I finally gave up on revenge. Nothing will ever bring my parents back. But this thing with Curtis has me all twisted up inside. I feel those old feelings growing in me again."

"Shh…" Dane soothed. "It's all right to be scared and protective of those you love. That doesn't make you a bad person. There's a big difference in wanting to kill someone and wanting them dead."

Emma sat up and turned her face to Dane. She laid her hand on Dane's chest, seeking reassurance through the touch. She pressed her lips to Dane's mouth in a gentle kiss. Dane's lips were warm and tender. Her arms were strong wrapped around her shoulders, offering Emma strength she didn't have on her own.

"Thank you for being here," Emma whispered.

"Where else would I be?"

Emma shook her head, not wanting to talk about the future and the time when Dane would leave. She pulled away. "We haven't talked about what happened between us."

Dane didn't move. She just looked into her eyes waiting for her to say more.

Emma held her hand out to Dane. "I know we need to talk, but right now I just need to sleep, and I don't want to be alone."

Dane took Emma's hand, lacing their fingers together. She pulled Emma to her until Emma's head rested on her shoulder. "You're not alone, Emma. I'm right here."

Dane held Emma in her arms, listening to her breathing as she drifted off to sleep. The thought that it was her family hurting Emma made her sick to her stomach. She thought about everything she'd learned about her family since coming to Jellico. If Thomas was Trevor's father, then that meant they were related, no matter how she looked at it. She could never escape the truth of what Thomas had done to her mother. She had come here wanting to be a part of a family. But these people would never be her family. Her mother had been better than them, and she'd chosen a different life. Dane pictured her mother's smile and remembered the sweet sound of her laughter. Her mother was better than all of them. She was her mother's daughter. That was the legacy that mattered.

Emma moaned softly and shifted in her arms. Dane pressed a kiss to Emma's head. Emma didn't deserve to be dragged into the evil web her family had created. She had already been hurt enough.

CHAPTER ELEVEN

Dane looked out over the mountain through the lens of her camera. The hill where she sat looked down over the valley, offering a unique window into the scene below. She set her gaze on a small white church with a blue metal roof nestled in among the trees. The first of the autumn leaves had turned and were starting to fall. It reminded her of old fairy tales where the ornate little cottage in the woods lured children in for the witch to eat for dinner. She laughed at the thought, then shivered, deciding that was a little too close to true.

A glint of light caught her eye. A faint trail of smoke drifted up from a stand of trees down by the river. She studied the spot, trying to make out the source. She trained her camera on it, using the lens like a scope. Whatever it was lay hidden among a thick grove of trees. She glanced back to the farm. The spot was only a couple of miles' walk through the woods from Emma's place. Dane frowned, her curiosity growing.

She gathered her things and jumped into the Jeep. She had a hunch, and if she was right it would answer a lot of questions.

She slowed the Jeep at the farthest point she could safely take it along the overgrown path. She looked around the area for signs that anyone had been there recently, but the rain, walnut husks, and falling leaves had hidden any traces that might have been there. She would have to go on foot from here.

She pulled her pack onto her back. She couldn't risk leaving her camera gear here. She looked around and listened to see if anyone was nearby. Satisfied she was alone, she set off. The path was little more than a dry riverbed, the rocks paving the way through the woods, the hillbilly version of the yellow brick road. The thought made her laugh. She was no Dorothy, and she knew her destination would be a far cry from Oz. Her skin prickled, and she looked around, realizing she could be getting herself into trouble if she stumbled onto something someone didn't want her to see. She pushed off the road, choosing to follow a deer trail across the ridge, which made it less likely she would be seen and gave her a better view of the river.

Slowly she began to make out the shape of a camper. She walked closer. No, it wasn't a camper. It was an old school bus someone had painted over in a camouflage pattern. Her skin prickled. Her pulse raced. She remembered Curtis saying something about an old bus the night they met. Could this be the place he was talking about? Most of the windows were painted over or boarded up. A small fire ring had been built close to the river, and the area around the bus was littered with trash. Tendrils of smoke still wafted up from the dying embers of a recent fire.

A rock dislodged beneath her foot, sending her stumbling down the bank, and she tumbled down the hill until she crashed against the shore below. So much for keeping quiet. She groaned and dragged herself to her feet, brushing leaves and dirt from her clothes. She rubbed a sore spot on her hip. That was going to leave a bruise. She heard a noise from the bus and thought she caught a glimpse of a shadow moving inside.

"Hello?" she called, pulling her pack off her back, hastily looking inside to make sure her camera was okay. She glanced around nervously. She was sure she'd heard someone. "Hello." She tried again. "Curtis, are you in there?"

The back door opened. A boot appeared on the makeshift steps with a faint thud. Then came another. Dane held her breath, hoping she hadn't made a mistake by coming here. At last the figure made the final step to the ground. The door swung closed and Curtis stepped into view.

Dane let out a relieved breath. "Dammit, Curtis, you scared me half to death."

Curtis grinned at her. "What are you doing here?"

Dane shrugged. "Looking for you, of course. Do you have any idea how worried your sister is right now?"

Curtis looked at the ground.

"Look, man, I didn't come here to give you a hard time. I want to help, but I need to know what's going on if I'm going to be able to do that."

Curtis sighed. "I can't go home right now. Emma will be okay if I just stay away."

Dane put her hand on his shoulder. "That isn't true. Every day she doesn't know where you are, or if you're okay, hurts her. If you won't go home, at least let her know you're all right."

Curtis shrugged. "It isn't like I have a phone. The cell service is dead here."

Dane looked at her phone. Sure enough, there was no signal. "Okay, then tell me what I can do to help. Why are you staying out here?"

Curtis sat on a large rock and rubbed his head. His shoulders were slumped. "I tried to make things right with Trevor, but he didn't believe me that the cops had taken all the stuff he gave me. He got real mad. I've never seen him like that before. I asked him about those people that died, and he went off. He said he needed to know who had been taking from him. He said he had to let people know he meant business. He said he was taking care of the bad seeds."

"He killed those people because they were skimming from him?"

Curtis shrugged. "I told him I didn't take nothin', that he could trust me. He hit me and threw me on the floor." Curtis looked away. "He never hit me before. We were friends. But Trevor said it didn't matter now."

Dane decided to push Curtis a little. "I'm sorry he hurt you." She hesitated. "You still have the drugs, don't you?"

Curtis looked up.

"The police didn't find everything, did they?" Dane guessed.

Curtis shook his head. "No. I hid it before I went out that night. I don't like to carry that much around. Something seemed different about this drop, so I only took what I had to. I was going to deliver the weed, but he gave me some other stuff that was different. I just didn't think I should carry it around."

Dane sighed. "What do you mean it was different?"

"It was a dirty looking wax, kinda oily. It didn't make sense."

"What do you plan to do now?" Dane asked, hoping Curtis was ready to go to the police.

Curtis shrugged again. "Trevor said if I don't come up with it, I'll have to answer for it. Said he couldn't have people thinking they could rip him off and get away with it."

Dane shook her head. "You have to go to the police. That's the only way out of this."

Curtis frowned and looked away. "I can't. They'll think I killed those people."

Dane wanted to argue, but he was right. He had played a part in this mess even if he hadn't known about the fentanyl laced in the K2.

"What if you give the drugs back to Trevor?"

Curtis frowned. "I can't do that. What if he sells it to more people and they die too?"

"Maybe you can do it in a way that he can't. You can work with the police to set him up. If you lead him to the drugs, the police can catch him red-handed."

"I don't know, Dane. Things are really messed up. I can't figure out how Trevor knows the cops don't have all the drugs. That night they got me didn't feel right. I swear someone told him something. I can't trust the cops with this, and I don't want to put it on you or Emma."

"You're going to have to trust me, Curtis. We have to do something before Trevor finds you. I don't know much about this place, and *I* figured it out. It's only a matter of time before he shows up here."

Curtis kicked rocks around with the toe of his boot. He wouldn't look at her.

"Come on, Curtis. I know you're scared, but we have to do something. Trevor has threatened Emma. You're running out of time. You can't hide from this and you can't do it on your own."

Curtis looked up at her, his eyes heavy with sorrow and regret. "Promise to leave Emma out of it. I don't want this getting to her. I don't want her to get hurt."

"I'll do my best to protect Emma. I promise." Dane clasped her hand on his shoulder and squeezed. "I'm your friend. You can trust me. I won't do anything to hurt you or Emma."

Curtis looked hopeful for the first time. "Okay, but I can't go home. I can't do that to Emma."

Dane nodded. "Do you need anything? Food, water, anything?"

Curtis pointed to a trail a few feet up the creek. "I sneak into the house sometimes when Emma isn't there and take a shower and get food."

Dane nodded. "I'll put some things together for you and leave them in the hayloft."

This made Curtis smile. "Thanks."

"Don't mention it." She held his gaze. "You should tell me where the drugs are hidden."

His brows knitted together. "I can't." He started to pull away.

"Hey, it's okay. I thought you'd say no, but I had to try. I'll do what I can. Okay?"

Curtis nodded.

Dane pulled him into a hug. "Hang in there. We'll get through this."

"All right," Curtis said sheepishly as he stuffed his hands into his pockets.

Dane hated to leave him, but the longer her Jeep sat at the end of the road, the more exposed he was.

"I'll leave some things in the barn tomorrow. I've got to go before someone sees my Jeep. We'll use the path through the woods from now on."

He nodded again.

Dane dug into her bag and pulled out the handful of granola bars she kept around in case of emergencies. The truth was, they were there to curb her sweet tooth. She handed them to Curtis.

"This is all I have for now."

He grinned. "Thanks."

She took off down the river path, turning once to wave back at Curtis. She looked back once more before stepping out of view, but Curtis was gone. Dane took a deep breath. She had a vague idea how she was going to get Curtis out of this, but she had a bigger worry on her mind now. What was she going to tell Emma?

Dane stored the food and supplies in the barn like she promised, but the more time she had to think, the more uncertain she became about her plan. She didn't know where to turn or who they could trust. She would have to tell Emma. It was the only way, but she had some work to do first.

The weeks she had spent researching her family tree had paid off. She found it much easier to find information on the living than for the dead. It only took a few hours' searching and she'd found everything she ever wanted to know about Thomas Stewart and the seven children he had sired. Trevor has already made his claim, but the other six had been a mystery. She was just happy not to find her own name on the list. That didn't mean she was free of him—it just meant there could be more children out there that no one knew about. She ran a quick search of the names through social media sites to see what she could learn. She was shocked at what people would post about their lives on the web for the world to see. She was particularly interested in one name that popped up with some photos that matched the description of the man who attacked her and Curtis. Milton Grimes. She printed copies of the photo. It looked like she was going on a little road trip.

Rain pelted against the windshield as Dane pulled the Jeep into the muddy gravel parking lot of the Miner's Light Bar. There were more ATVs parked in the lot than trucks, and even they were equipped for off-road use. She shook her head. Coalfield made Jellico look civilized.

She took a deep breath and stepped out into the rain, pulling her cap down over her eyes and tugging the hood of her jacket up.

As expected, the noise level dropped a notch the moment she entered the bar. She shook the rain from her shoulders and took a good look around. She didn't recognize anyone, so she went to the bar and ordered a beer.

The bartender peered at her through dark distrustful eyes. He scanned the room behind her as he handed her the beer. The hairs on the back of Dane's neck prickled as if she was being stalked by a deadly predator. She glanced over her shoulder to see the men behind her watching.

Dane reached into the inside pocket of her jacket and pulled out a photograph, then slapped it onto the bar in front of her. "Do you know where I can find this guy?"

The bartender paled. He worked his jaw from side to side as if he was chewing on his tongue. She could tell by his expression he knew exactly who she was looking for. He shook his head. "Nope."

She took a drink from her beer. "Hmm, I was told I'd probably be able to find him here."

The bartender shrugged. "You were told wrong."

Dane picked up the photo and put it back in her pocket. This was her third stop and she hadn't found anyone willing to talk to her. Not that she really expected them to. But by the way this guy was acting, she figured he'd be on the phone with her guy before she left the parking lot.

She tossed a five onto the bar as she stood. She glanced around the bar as she zipped her rain jacket and lifted the hood. She needed to keep her eyes open, but mostly she wanted to make sure everyone got a good look at her. She wanted to make sure Milton knew she was looking for him.

Once back inside the relative safety of her Jeep, she checked her watch. The sun was already hanging low. She had to get moving. She had a promise to keep.

Emma would be at work already. It was delivery day. With any luck she'd catch her before things got too busy.

As she'd hoped the bar was empty. The Budweiser truck sat in the back, and a young man wheeled boxes of beer into the cooler. Emma was busy stacking the cases as quickly as the man could bring them in.

Dane waited until the last load was finished and watched as Emma signed the invoice. Emma smiled at her as she entered. Dane swallowed the lump of guilt that was quickly growing in her throat.

"Hey, do you have a minute. I need to talk to you about something."

Emma's face paled, and Dane could see her body stiffen, readying for bad news. She knew Emma was going to be mad, but there was no other way around this. She stuffed her hands into her pocket to ward off the chill of the cooler and the icy darkness that had clouded Emma's eyes.

"What is it?"

"Can we talk somewhere else? It's freezing in here."

Emma's lips thinned as she pressed them tightly together. "Sure." Dane followed Emma into the bar. "Out with it. What's wrong? Has something happened to Curtis?"

"No."

Emma braced herself with a hand on the edge of the bar. "You leaving?"

Dane frowned. "No."

"What is it then?"

"I found where Curtis has been hiding. I talked to him."

"What do you mean you talked to him? Where is he? Why are you being so secretive?" Emma demanded.

"I can't tell you yet. But I promise he's safe for now." Dane bit her tongue, hoping that was true.

Emma pinned Dane with the weight of her furry. "Dane, so help me God if anything happens to him—"

"I know. I'm sorry. But it's the only way I could get him to go along with this. I think I figured out who beat him up. If my plan works, we may be able to get him out of all of this and put Trevor behind bars."

"What plan?" Emma could feel the heat burning her face. She was so mad she could hardly hear what Dane was saying.

"When I first came here, you told me that even the police here are protective of family secrets and would never sell out family. Is there anyone you know in your heart you can trust? Anyone on the force who will be true to the law and help us?"

Emma ground her teeth together trying to make sense of what Dane was saying.

"Curtis thinks someone on the inside has told Trevor that he didn't have all the drugs on him. He's afraid to turn to the police with what he knows and won't tell me where the drugs are."

Emma pulled out a chair and fell into it with a thud. "What the hell?"

"Who do you trust?"

Emma shook her head. "If Trevor has someone on the inside, there's no way to know who is and who isn't involved in this."

"That's why it's important for us to get this right. If we trust the wrong person, Curtis could take the fall for everything."

Emma dropped her head, burying her face in her hands. "I don't like this."

"I need you to think about it. Curtis is pretty certain someone on the force is involved. And I started thinking about the day he was beaten. He said he just came from a meeting with his probation officer. That's a big coincidence, don't you think?"

Emma sighed. "Or it's Curtis trying to put the blame on everyone except Trevor."

Dane frowned.

"I told you, Curtis has a way of twisting things around," Emma said, brushing a strand of hair out of her eyes. "You can't always believe him. He convinces himself of his own lies when he doesn't like the truth. He spent three years after Momma and Daddy died pretending they were on vacation and would be back for him. He made up elaborate stories about phone calls and letters that never happened."

"That was a long time ago. He's a gown man now."

"No, he isn't. He still does it all the time. A few months ago, he convinced himself he had a girlfriend. Come to find out he had been sitting in the parking lot of the diner in town watching some girl who had been nice to him and gave him a free ice cream. She had no idea he even had a crush on her."

Dane remembered the night Curtis had said he was going to meet a girl. Had that been real? She shook her head, confusion clouding her reasoning. "So what do you think we should do? Just turn him in to the police?"

"It's the only thing we can do."

Dane frowned. Emma was right. They would have to turn Curtis in, but there had to be something they could do to sort things out, so he wouldn't take the fall for everything. She knew there was no way Curtis would testify against Trevor.

"What if we got Curtis to tell Trevor where the drugs are hidden? Couldn't the police just pick Trevor up when he goes to get the stuff?"

Emma shook her head. "Who's to say Trevor will be the one to go? He could have another kid like Curtis do it for him."

Dane's head hurt. There had to be a way.

"Dane," Emma said softly. "I appreciate you trying to help Curtis, but you have to let this go. Tell me where he is. He's my responsibility."

Emma was right. She had been so determined to help that she hadn't been willing to admit the obvious.

"You're right," she conceded. "I'll go get him."

"Wait. I want to go with you."

Emma turned out the lights and put a closed sign on the door.

"You don't have to, I can go—"

Emma cut her off. "He's *my* brother."

Emma held her breath as Dane took a narrow curve a little too close to the edge. She was anxious to get to Curtis, but she wanted to get there in one piece.

"Slow down, you're making me nervous."

Dane slowed, and Emma loosened her grip on the handle attached to the roll bars above her head. Dane had been quiet on the drive and Emma regretted snapping at her. She was only trying to help.

Emma's nerves were getting the best of her and she couldn't stand the silence any longer. "How did you find him?"

"It was an accident really. I remembered something he said the day we met and had a hunch. It paid off."

"When did you see him?"

"Yesterday."

Emma clenched her teeth. "You knew where he was yesterday, and you didn't tell me." It was not a question. Emma was pissed.

"I know you're mad, but I didn't want Curtis to run again. He said he wanted to protect you."

"I can take care of myself. I can't believe you. You know how worried I've been, and you still didn't tell me."

"I know. I really was trying to help."

Emma stared out the windshield refusing to look at Dane. She had to get a grip on her anger before she saw Curtis, or she'd just scare him off again. It wasn't like Dane had kept this from her entirely. Anger burned her throat like acid, but she was mostly scared. She didn't know what was going to happen to Curtis, but she'd rather take her chances with the law than leave him at the hands of someone like Trevor.

She looked at Dane. Her hands were clenched tight around the steering wheel, and a muscle jumped at the side of her jaw as she clenched and unclenched her teeth.

"Thank you for telling me. I know you're trying to help." Dane glanced at her. She could see the turmoil rolling in Dane's eyes. "As soon as we get back to the house, I'll call the lawyer. We can run all of this by him and see how he thinks we should handle it. I think it will be better if Curtis comes forward before they have to come looking for him."

Dane nodded. She turned down the old river road that backed up to the farm.

Emma frowned. Had Curtis been right under her nose this whole time?

"We'll have to walk the rest of the way."

Emma nodded as she slid off her seat belt. Adrenaline coursed through her making her jittery, and her stomach was in knots. She felt like running the rest of the way but made herself stay calm. It wouldn't help if she lost control and pissed Curtis off. If she didn't play this right, she knew he wouldn't come home with her. He could be as stubborn as a mule sometimes.

She reached for Dane's hand, seeking the comfort of her touch to calm her worry and fear.

Dane gave her hand a squeeze. "Let's go get him."

Emma gasped at the sight of the bus when it came into view. All the windows were broken, bullet holes riddled the tattered metal, and the back door hung open.

Dane clasped her hand over Emma's mouth and pulled her into her arms, rushing for cover behind a stand of mountain laurel. She scooted close to the ground until they were safely tucked behind a sycamore tree. She held her finger to her lips, motioning for Emma to remain quiet. She took Emma's face in her hands forcing her to look at her. She shook her head. Emma's eyes were wide with fear. Dane could feel her muscles tight as bowstrings beneath her hands. Emma was ready to bolt.

"Wait." Whoever had shot up the bus could still be there. They would be easy targets if anyone wanted to take care of loose ends. Dane peered into the clearing, searching the area for any signs that someone was still there.

Tears streamed down Emma's face. Dane shook her head again, trying to tell Emma not to give up hope. She looked around again. There was no sign of anyone except the faint smell of gunpowder lingering on the air. Everything was quiet.

Dane held Emma's face in her hands, forcing her to look at her. "Wait here. I'll go check. You have to be quiet," she whispered.

Emma put the pad of the palm of her hand in her mouth and bit down, nodding. Tears glistened in her eyes.

Dane kissed her forehead. She pressed her finger to her lips, reminding Emma to be quiet. She slithered down the bank onto the road. She approached the bus slowly, praying no one was there and dreading what she might find inside.

The bus was in shambles. Whoever had been there had meant to make sure nothing inside survived. Broken glass littered the floor and fragments of old camping equipment had been ripped to shreds. She lifted a cot that had been turned over on the floor expecting to find Curtis among the remains, but he was not there. There was no blood, no sign of him at all.

She stepped back outside, waving her hand to motion Emma out.

Emma staggered onto the rocks like she was having trouble working her legs.

Dane shook her head. "He isn't here. There's no sign of him."

Emma slumped to the ground. "Thank God."

Dane kneeled on the ground beside her.

Emma's hands shook. Dane could see the imprint of teeth marks in her palm.

"Where is he? They've got him. Oh God, what are they going to do to him?" Emma asked.

It was obvious whoever did this was sending a message. "I don't know, but I don't think Curtis was here when this happened."

Emma looked at her hopeful. "Why?"

"This is overkill. Why shoot the place up if they found what they were looking for?"

Emma took a deep breath. Some of the color was returning to her face.

"Come on, let's get out of here."

Dane helped Emma to her feet. As they stood Emma's gaze moved to something in the distance and her mouth fell open. Dane turned to see what it was that had put this new fear in Emma's eyes.

"Shit," Dane said when she saw the smoke billowing above the trees overhead.

"That's coming from the farm," Emma choked out.

Dane grabbed Emma's shoulders once more and forced her to look at her. She pressed the keys to the Jeep into Emma's hand. "Go back to the Jeep, and as soon as you get a signal, call for help." Dane turned to run but Emma held her in her grasp.

"Where are you going?"

"I'll take the path through the woods just in case Curtis is hiding or hurt out there somewhere. I'll meet you at the farm. It'll be okay. Go," she commanded and pushed Emma toward the Jeep. As soon as Emma began to run, Dane bolted into the woods.

Dane sprinted across the field, her feet pounding against the earth, each step bringing her closer to the thick cloud of smoke growing in the sky ahead of her. She could see the barn ahead. She was almost there. She drank up the adrenaline fueling her to push harder, run faster. She had to get to the farm. She had to save Curtis. She tagged the fence, her hands grabbing the rails, and she pushed her body up and over in one swift vault. She burst out of the barn into the yard just as the Jeep jolted to a stop and Emma jumped out.

"No," she shouted as Emma ran into the burning house.

Samson barked frantically, running past her the moment she pushed through the door.

A wall of heat and smoke hit Dane full force as she burst through the door. She coughed, covering her mouth with her shirt and her hand.

"Emma. Curtis," she called. She couldn't see anything. She followed the sound of Samson's barks, calling out to Emma between coughs.

"In here," Emma's voice called from the center of the living room. Heat and smoke burned Dane's eyes, making it hard to see. She crouched as low to the floor as she could as she stumbled along the hall.

She fell to the floor in the doorway of the living room. Emma was crouched next to Curtis who lay in a heap on the floor. Flames snaked up the walls, the curtains and antique sofa already engulfed in fire. Dane grabbed Curtis and helped Emma roll him over. Blood seeped from a wound on the side of his head and from a hole in his chest.

Curtis looked up at her, his steel gray eyes pleading. "I'm sorry," he said weakly.

"Don't you give up. Do you hear me? Don't you leave me," Emma yelled.

Dane's head swam. The fire was so hot she could feel her skin blistering. She pulled Curtis upright and looped her hands under his arms. "Grab his legs," she yelled to Emma.

She struggled for air. Her lungs were burning—she was burning. They made it to the kitchen, but the smoke was too thick to see anything, and she coughed and gasped for air. Emma had Curtis by the feet leading them out. She was at the door. They were going to make it. Dane heard a crash and looked up as the rail of the staircase fell. She instinctively put her arm up to brace against the fiery impact and threw herself away from the emblazoned timber.

The pain seared through her skin and she screamed. With one last push she shoved Curtis and Emma through the door.

Dane choked on the thick smoke and the searing pain. She panted and gasped, trying to get her breath. The doorway was blocked now. She heard barking and peered back down the hall. Samson grabbed her pants leg and tugged. She crawled on the floor through the house, Samson at her side. He whined and barked as if he could frighten the flames away. The smoke was too thick and the flames too hot.

Dane blinked rapidly trying to see through the black cloud stinging her eyes. The memory of the terror she'd seen in Michelle's eyes flashed through her mind. This was her destiny. Michelle had come back for her. It was always supposed to be her. Dane fell to the floor, coughing. She laid her head on her arm, gasping for breath. Samson barked again, drawing her back to the present. Rage boiled up in Dane's heart. "Not today," she murmured. Samson had fought for her. She wouldn't give up on him now.

❖

Emma tumbled down the few steps to the ground, frantically dragging Curtis through the yard to get him away from the blaze. Smoke and tears burned her eyes and she coughed, trying to clear the acrid smoke from her throat. Her hair was singed but she was alive. They were both alive.

Emma peered into the flames. "Dane," she screamed. "Dane." She held her hand over the wound in Curtis's chest. She couldn't leave him, but she desperately needed to get to Dane. The sound of sirens grew closer and she prayed help would get there soon.

What was taking so damn long? She looked down at Curtis. His eyes were closed now, and he wasn't moving. No. She couldn't lose him. She couldn't lose them both. She screamed as her heart ripped to shreds.

She heard a crash at the back of the house and snapped her head up as a chair flew out her bedroom window. Glass and shards of wood scattered to the ground as smoke billowed out of the window. She held her breath. "Please. Please get out, Dane. Please."

She could hear glass breaking and saw the comforter from her bed thrown over the windowsill. Then she saw Dane throw one leg over the sill, then the other. She jumped from the window holding a large bundle in her arms.

Emma clutched Curtis to her chest, choking on her tears. "Dane," she croaked.

Dane stumbled to her feet still clutching the bundle in her arms. She fell to her knees beside Emma. Samson was wrapped in her mother's old quilt and her father's robe. Samson lifted his head and whined at her. He wiggled closer and licked her face. They had made it. They had all made it.

Dane coughed in violent fits and was clearly having trouble breathing. She lay back on the ground next to Emma, her burned hand clutched tight to her chest. New burns marked the surface of the old scars. Her face was black, and tears streamed from her swollen red eyes washing through the soot clinging to her cheeks, cutting trails of pain onto her face.

Emma's lungs burned with every breath. Everything she loved was in ruins. Lights flashed around her. Hands grabbed at her, pulling Curtis from her arms. She watched the firefighters in their bright yellow gear spray rivers of water onto the fire burning up her life.

Someone shoved an oxygen mask over her face, and she held it firmly in place, the air battling the darkness filling her lungs, trying to free her from the burning smoke that was slowly suffocating her.

She watched a woman place another oxygen mask over Dane's face and then insert a long needle into Dane's arm. Dane turned her head toward Emma. She nodded and closed her eyes.

Emma turned back to Curtis. The paramedics were pushing him toward the ambulance. Emma ran after them. "Please, let me go with him. I'm his sister."

The driver nodded and helped her climb into the back before slamming the heavy doors shut. Emma was silent as she watched the medic work on her brother. She remembered the day he was born and the love she saw in her mother's eyes. She remembered pushing him in his swing and teaching him how to ride a bike.

She remembered the day she left for college. He had cried after her, not wanting her to go. Then there was her father's funeral when Curtis had clung to her hand, refusing to let her out of his sight. She relived the day she had found him in the loft crying after their mother had died. He had been afraid she would leave him too and go back to the city.

She had promised she would never leave him. She had promised her mother she would take care of him. He was her responsibility. She had lived for years with anger for everything she had given up, but as she looked down at him, his clothes soaked with blood, tubes running into his arms, his skin pale and lifeless, she realized she hadn't given up her life. She realized she needed Curtis just as much as he needed her. She let the oxygen mask slip from her face. New tears flowed from her eyes and panic rose in her chest. She couldn't lose him.

The paramedic took her hand and guided the oxygen back to her face. "You need to keep this on. Don't worry. We're doing everything we can."

Emma nodded. "Thank you," she croaked, cringing from the searing pain in her throat.

"You probably don't want to talk if you don't have to. Your throat will be sore for a few days. The doc will want to check it out when we get to the hospital."

"What about Dane?" she rasped.

The woman looked at her. "The other woman at the scene you mean?"

Emma nodded again.

"She'll be in the ambulance right behind us. She'll be at the hospital within minutes of our getting there." The woman gave her a faint smile. "I know this is hard. Just hang tight. We're going to take good care of you."

The woman picked up a radio and began speaking into it, relaying information about Curtis, his age and vital signs, identifying the laceration to the head and a gunshot wound to the chest.

Emma felt her head spin. The full understanding of what had happened hit her like a ton of bricks. Someone had shot Curtis and then set her house on fire. Someone wanted Curtis dead.

CHAPTER TWELVE

Emma watched the lines on the monitor change pattern with every beep of Dane's heart. Her own heart was breaking, and she had no idea what she was supposed to do next. Curtis was in surgery, and Dane had been asleep since they gave her pain medication. The nurse had explained about the morphine, but Emma needed to see Dane's eyes before she could believe she would be okay. They had explained that the oxygen tube in her nose was to help her breathe until the swelling in her nose and throat improved.

She rested her head on Dane's bed waiting for something to change. A hand on her shoulder drew her up.

"Hey, sweetheart."

Emma stood, wrapping her arms around Aunt Lily. The old woman enveloped Emma in her arms, holding her as she cried.

"Are you okay?" Lily asked, brushing a tear from Emma's cheek.

Emma nodded, pulling away to wipe her face.

"You look awful. Are you sure? You look like you should be lying in a bed just like that one."

Emma shook her head. "I'm okay. The oxygen they gave me helped, and I guess I'm in the right place if anything goes wrong. Other than the rawness in my throat and a headache, I'm fine."

"How about our boy?"

Emma shook her head. "I don't know anything yet—he's still in surgery. Someone shot him. They shot him right there in our living room. They tried to burn down the house around him." Her chin quivered as she tried to hold back another wave of tears. "What kind of monster would do that?"

Lily pulled her into her arms, rocking her gently. "Shh. Hush now. It's all going to be okay. We aren't going to let anything else happen to you or our boy." She brushed her hand over Emma's hair. "James called from the house and said he had Samson. Said he was banged up a bit, so he took him out to see the vet. Everyone is in good hands now."

"Thank you," Emma sobbed.

Lily pulled back and looked down at the sleeping woman in front of them. "How about Dane? Is she okay?"

"I think so. They gave her something for the pain. They said she had some damage to her upper respiratory system from the smoke and heat, so they want to keep her sedated for a little while."

Lily continued to stroke Emma's hair the way she used to do when she was a little girl. "Good thing she was around, or I might have lost you both."

Emma nodded and buried her face in Lily's neck as the tears began to flow again. She lifted her head and turned at the sound of a knock at the door.

The sheriff cleared his throat and nodded to Emma. "Ms. Reynolds." He nodded to Lily. "Ma'am."

Emma sighed. She had wondered how long it would be before she had to start answering questions. "Sheriff."

"I know this is a bad time, but I need to talk to you if I can. The sooner we get on this, the sooner we can catch whoever did it."

Emma frowned. "I'm pretty sure we all know who did this, Sheriff."

He pursed his lips in silent refusal to agree with her statement. "I have to get the story, Emma. I need to know what happened out there today."

Emma glanced at Dane and then turned to Lily. "Will you stay with her? I don't want her to be alone when she wakes up."

"Of course, honey. I'll be right here when you get back."

The sheriff led Emma to the chapel. "I thought maybe we could talk in here if that's all right. It's a lot more private than just pulling one of those curtains, and I didn't think you'd want to go to the station."

"This is fine."

Emma told him what she knew, starting with the man beating Curtis up in the yard, Trevor meeting with Curtis at the bar, then Dane finding Curtis at the river, someone shooting up the old bus, and then finding Curtis in the burning house.

"Did Curtis say anything when you found him? Was he able to tell you who did this?"

"No." Emma stared down at her hands folded in her lap. She felt helpless. She knew it wasn't much to go on, and she didn't have any proof it was Trevor who did it. He had most likely sent his bear to do the dirty work.

"I'm really sorry, Emma. I know this is hard."

"Thanks."

"I'll have someone here at the hospital to watch out for Curtis until he's better or we catch whoever did this."

Emma looked at him, surprised. She hadn't thought to ask. "I have to tell you something, Sheriff, and you're not going to like it."

"I'm listening."

Emma met his eyes. "Curtis believes someone in your department is passing information to Trevor. The guy who beat him up showed up at the farm right after his meeting with the probation officer. It may be nothing, but if it's true, you've got a problem. Dane was trying to explain all of it to me. She might know more than I do."

He nodded. "I'll look into it. Did anyone see anybody at your place?"

Emma shook her head. "I have no idea. I was at the bar until Dane came in, and then we went straight to the river to get Curtis."

"How well do you know Dane?"

Emma squinted at him. "Dane didn't do this. She risked her life going into that fire after us. She wouldn't even leave Samson. I hardly think she would have done that if she was trying to kill Curtis."

The sheriff put his hand up. "I'm not saying anything like that. But it's worth asking. She's not from around here, and I don't recall any trouble like this before she showed up."

Emma wanted to scream at him. How could he even consider Dane? "I assure you this isn't about Dane. If you remember, someone beat her up a few weeks back outside my bar."

"I do recall. That just leaves more questions, doesn't it? Who has she crossed that would do something like that?"

Emma sighed. "I understand why you have to ask these questions, Sheriff, but please promise me you won't spend all your time trying to pin this on the outsider just because it fits in a nice little package. Don't fall for the small-town stereotype and cover up something, just because the outsider is easy."

"Now, Emma..."

"Don't *now, Emma* me," Emma said, her voice steadily rising. "This is my family. Someone already killed my father and got away with it. I won't allow you and this town to let the same thing happen to my brother. Look into Dane all you want, but I want the real person responsible for this to pay. I'm tired and I won't stand for this any longer."

The sheriff dipped his head in agreement. "I'll do all I can, no matter who it is."

"Then we understand each other."

The sheriff smiled. "We do."

Emma stood to leave.

"One more thing, Emma."

She turned to face him.

"Did Curtis ever tell you if there were more drugs?"

She held his gaze. "No."

He stared at her a moment longer as if assessing her. "Okay. I'll have an officer stationed outside your brother's door within the hour if he makes it out of surgery."

Emma flinched. She closed her eyes, trying to stop the buzzing in her ears. The room was spinning, and she felt her chest tighten.

She clenched her fist. "He'll make it." He had to.

❖

Emma jerked her head up at the sudden movement of Dane's arm. She hadn't meant to fall asleep. Dane's eyes were wide with fear as she raised her hands, trying to get to the tube protruding from her nose.

Emma stood and grabbed Dane's arm before she could do any damage to herself. She leaned over so Dane could see her. "Shh," she soothed as a nurse scurried into the room to attend to her. "It's okay. You're okay. You have to leave that there for a little while, just until the swelling in your throat goes down."

Dane stared up at her, her eyes pleading. Her nostrils flared as she struggled, and tears leaked from the corners of her eyes onto the red swollen skin scorched by the heat of the fire.

Emma leaned closer so that her mouth was only inches from Dane's face. "I'm right here. I'm not leaving you. I won't let anyone hurt you." She slid her hand into Dane's and felt her fingers clamp around hers.

"Cur—Curtis?"

The words tore through Dane's throat like they were too big to squeeze through the narrow opening. But Emma could see the question in Dane's eyes and knew what she wanted. "He's in surgery. We just have to wait and see."

Dane blinked. Her eyes opened wide and she searched Emma's face then looked down. She squeezed Emma's hand.

"I'm fine. My throat is a little sore from the smoke and I have a small burn or two. My skin is tender, but nothing to worry about. You saved us."

Dane frowned and shook her head from side to side. Her brows furrowed together, arguing against the statement.

"You did. You saved us. I wouldn't have been able to get him out without you. I would have died trying."

The nurse moved around them, pushing buttons on the beeping machines and adding medicine to the tube running into Dane's arm. Dane relaxed, and her eyes became glassy and her lids heavy. The machines quieted as the medication worked its way into Dane's veins.

Emma looked to the nurse.

"I gave her something for the pain. She'll sleep for a while, and she may not remember this the next time she wakes up. You may have to explain everything again. She's responding well, though."

Emma nodded. "Thank you," she said, turning back to Dane. She looked down at their joined hands. The fingers that had held her so fiercely only moments ago were slack against her palm. She glanced at the clock. How much longer would they take with Curtis? Why hadn't she heard something? She gripped Dane's hand, finding comfort in being close to her, even if Dane didn't know she was there most of the time.

She sank back into the chair and rested her cheek against their joined hands, the words the sheriff spoke coming back to her. How well did she know Dane? The moment she laid eyes on her she'd thought Dane was trouble. None of this started until Dane showed up in her life. Could Dane be involved? She remembered Dane talking to Trevor and the piece of paper he had given her. What had that been about? She watched the sleeping woman, letting the questions tumble around in her mind. She hated herself for doubting Dane after what she'd done to save her and her brother. She closed her eyes and let her mind drift to memories of Dane flirting with her, the day at the creek, sharing her body with Dane, and Dane holding her when she felt weak and vulnerable.

Emma brushed a kiss to the back of Dane's hand. Her head might be full of questions, but her heart had no doubts.

Lily shuffled into the room gripping a metal cane in her hand.

"Lily, where's your walker?" Emma asked, concern breaking through her weariness.

"I left it in the car. If I need it, one of the boys can go fetch it for me."

Emma shook her head at the stubborn old woman she loved so dearly, thankful she was there with her. "You need your walker."

Lily huffed. "As long as I'm on even ground, I'm fine."

Emma pulled up a chair for Lily and made sure she was securely settled before returning to Dane's side.

"You need some rest, honey. You look tired."

Emma sat back, resting her head against the chair. "I am tired. I'm tired to my bones. Every minute I watch tick by on the clock feels like an eternity. I feel so helpless."

"We'll know something soon. Right now, no news is good news."

Emma nodded.

"Then let us help you, sweetheart. James, Sue, John, Marshal, and all the rest are waiting outside. You don't always have to do everything on your own."

Emma took Lily's hand. "I know. I just don't know what to do. Everything Momma and Daddy worked so hard for is gone."

Lily shook her head. "No, Emma. The house can be rebuilt, the things inside replaced. You and Curtis are what they worked for, what they loved. You are what matters."

Emma fought back the tears that welled up in her eyes. She didn't want to cry anymore. Her eyes were sore, and she wasn't sure how much more crying she had left in her. Each tear drained a little of her hope.

Lily squeezed her hand. "I want you to tell me everything. Start from the beginning."

So Emma did. She told the whole story, starting from the moment Dane walked into her bar. She did leave out the part about having sex with Dane—she was talking to her aunt after all, and she wasn't about to share those details with anyone.

Lily listened intently. When Emma was done, Lily patted her hand like she was a child. "She cares about you."

Emma glanced at Dane.

"How do you feel about her?"

Emma didn't answer.

"I've been watching you two. I might be old, but I'm not blind, Emma. Any old fool can see you have feelings for that girl."

Emma drew in a deep breath. She wasn't ready to talk about her feelings for Dane. She couldn't bear the thought of letting her go.

After all that had happened, she wouldn't blame Dane for packing up and leaving the moment she was able.

"She has a life somewhere else."

"Yes. But she also has a life here."

Emma shook her head. "No one has a life here."

"Oh, sweetheart, your life is whatever you choose it to be. I think it's about time you stop living for everyone else and start living for you. If love is at your door, don't close it."

Emma couldn't see it. "I'm going to go get a cup of coffee. Will you stay?"

"Of course."

"Can I get you some?"

"I'd like that."

Emma went to the lobby where most of her family sat waiting for news. Sue's eyes widened and she stood as Emma entered.

Emma shook her head. "I don't know anything yet."

Sue put her arms around Emma. "He'll make it. He's a tough kid."

"I don't know. It was bad, Sue. Really bad."

Sue patted her hand against Emma's cheek. "What about you?"

Emma was about to answer when her gaze caught on the figure walking toward her. She clenched her teeth and her shoulders stiffened.

"What?" Sue asked, turning to look behind her.

"What the hell are you doing here?" Emma said through gritted teeth.

Trevor held Emma's gaze. "I heard what happened. I came to see about Curtis. How is he?"

Emma slapped Trevor, pouring every ounce of hurt and pain and anger she had into the strike. "He's not dead, if that's what you mean."

Trevor's head snapped to the side at the impact. He rubbed his cheek with his hand and glared at her but didn't respond. Everyone in the room stood and gathered around them.

"Get out," Emma demanded.

Trevor put a hand up. "This is a public place. I have a right to be here."

"You don't have the right to be anywhere near my family."

Trevor shrugged. "Fine. But I have a right to know what's happening with mine."

Emma frowned. "What are you talking about?"

Trevor shrugged ignoring her question. He glanced around the room at the men and women glaring at him. He pursed his lips in a tight line, his anger close to the surface.

"I can see this is a bad time. I'll check back later."

"Don't bother."

Trevor stared at her for a moment, his smug smile goading her. He looked like he was about to say more but stopped, as if thinking better of it. He took a step, then turned back to Emma. "Tell Dane I was here." He turned and walked out.

Emma was seething mad. She wanted to pound her fist into his face. Her anger was quickly doused when the doctor walked into the room.

"Ms. Reynolds?"

"Yes," she answered, breathless. Her heart felt like it was lodged in her throat. It was hard to breathe.

He nodded to her and the family as everyone drew closer. "He's stable. We were able to fix the damage to his chest, but he lost a lot of blood. He's not out of trouble yet, but he has a chance. It will be a while before you can see him."

"Thank you."

He dipped his head slightly toward her.

Sue gripped Emma's shoulder. "Thank God."

Everyone smiled and hugged her. Murmurs of gratitude filled the room as the rest of the family took in the news. Emma felt like a weight had been lifted from her chest. New tears stung her eyes. She hadn't lost him.

Emma gathered the coffee and hurried back to Dane's room to tell Lily.

She was surprised to see Dane awake talking to Lily as she entered.

"Look who's awake," Lily announced.

Emma smiled, feeling another piece of her heart mend. It had been a long night, and she hadn't believed Dane was okay until she looked into her clear blue eyes that always reminded her of the ocean.

"Hey," she said to Dane.

"Hey," Dane croaked.

Emma set the coffee down on the table and turned back to Dane, placing a hand on Lily's back. "I just saw the doctor. Curtis is out of surgery. He made it. He isn't out of the woods yet, but he has a chance. It will be a while before we can see him."

Lily wrapped her arm around Emma and kissed her cheek. "Oh, that's wonderful news."

Emma nodded. "Yeah." She looked down at Dane. They had come out of the flames, but the danger wasn't over yet. Trevor's visit said as much. The vultures were circling.

CHAPTER THIRTEEN

Dane sat on the edge of the bed and tried to figure out how she was going to manage her escape when she didn't even have a pair of pants. She was certain her bare ass hanging out the back of the hospital gown was a dead giveaway.

"Don't even think about it."

Dane looked up to see Emma standing in the doorway watching her. Her arms were folded across her chest, and the look on her face told Dane not to argue.

"I hate these things," Dane said tugging at the thin white cotton with little blue diamond patterns scattered about. "This is worse than wearing a dress. I think I at least deserve a pair of pants."

Emma smiled. "If you're good, I'll see what I can do."

Dane took a moment to study Emma. She looked more refreshed after her shower and clean clothes. But the dark circles under her eyes gave away her fatigue.

"You look better today," Emma said stepping closer and tossing a bag onto the floor.

"I was about to say the same thing about you. Did you get any rest?"

"A little."

"Any changes with Curtis?"

Emma shook her head. "He's stable. He woke up for a little while earlier this morning. It was good to see his eyes open and know he's going to be okay."

"This morning?" Dane looked at the clock. What time had Emma come back to the hospital? Had she really slept at all? Emma was a rock on the outside, but Dane knew she was a mess on the inside.

Dane clenched her teeth. Why had she left Curtis? If she'd only brought him home and made him—made him what? He wouldn't tell her where the drugs were. He wouldn't go to the police. He wouldn't even face the fact that Trevor would hurt him. She looked hard into Emma's eyes. "I'm sorry. I'm sorry I didn't tell you sooner. If I had only—"

Emma stopped Dane by placing her fingers against her lips. "I don't blame you for any of this. It isn't your fault. There's no way you could have known any of this would happen. I know my brother. I know how stubborn he can be."

Dane looked away. She had screwed up again, and once again someone else was paying for it.

As if reading her mind, Emma placed two fingers under Dane's chin and turned her head toward her. "Look at me."

Dane looked at her. Instead of the hurt, rage, and disappointment she expected to find, she saw worry, gratitude, and understanding. Tears glistened in Emma's eyes.

"Don't blame yourself for this. Curtis got himself into this mess. And whoever did this to us is the one responsible for what happened, not you. I wouldn't be standing here right now if it wasn't for you."

Dane squeezed her eyes shut to push away the thought of anything happening to Emma. When she'd seen her run into that burning house, she'd lost her mind. She would have walked through the fires of hell to get Emma out.

Dane kissed the tips of Emma fingers, relishing the feel of her touch.

Emma moved her hand to Dane's cheek and kissed the spot where her fingers had been. Dane's skin didn't look as red and angry as it had the day before. The soot and grime had been washed away, and with the exception of the tender pink skin around her nose and the bandages to her arm, Dane was beginning to look more like herself again.

Someone knocked at the door. Emma pulled away, making room for the young man pushing a cart.

"Time for your breathing treatment."

Dane sighed. "How many more of these do I have to take before you guys will let me out of here?"

The young man shrugged. "That's up to the doc. But I'd take these things as long as they tell you to. The last thing you want is to set up an infection in your lungs."

Dane's shoulders slumped. "Fine."

Emma regarded Dane with a faint smile. She was definitely getting back to her old self. One more day of this, and she was sure Dane would make a run for it.

Emma waited until the young man left the room before returning to Dane's side. "So, what's your plan?"

"Plan?"

"You can't tell me you weren't sitting here planning your escape."

Dane laughed. "Know me that well, do you?"

Emma shrugged. "I know you hate hospitals."

"Yeah, well, at least as long as I'm here, I can keep an eye on you and Curtis."

Emma was surprised by the answer. "I thought that after all of this you'd be ready to get as far away from us as possible."

Dane took Emma's hand, lacing their fingers together. "You aren't going to get rid of me that easy. I'm not going anywhere."

A faint sigh slipped from Emma's lips and she wouldn't meet Dane's gaze.

"What is it?"

Tears stung Emma's eyes. "I was scared. I was scared when you were hurt. I was scared you would leave."

Dane wrapped her arm around Emma's waist and pulled her close. "Hey, I'm okay. All they've done is piss me off. There's no way I'm backing down now."

"What are you going to do?"

Dane shrugged. "I'm good at asking questions. I'll start by shaking a few bushes. You never know what will fall out if you shake hard enough. The sheriff was in here earlier. I told him what I'd found. You wouldn't believe how many guys on the force are related to Trevor."

Emma shook her head. "I don't think that's a good idea. Trevor has already been here. I don't want you getting hurt. They tried to kill Curtis. I don't want them coming after you too."

"What do you mean, Trevor was here?"

"He was in the lobby just before the doctor came out to tell us Curtis was out of surgery. He said he heard what happened and wanted to check on him."

Dane clenched her teeth together so hard Emma thought they would break.

"I slapped him and told him to get out."

Dane jerked her head up, surprised. "Good for you." Then she frowned. "Oh, shit."

Emma smiled, then looked down at their joined hands. "He said something before he left. He said he had a right to check on his family. Then he said to tell you he was here." Emma looked up into Dane's eyes. "Is there something you should tell me about you and Trevor?"

She nodded. "That night Trevor talked to me at your bar, he told me something I didn't want to hear." Dane's skin turned cold as the icy tendrils of dread spread throughout her body. "Thomas Stewart is his father. He wanted to rub it in my face."

Emma gasped. "He's your brother?"

Dane shook her head. "No. I don't believe it. But if Thomas is his father, we are at least cousins. And from what I found, Trevor is just one of many bad apples from that tree."

Emma swallowed. She looked shaken.

"See, you were right. I am trouble."

"You aren't anything like him."

Dane blew out her breath. "I've got to do something to stop him. I can't just sit back and do nothing."

Emma gripped her hand like a vise. "Then let the police handle it."

Dane smiled. "I intend to do just that. But I can at least shake the bushes."

Emma rolled her eyes. "This is serious, Dane."

"I am very serious."

Emma pulled away and sat in the chair next to the bed, as if needing a little distance between them so she could think.

Dane changed the subject. "Have you been to the house?"

Emma nodded. "It's all gone. The house, all of Momma's things. It's all gone."

"I'm sorry. I know how important that was to you. I can't imagine."

A tear fell from Emma's lashes to her lap. "Aunt Lily has been great to take me in. Her place is small, and she doesn't have much room, but it's been good to be with her."

Dane picked up on some of Emma's worry. "I was thinking I'd get a room at the hotel when they let me go. At least for a few days, until I can figure something out."

Emma shook her head. "That place is dangerous. You can't go there. Let me talk to James and see if he has room."

"I don't think I have to worry about it right this minute," Dane said, lifting her arm, the IV tube dangling from her wrist. "I'll figure something out. Right now, I have bigger worries."

Emma frowned. "What?"

"Where am I going to get pants?"

Emma laughed and kicked the bag she had tossed onto the floor. "I think I can hook you up, but only on one condition."

"What's that?"

"You will stay here until the doctor says you can go, and you won't get into any trouble."

"I think that's two conditions," Dane teased.

"Promise me."

Dane pressed her hand over her heart. "I promise."

Emma narrowed her gaze at Dane, using her *I mean it* look.

"Come on, Emma, help me out here. That blond nurse with the red lipstick keeps looking at my ass. Do you really want that?"

Emma laughed. "I don't know—maybe she's just what you need."

"*You* are what I need. You and pants."

Emma unzipped the bag and handed Dane a pair of black sweatpants. "And since you've been such a good patient, I even brought you a T-shirt to match, but I'm not sure they'll let you wear it."

Dane took the shirt. "I'd like to see them try to stop me."

"Be careful. I saw how swift the nurse was to give you those knockout drugs."

Dane stopped and looked at the door half expecting the nurse to walk in on her. She shrugged and started tugging on the sweats. She pulled the strings free and tried to slide out of the gown, realizing too late that there was no way she could get the T-shirt on with the IV in her arm. She sat with her bare breasts exposed as she tried to figure a way out of the mess.

Emma stood and took the shirt from her. "Here, let me help." She couldn't stand to see Dane like this, but it could have been so much worse. She stared at Dane's bare chest, the tender skin of her breasts. She wanted to reach out and touch her. The memory of Dane's skin on hers made her hot, and she felt her cheeks burn. The reality of how close she had come to losing her was overwhelming, and Emma wanted to touch Dane just to know she was real.

Emma slowly worked the gown back over the bandages. She wrapped her arms around Dane to tie the strings in the back, gently brushing her fingers against Dane's skin. She felt Dane shiver at the touch. Dane slid an arm around Emma and rested her head on Emma's shoulder.

Emma drew in her breath. It seemed like an eternity since they had held one another, since she had felt Dane's skin on hers, and now even the slightest touch had her longing to be alone with Dane. She needed to inspect every inch of her to know her hurts and heal her with her kiss.

"Emma."

Emma took a step back. "Sorry. I didn't mean to."

Dane grasped her arm as she backed away.

"Oh no. I'm already having a hard time not touching you. I can't," Emma said putting her hand up between them.

"Tell me what's wrong?"

"Nothing. I just can't do this here." She picked up the bag and handed it to Dane. "I also got you some other things I thought you might need." She glanced toward the door. "I'm going to go see if they'll let me see Curtis. Maybe he'll be awake this time."

"Will you come back later?"

Emma stopped at the door. "I'll be here."

"Thanks for the clothes."

Emma looked at her, trying to defuse the tension with playfulness. "You promised, remember."

"Yeah. I promised."

CHAPTER FOURTEEN

Dane sat in a chair across from Curtis, watching him sleep. She had been released earlier but didn't know where else to go. She had plenty she needed to do, but for the time being she couldn't pull herself away. They still didn't know if Curtis would survive, but every day gave hope. She hated to think of what would happen to him if he did. Whoever shot him wouldn't want him living long enough to identify them. She pondered every memory she had of Curtis. He was like a puzzle. She thought if she looked at him long enough, she'd figure it out.

Curtis stirred. His eyes slowly fluttered awake. He looked confused when he saw her sitting at his side.

"Hey, Curtis."

"Hey." He looked around as if expecting someone else. "Where's Emma?"

Dane leaned forward and rested her elbows on her knees. "She's getting some rest. I told her I'd stay with you today."

"Did you really drag me out of that fire?"

Dane nodded. "Emma and I did it together."

Curtis let out a sigh. "Emma's still mad at me. Are you mad too?"

"No. I'm not mad. And I don't think Emma is mad at you either. She's worried and she's scared." Dane picked at the soft bandage covering her arm. "What do you remember?"

"Not much."

"Look, man, you can't keep doing this. You have to give me something. I can't help you if you don't talk to me. Emma deserves better than this. You have to stop thinking like a kid and act like a man. They can't get to you in here, but you'll go home eventually. Do you really want these guys getting to Emma or Aunt Lily?"

Curtis flinched. He looked to the door as if he expected someone to come through it and finish him off.

"I was up the creek by the bus when I heard Trevor call my name. I could hear things getting thrown around in the bus. I ran up the trail to the farm when I heard the gunshots. It sounded just like in the movies, only this time it was real, and I was scared. I ran to the house. I didn't know where else to go. But the big man was waiting there. He pointed a gun at Samson and told me to call him off or he'd shoot him. I told Samson to go check the chickens. The big man didn't like that I wouldn't tell him where the rest of the drugs were. I tried to tell him the police took 'em, but he wouldn't believe me. He hit me in the head with the gun. He searched around the house for a bit and got real mad when he didn't find anything."

Dane reached into her pocket and pulled out the photo she'd printed out before the fire. "Is this the guy that shot you?" she asked, holding the picture up for him to see.

Curtis stared at the picture, his eyes widening with recognition. He nodded. "That's him. That's the guy, the same guy that came to the farm and beat me up."

Relief flooded Dane. She was glad they were on the right track. Once they could get an identification to the sheriff, they could get this guy before he could come back for Curtis.

"Why didn't you just give him what he wanted?"

"I couldn't. Those drugs are killing people. They killed my friends. I couldn't let them have it back."

Dane nodded. "Did this guy say who sent him?"

"No. He just said he wanted his stuff. He said he was tired of playing games with me. But that didn't make sense because he didn't give me the stuff, Trevor did. I figured this guy was trying to pull one over on Trevor and get him in trouble. The next thing I know he's pointing a gun at me. I don't remember anything after he shot me."

"I'm sorry, Curtis, but this guy wasn't trying to get Trevor in trouble. He's Trevor's brother. Trevor knew he was there."

Curtis bit his lip. His eyes brimmed with tears. "What do you want me to do?"

Dane moved close to Curtis, so she could keep her voice low. "I want you to tell the sheriff everything you've told me. Answer all of his questions with the truth." She waited until he nodded his agreement.

"You need to tell me where it's hidden."

Curtis pursed his lips in a thin line. He pressed a button on the small wand he held in his hand. "I don't think that's a good idea." He motioned Dane closer. "I need you to do something for me."

When he spoke, his voice was barely a whisper. Dane listened carefully, trying to grasp what he said.

She raised her head and looked down at him with a slight nod. "I'll take care of it."

"I'm tired."

She patted his shoulder. "It's okay. Get some rest. I'll stay with you until Emma or Aunt Lily gets here."

Curtis closed his eyes and went back to sleep.

Dane opened the drawer to the small table next to his bed and sifted through the contents. She picked up his phone and turned it on, happy to find there was no access code. She read through his text messages, his call log and contacts. It didn't take long to find what she was looking for.

Dane was still sitting next to Curtis watching him when Aunt Lily stuck her head in the door.

"There's that handsome girl I'm looking for. How's my boy?"

"Good," Dane answered as she stood to give the old woman her chair. "He's been asleep most of the time. The morphine really knocks him out."

"Has he said anything?"

"Yeah, he told me what happened. He had to be scared to death, but he never gave in to them."

"Who was it?" Lily asked.

Dane shook her head. "Trevor was the one who shot up the bus. He said the big guy that beat him up before was the shooter." Dane handed the picture to Lily. "His name is Milton Grimes. He's Trevor's brother."

Lily puckered her lips as if she'd just tasted something sour. "The police will be able to pick him up on that. But we can't nail down Trevor."

"No. But it's a place to start."

The old woman shook her head. "I don't like it. This is too much like what happened to their father."

"I don't like it either. This isn't over. He knows too much. These guys won't stop until they get to him. We have to find a way to stop them."

"You know where he hid it, don't you?"

Dane couldn't lie to Lily. She met her gaze. "I think I figured it out. I still have to check a couple of places. I went snooping around looking for Milton before all of this happened. I wanted to rattle the cage, but I didn't see any of this coming. I figure the minute I walk out those doors Trevor and Milton will know about it. We don't have a lot of time before they come back."

Lily sighed. "Tell me everything."

Dane did her best to fill Lily in on what she knew and what she suspected. Besides Emma, Lily was the only person she could trust.

When she finished, Lily patted her hand. "You're going to need help. This is a family matter now."

Dane started to argue, but Lily stopped her. "You listen to me. I've lived in these hills a long time. Sometimes things are just outside the law. It's time we settle this the old way."

Dane shook her head. "We can't do anything illegal, Lily."

Lily smiled. "You have to trust me. That child lying there is as good as mine, and Emma has been through enough. I think Curtis needs to have a little chat with the sheriff to start."

Dane sighed. "Do you know where I can find Emma?"

"I'm not sure, but I'd bet she's at the bar or at the farm. That girl has a lot to sort out."

Dane nodded. "Thanks, Lily."

Lily dug around in her purse and pulled out a set of keys. She pulled one from the ring and handed it out to Dane. "This is to my house. I suspect you could use a place to stay until you figure out what's next. You can stay with me as long as you like. It's been nice having company. That old place has been too quiet for too long. You and Emma will be good for me."

Dane smiled. "Thanks." She leaned down and kissed Lily's cheek, closing her hand around the key Lily offered. "Do you need anything before I go?"

"I'm fine. You go on and see about Emma and don't you worry one bit. I'll be right here."

Dane nodded.

"Dane," Lily said before she reached the door.

"Yeah?"

"Do what you have to do."

Dane took a deep breath. "I'll call you tomorrow."

Emma was standing in front of what remained of the house when Dane pulled up at the farm. Someone had been there with a dozer and had leveled what had been left of the house to a pile of smoldering rubble. Remnants of the crime scene tape tied to a small maple flapped in the breeze.

Emma looked lost.

Dane stepped out of the Jeep and went to her. She wanted to wrap her arms around her and tell her it would all be all right. But she knew it wasn't that easy.

Emma looked up as she approached.

"I thought I might find you here."

Emma shrugged. "Where else is there?"

Dane pressed her hand lightly against Emma's back. "Come here."

Emma slid into her arms, burying her face in her neck. She could feel hot tears against her skin.

"I'm so sorry, Emma. I know things can never be what they were, but I promise things will get better."

Emma squeezed her arms tighter around Dane's waist. "I know. It's just so hard."

Dane brushed her hand against Emma's hair. "What can I do? What do you need?"

"I don't even know where to start."

"Do you think you'll rebuild?"

Emma looked around at the ruins. "I guess I will. I can't live with Aunt Lily forever. The sheriff said he had everything he needed, so I decided it was better to take it down than look at it the way it was. It doesn't look like there will be any problem with the insurance, but I don't know how I'm ever going to get everything done."

Emma's voice was thick with tears as she spoke. Dane wished there was something she could say to make this easier for Emma. "You don't have to do it all by yourself, you know. Let people help you. Your family is just dying to chip in. You have some really good people around you."

Emma smiled. She placed her hand to Dane's cheek. "Do I?"

Dane felt her skin heat beneath Emma's touch. "Yes."

Emma laid her head against Dane's shoulder, relishing the feel of Dane's arms around her. She was so tired. She just wanted to lie down and sleep. Maybe Dane was right. Maybe she didn't have to do everything alone.

She looked up and peered into Dane's eyes. "I'm tired. Will you come back to Lily's with me?"

Dane pulled the key from her pocket. "Lily insisted."

Emma smiled. "I love that woman."

"Let's go then."

Emma had a feeling the next few hours would determine their fate. She unlocked the door and pulled Dane inside. "The house is small, but it is totally Aunt Lily."

Dane smiled as she looked around the living room. "That's okay. I can sleep out here on the couch."

Emma wrapped her arms around Dane's neck and pressed her lips lightly against Dane's mouth. Dane softened at her touch. Emma pulled Dane's shirt out of her pants and ran her fingers along the smooth skin of her sides.

Dane shivered.

"I don't want you to sleep out here. I want to feel you next to me. I want you to hold me while we sleep together."

"Are you sure?"

Emma smoothed her fingers against Dane's face. "I'm afraid I won't be able to sleep at all if you don't."

Dane nodded.

Emma closed the bedroom door and stripped off her clothes down to her underwear. She slid into a T-shirt she pulled from a drawer in the dresser. She handed another one to Dane before pulling back the covers and sliding between the sheets.

Dane peeled off her clothes and stood naked beside the bed.

Emma watched Dane, her eyes lingering on the bandages covering her arm. There was a hollow look to Dane's eyes like she'd never seen before. Dane had fought to save her. She had stayed when she didn't have to. She had given more than Emma could ever ask. She held out her hand and invited Dane in.

Dane climbed into bed, sliding next to Emma until their thighs met. Emma pulled the covers over them and slid her arms around Dane, pulling her close until she felt the soft brush of Dane's breasts against hers. She raised her head and kissed Dane, tentative kisses to soothe and comfort at first, then deeper as Dane slid her hand between them and cupped her breast.

Dane gripped her hips and parted her thighs as she slid her leg between them. Emma closed her eyes and lost herself in Dane's touch. She didn't know what tomorrow would bring, but today she would give herself to Dane. She would shut out the world in this moment and believe for a little while that Dane would stay.

Emma pushed Dane onto her back and straddled her hips, pressing against Dane's pubic bone.

Dane's eyes widened, and her breath hitched as she gripped Emma's thighs and thrust her hips up to meet Emma. She slid her hands beneath the thin fabric and tugged her panties down. Emma lifted herself, allowing Dane to slide the silk down her legs then toss it to the floor.

Emma smiled down at Dane as she straddled her, reaching behind and stroking Dane's clit as she rubbed against her.

"Look at me," Emma whispered.

Dane locked on to Emma's eyes. The intensity of Dane's gaze sent a surge of arousal straight to Emma's clitoris. Dane pressed the palm of her hand against Emma's stomach and slid the pad of her thumb through her folds. She pressed firm strokes against Emma's clitoris, coaxing her need, calling her to her.

Emma groaned, and the pleasure surged through her as she swelled against Dane's touch. Tendrils of pleasure coiled in her belly as Dane rocked her hips, increasing the pressure against her clitoris. With each thrust Emma slid her fingers up and down the length of Dane's clitoris.

"More," Emma said as she raised her hips and guided Dane's fingers inside. She lowered herself on Dane's hand, groaning as Dane filled her. She rocked her hips, continuing to stroke Dane with her hand. Each thrust of her hips pushed Dane deeper inside, increasing the pressure of her thumb against her clitoris. "Dane…"

Dane locked her gaze on Emma's, glorying in the beauty of the woman touching her. Emma's fingers stroked the length of her with every thrust of her hips. Dane clenched her teeth. Pleasure surged through her with every stroke of Emma's hand until she could hold no more. Her legs stiffened, the nerve endings beyond what she could hold. Tendrils of pleasure seeped out through her nervous system, filling her entire body with pleasure. Her skin tingled. Her vision dimmed. She reached deeper, pushing herself into Emma as her orgasm exploded in a rush of pleasure unlike anything she had ever felt. "Emma," she groaned as she erupted against Emma's hand.

Emma continued to press against her, taking her fingers deeper with every thrust.

"Emma," Dane repeated, never taking her eyes from Emma's.

Emma smiled down at her as she settled herself onto Dane's hand, her fingers sliding in and out with every thrust. Dane filled her over and over until the swell of orgasm, like tendrils of electricity, sparked in her depths. Emma shuddered and tightened her thighs against Dane's sides. The walls of her sex clamped down on Dane's fingers. Emma trembled as she rode out each wave of pleasure, lifting her hips just enough to slam back against Dane.

"Yes. Oh God, yes." Emma's breath came in short gasps as she leaned forward. The pressure of Dane's thumb against her clitoris ignited a second eruption. She rode wave after wave of pleasure, pushing herself down against Dane's hand, holding her inside her.

Emma collapsed against Dane's chest, spent. She lifted her hips and let Dane slip out of her as she nestled close against her.

Dane pressed a kiss to her head and pulled the sheet up over them. She circled her arms around Emma and felt her drifting off to sleep. She took in the warmth emanating from her and the soft glow of her skin. She realized in that moment that she had never felt this close to anyone. She felt connected to Emma. Emma made her feel like she could do anything, be anything. Emma filled the emptiness in her heart. And someone was trying to take her from her.

Dane slipped out of bed. If she was lucky, she would be back at the house before Emma woke. She didn't like leaving her like this, but she had a shot at putting an end to all of this trouble and she had to take it.

CHAPTER FIFTEEN

Despite her best efforts, it was getting dark when Dane pulled up at the farm to find Emma's truck parked in front of the barn. She could see Emma moving around putting the chickens in the coop for the night. Everything was quiet. Dane stared out over the ruins of the old house, remembering the night Emma and Curtis first brought her into their home. The house and everything inside had been old, weathered, and worn, but it had been comforting and warm.

She dialed Lily.

"Hey. The first place didn't turn up. I'm at the farm. Emma's here. I'll call back in a few minutes to let you know what we find."

She hung up and climbed out of the Jeep, peering into the shadows to make sure they were alone.

"Hey, look at you in your fancy new Wranglers," Emma called as she walked toward her. "What are you doing out here?"

Dane smiled. She brushed her hand over her new jeans and tugged at the fresh shirt. "Fresh off the rack at Tractor Supply. What do you think, do I pull off the farmer look?"

Emma laughed. "Not exactly. You are cute, though."

Dane pulled Emma into her arms the moment she was within reach. "I'm sorry I left earlier. I missed you today." She kissed Emma's cheek. "How are you?"

Emma's gaze flickered to the empty void where the old house had stood. "I'm thankful for what I do have. I'll worry about the rest tomorrow."

Dane smiled.

"Now answer me," Emma said, her brows furrowed, "what *are* you doing out here?"

Dane let Emma go and stepped away, putting a little space between them. Her skin pricked with uncertainty. "I need to check something."

Emma's frown deepened.

"Come on, you'll see."

Dane quickly led Emma to the back of the property, stopping outside the old cellar. It looked like a tomb. She wasn't looking forward to seeing what kind of creepy crawlies made their home in there. She pulled out her phone and activated the flashlight.

"Dane, what are we doing?"

Dane looked around nervously. Gathering all her courage, she sighed and opened the old wooden door and stepped into the cavern. Emma was so close to her she could feel her breath on the back of her neck.

The smell of dank earth hit her the moment she stepped inside. Spiderwebs covered old jars and plastic milk crates that had been stacked on end and used as shelves. Dane rubbed the back of her neck, imagining spiders crawling on her skin. She shivered at the thought. *Focus.* She had to focus so she could get what she came for and get the hell out of there. She didn't know where to start.

"Tell me what we're looking for, and maybe I can help, since this is my cellar after all."

Dane took Emma's hand. "A couple of days after you let me come stay here, Curtis took me to meet a guy named Mark. I was shocked that Curtis made a drop with this guy. He gave him marijuana," she explained.

Emma nodded. "Yeah, I remember you told me about that."

"Well, just before we left that day, Curtis said he had to go get something, and I saw him come in here. I hadn't even noticed the cellar was here until then. I remember thinking it was odd, but then so is Curtis, so I brushed it off. I've been racking my brain trying to figure out where he would hide those drugs no one can find. Then I remembered this place."

Emma looked around the cellar. "That little shit. You're telling me he's been hiding drugs in here."

Dane shrugged. "That's my hunch. I figure there's only one way to find out." She moved the light around. "Look for a place that looks more used than the others. You know, less dirt, spiderwebs that have been cleared away, things like that."

Emma pointed to a box in the corner. There was a handprint on the side where the dust had been wiped away.

Dane handed Emma the light and shifted the box to the side, exposing a hole where one of the stones in the wall had been removed. She reached into the opening and closed her hand around a metal box. Her heart raced. "I've got something," she whispered. She pulled out the box and lifted the latch to an old Ninja Turtles lunch box. She opened the lid. A pile of small plastic bags littered the bottom of the box, each filled with a greenish-brown waxy substance. "Bingo."

Emma sighed. "If Curtis lives through this, I think I might kill him myself."

Dane shook her head that such a little thing had brought so much pain. Well, this bit was going to end here. She slammed the lid closed and fastened the latch. They had what they were looking for, and it was time to get out of there.

"What is that stuff, anyway?"

Dane glanced at the box in her hand. "I think they call it dab. It's a concentration of oil from marijuana plants. Let's just stay a little of this goes a long way. And if I'm right, this stuff has been laced with fentanyl."

"Shit. I can't believe he would bring that here."

Dane stopped, listening. She held up her finger in front of her mouth. Emma froze. For a moment Dane thought she heard something.

"Let's go. This place gives me the creeps." Dane dialed Lily as she stepped out of the cellar. "Hey, we found it." As they stepped into the clear night, they came face to face with two dark figures.

"That's far enough," a deep voice said.

Dane let her hand fall to her side, cupping the phone without ending the call. She quickly surveyed the situation, contemplating her options. She might be able to get past them on her own, but there was no way she could let them get to Emma. Running wasn't an option. She just hoped Lily could hear what was happening and send in the troops.

"What are you doing here, Trevor? Haven't you caused enough trouble already?" she said defiantly.

Trevor walked closer, pointing a gun at her chest. The big man beside him mirrored his every move.

"Not really. I'll take that now," he said pointing to the box.

Emma lunged toward Trevor. "Curtis trusted you." Dane threw up her arm, catching her. "You were supposed to be his friend. How could you do this to him?" Emma shouted.

"Curtis knew the rules. He stole that from me. I only came for what's mine."

"So you sent your muscle after him." Dane nodded to the big man. "It's Milton, right?"

Trevor laughed. "I heard you've been barking up the family tree. I guess you just can't get enough. Say hello to your brother."

Dane flinched. "I don't have a brother."

Trevor laughed again. "That's not how I hear it. Even if Dad didn't get that little bitch pregnant, you're still family, like it or not. Maybe we should all get to know each other a little better, let you get a taste of how the family works." He grabbed his crotch and jerked his hips toward her. "Maybe we should have worked you into the family business. Emma seems pretty sweet on you. You could have done some good business for us at the bar."

"Keep dreaming, asshole," Dane said through gritted teeth. "I'll never work for you, and if you touch me, I'll make sure you eat your dick."

Both men laughed at her.

Trevor took another step closer. "Suit yourself." He looked pointedly at Dane. "We have what we wanted. We don't need Curtis or you anymore. He knows too much, and you really aren't any use to me." He turned back to Emma. "It's too bad you had to learn all this the same way your father did. None of this would have happened if you had just played along."

Emma gasped.

Dane frowned. "What are you talking about?"

Trevor sneered at her with a smug grin. "How does it feel, Emma? What's it like knowing you bedded the daughter of the man who killed your father?"

Emma stared at him, her mouth slightly ajar. All the air had been sucked out of her chest and she couldn't think. "What?" she choked.

Dane cringed. "Thomas killed Emma's dad?"

Trevor laughed. "It looks like we've all come full circle. First the old man, then Curtis, and now the two of you. Seems my family is destined to destroy yours, Emma. Maybe we should have a go with you first. Teach you a little lesson."

"Stay the fuck away from her," Dane demanded, stepping in front of Emma.

"Ha." Trevor shook his head. "You don't get to make the threats here. Now, hand me the box." He pointed the gun in Dane's face. He reached for the box, taking it from her hands. He raised the gun to her head. "Start walking," he said, herding them to the truck like animals.

Dane jerked her arm away as Trevor tried to shove her into the truck. She froze as she stared down the barrel of the gun. She had to buy some time. She knew if they got in that truck they were as good as dead. She glared at him. "What's with those drugs anyway? Why are you killing people? Isn't that bad for business?"

Trevor flipped the box open and peered inside. "It was time to shake things up a bit. I needed to know who was skimming from me. This way my guys learned not to cross me. I'll put the word out that the drugs were from a competitor, and everyone will be looking to buy my stuff instead. Deal with the devil you know and all that."

They heard a car speeding up the drive, kicking up gravel and mud. They all turned to see who it was.

"Son of a bitch, it's the cops," Milton said, speaking for the first time. "What the fuck? I don't like this, Trevor. Do something."

"What? What do you want me to do?"

"I don't know, but I'm not going back to prison." Milton jumped into the truck.

Trevor kneed Dane in the stomach, knocking her to the ground. He grabbed Emma around the neck, holding the gun to her head as the police cruiser slammed to a stop a few feet away.

The sheriff jumped out of the car, bracing himself behind the door, his gun drawn. "Drop your weapons," he yelled. More sirens wailed in the distance. In a few more minutes they would be outnumbered.

Milton stuck his arm out the window and fired at the sheriff. An instant later a second gunshot rang out and blood spurted from Milton's arm.

"Fuck," Milton screamed.

Trevor dragged Emma to the truck. He had her hair gripped in his fist and the gun pressed below her ear.

Dane scrambled to her feet. As Trevor moved his gun hand to open the door, she grabbed his arm, desperately trying to wrestle the gun from him.

Emma screamed as Trevor shoved her against the truck, letting her go.

"Run," Dane yelled as she struggled for the gun.

Emma ran.

Dane could hear the sheriff yelling, Trevor cursing. The big engine in the truck roared, and her own breathing amplified, but time moved in slow motion as Trevor yanked his hand away and slammed the gun into the side of her head. There was a loud crack and fire exploded in her shoulder, ripping a path through her back.

Trevor jumped in the truck, and gunfire erupted all around her as the truck roared to life. The big tires spun, churning the gravel into a storm of projectiles beating against her skin like an angry swarm of hornets.

Dane turned to her side and rolled into a ball, trying to cover herself. The roar in her head faded. She could hear the sheriff yelling for an ambulance. She closed her eyes against the pain and lifted her head. Where was Emma?

Footsteps pounded the gravel rushing up behind her.

"Dane," Emma yelled.

Dane rolled to her back, clutching her arm.

Emma fell to the ground beside her, her eyes wide with fear as tears streaked her face.

"Oh my God. No." She pushed her hand against the wound in Dane's shoulder.

"I'm okay," Dane said through gritted teeth, the stabbing blade of pain ripping through her shoulder. She groaned. "Damn." She let her head fall back against the ground. "I hate hospitals."

Emma choked out a laugh through her tears.

The sheriff kneeled beside Dane. "The ambulance is on the way."

Emma stared at the monitors, watching the lines streak up and down with every beat of Dane's heart. She hoped she would never have to watch those lines define the life of someone she loved again. The adrenaline had burned away long ago leaving her feeling hollow and tired. She was afraid to close her eyes, afraid if she looked away, Dane would be taken from her.

They told her the surgery had gone well. The bullet hadn't damaged anything vital, but there was damage to her scapula. It would be a long recovery. Emma was just glad she was alive.

"Hey." Dane's voice ripped her from her thoughts.

She grasped Dane's hand and squeezed. "Hey, you."

"How long have I been out?"

Tears filled Emma's eyes. "Two days."

Dane raised her eyebrows in surprise. "Funny, I don't feel like I've slept at all. It's all just a big void."

Emma let out a long breath, relieved to see Dane's baby blues again. "You know, for someone who doesn't like hospitals, you sure spend a lot of time here."

Dane smiled. "How are you?"

"Better now."

"What about Trevor and Milton? Did they get them?"

Emma pressed her lips into a thin line and frowned. "Not yet. They disappeared into the mountains. There's no telling where they're headed. But there's no way they'll come back here. The sheriff called off the search, but they have people all over the state watching out for them. If they show up anywhere, they'll get them. It's just a matter of time." She paused, questioning if she should tell Dane the rest.

"What?"

"Paul and the guys have gone out...hunting."

Dane frowned. "Hunting?" she echoed, not understanding what Emma was trying to tell her. Then it dawned on her. "You mean...?"

Emma nodded.

Dane studied Emma's eyes, reading all the hurt and fear that had ravaged her for weeks. So much had happened. She didn't know how Emma was keeping it together.

"What are they going to do?"

"I don't know. I don't think I want to know. Lily called a family meeting and said something about family business and that was the end of it. They all took off. Trevor is a fool if he thinks he can hide from those boys. I think they're all part goat, and they know these mountains better than anyone. I don't know what's going to happen."

Dane didn't know what to say. Wasn't this what Lily had spoken to her about? "How's Curtis?" she asked needing a change of subject.

Emma's eyes brightened. "He's better. They moved him to a regular room and he'll likely go home by the end of the week."

Dane lifted her hand to the bandage on her head and looked down at her arm in a sling strapped across her chest. "Looks like we're a matched pair."

Emma laughed. "Yeah." She lifted her hand and brushed the tips of her fingers along Dane's cheek.

"Listen, Emma," Dane said peering into Emma's eyes. "What Trevor said about our families, your father—"

Emma pulled Dane's hand to her lips. "Our families may be linked together, but you had nothing to do with what they did. You aren't like them. I don't blame you."

Dane was grateful that Emma hadn't turned her away, but she wasn't so sure she could offer herself the same pardon. "I'm so sorry for all of this," she whispered.

Emma shook her head. "I'm the one who's sorry. Curtis got us into all of this, not you. Trevor took advantage of him. You didn't cause any of this. You've saved me twice now." She shook her head. "I don't know what I would have done without you." Emma leaned down and kissed Dane, letting the warmth of Dane's lips soothe her fear. "Thank you."

Dane had come to Jellico searching for a family, some moral fiber that she thought would redeem her. What she'd found instead was a level of hell that she never deserved. Dane had more than proven her moral fiber. Emma meant what she said. She didn't believe Dane was in any way to blame for the sins of her family.

"You should go get some rest," Dane whispered. "If you're not careful, you'll end up stuck in here with the rest of us."

Emma smiled. "I will. I just needed to be here."

"I'm glad you were here when I woke up, but now it's time to rest. Get out of here for a while before I have to call Lily on you."

Emma laughed. "Okay. But promise me you'll be here when I get back."

Dane heard the uncertainty in Emma's words, and she had the feeling they were about more than the gunshot. She lifted the edge of the sheet and peered down, shaking her head. She sighed dramatically. "It doesn't look like I'll get far without pants."

Emma grinned. Her eyes softened. She leaned forward and kissed Dane again. "Please don't scare me like that again. I don't think my heart can take it."

Dane threaded her fingers through Emma's hair and pulled her back in to a kiss. "I won't," she promised. She wanted to pull Emma into her arms and hold her. She wanted to chase away the fear and doubt that clouded her eyes. She wanted to burn away the images of Trevor clutching Emma, the gun pressed to Emma's head. She wanted the nightmare to end.

She flinched and pulled away as a stabbing pain ripped through her chest.

Emma pulled back. "I'm sorry."

Dane squeezed her eyes closed, trying to block out the pain. She shook her head. "I'm okay."

Emma smoothed the sheet over Dane's chest and sat in the chair next to the bed. "Maybe it's best if I stay over here." She took Dane's hand. "Do you want me to call the nurse?"

"No. It'll pass. I just moved wrong."

Emma bit her lip.

Dane could see the worry heavy in her eyes. "I think I'll get a little sleep for a while. You should do the same. Get out of here for a while."

"Okay. If you're sure you'll be all right."

"I'll be fine."

Emma stood. "I'll come back tomorrow morning." She brushed a gentle kiss against Dane's cheek. "Have a nurse call if you need anything."

Dane nodded. She closed her eyes, giving in to the sleep pulling her under.

Dane woke in the night disoriented and afraid. The nightmare that ripped her from her sleep lingered in the shadows, making her jump at every sound. The hours without Emma seemed slow, and the room felt cold without her there. Twelve hours had passed on the clock. She lay awake, listening to the beep of the monitors and the shuffling of feet as the nurses moved up and down the hall. She tried to move, but the pain in her back screamed a warning that she wouldn't be going anywhere anytime soon.

She thought about all she had learned about her family since coming to Jellico. What she'd learned about herself. She wished she had been a better friend to Michelle, and maybe if she hadn't been late that morning, Michelle would still be alive, or maybe they would have died together. Dane closed her eyes to shut out the memory. There were some things she would never have the answers to. She would never know about her mother's childhood. She would never get that time back. If the answers weren't in Jellico, what would she do next?

She turned her head at the sound of a knock at the door. "Are you up for a visitor?" the nurse with the red lipstick asked.

"Sure," Dane answered, happy to have a distraction from her thoughts.

The nurse opened the door wide and wheeled Curtis inside. He looked like a little boy in the wheelchair.

"Hey," Curtis said with a big grin on his face.

"Hey, nice wheels."

Curtis laughed. "It's kind of fun, but she won't let me drive."

Dane laughed.

The nurse pushed Curtis up beside the bed and set the brake. "I'll be back in a few minutes. You two try not to get into any trouble."

Curtis promised to be good.

When the door clicked closed, he turned to Dane. "I heard what happened." He shook his head. "You going to be okay?"

"Yeah," Dane answered.

"I made a real mess of things."

"Yes, you did," she said wanting Curtis to feel some responsibility for what happened, but then she relented. "But Trevor lied to you. He knew what he was doing was wrong."

"What's going to happen now, Dane?"

Dane felt sorry for him. His world had changed. She doubted anything could take away his innocence completely or change his heart, but she hoped from now on his trust would not be blind.

"I don't know what's going to happen, Curtis. The police are still looking for Trevor and his brother. I suppose there will be a trial once they're captured."

"What about us?"

"Well, Emma will have to decide if she wants to rebuild the house. You'll both have a lot of work to do."

"What about you?"

Dane pressed her lips together, contemplating her answer. "I don't know that yet either."

Someone tapped on the door. Emma stuck her head in. "I thought I might find you in here." She looked at Curtis. "There's a young lady outside who's been trying to see you. She says her name is Candice."

Curtis smiled, his eyes lighting up with excitement. "Yeah."

Dane smiled.

"I take it you know her?" Emma asked.

"Yeah," Curtis answered, his smile widening.

Emma opened the door and waved her hand. A young woman with long blond hair stepped into the room. She looked shyly from Dane to Emma and then to Curtis.

"Hey," she said stepping up to him.

"Hey," Curtis answered.

"You okay?"

Curtis nodded.

"Somebody named Dane called me a couple of days ago, but I couldn't get my dad to bring me here until today. He finally agreed to shut me up."

Curtis pointed to Dane. "This is my friend Dane. I asked her to call for me."

Candice nodded. She looked over her shoulder to Emma as if afraid she would bite.

"That's my sister, Emma."

Candice raised her hand chest high and waved at Emma.

"This is my girlfriend, Candice."

Emma's mouth fell open. "Girlfriend?"

Curtis blushed.

Emma shook herself and extended her hand. "It's good to meet you, Candice. I'm sorry I didn't know to call."

Candice shrugged. "It's okay."

The nurse came back, frowning at the sight of so many people in the room. She leveled her gaze at Emma. "Only two visitors at a time, please."

Emma stood. "Curtis, why don't you have Candice take you back to your room, so you can talk? I'll stay here with Dane."

The nurse nodded as she checked the IV. "I'll have someone come help you back into bed. Don't even think of doing it by yourself."

"Yes, ma'am," Curtis said as he was wheeled through the door.

Emma narrowed her eyes at Dane. "Were you ever going to tell me that my little brother had a girlfriend?"

Dane laughed. "I just found out myself just before all this happened. He asked me to get the number out of his phone and call her for him."

"Why didn't he tell me?"

"I don't know. She seems sweet, though."

"Yeah." Emma laughed. "I wonder what else he's keeping from me."

Dane wrapped her fingers around Emma's hand. "I think he's done with secrets."

"Let's hope so."

"Did you get any rest?"

Emma sighed. "Honestly, I think I could sleep for a week." She leaned her head in her hand and smiled at Dane. "You?"

"It's been a long night. I'm exhausted. Not to mention I don't even know where to begin sorting out my feelings about what happened."

Emma squeezed Dane's hand. "I'm sorry you got dragged into all of this. But I know what you mean. I've been thinking the same thing. I never would have imagined any of it. I don't recognize my life anymore."

"I guess we all have a lot to figure out."

Emma's heart ached. She had let Dane into her life and into her heart. She knew they were at a crossroads, and it was time for Dane to go back to her life. She had always known this time would come. She'd prepared for it, but she hadn't prepared for loving Dane. She hadn't been prepared for needing her.

"Curtis and I will stay at Aunt Lily's until I can figure out things with the house. Amy and her son Chris have been helping at the bar, and some friends have volunteered to help clean up the mess from the fire."

"I'm glad you're letting everyone help out."

"Yeah, I guess some change is good. Not that I really have much choice." She glanced at the door wondering how long she had before they would be interrupted.

"You look like you have something on your mind. What's up?"

Emma leaned close, speaking softly so no one could hear. "Paul and James came back this morning."

Dane sucked in a breath. "And?"

Emma smiled. "They said they had a productive trip. They had a nice bag of ginseng with them."

Dane frowned. "Is it over?"

Emma bit her lip and glanced back at the door. "They didn't give any details, but they said they found what they were looking for." She cleared her throat. "They came back alone."

Dane closed her eyes, letting the meaning sink in. She didn't want to know the specifics. It was enough just knowing the nightmare was over. Trevor and Milton wouldn't be able to hurt anyone ever again.

CHAPTER SIXTEEN

Emma stared out the window as Dane dressed. "What's your plan?"

"I don't really have one beyond getting through the next couple of weeks and starting physical therapy."

Emma turned to face Dane. "You could do that here." Dane looked stricken. Emma knew she was making this harder for Dane, but she wasn't ready to let go.

"We both know I can't stay at Lily's. I need some time to heal. I'll come back as soon as I'm back on my feet."

"I understand. You don't have to explain. The next few weeks are going to be hard for you. It makes sense that you would go."

Emma couldn't blame Dane for leaving. Why should she stay? There was nothing but heartache here. Dane had been beaten, burned, and shot in a matter of weeks. No matter what her own feelings were for Dane, it would never be enough to bridge the gap between their worlds.

"Promise me you'll do the physical therapy they ordered." She brushed her fingers against Dane's cheek. "And try to stay out of trouble."

Dane leaned in, closing the short distance between their lips, and kissed her. Emma savored the feel of Dane's lips against hers, the taste of her, the warmth of her touch. One last kiss. She felt the faint brush of tongue against hers, and the familiar sinking feeling as if she was being swept away.

Emma was the first to pull back. The moment Dane's lips left hers, she felt the weight of loss settle over her like the dark cloud of lost hope.

Dane pressed her palm to Emma's cheek. "What is it?"

"I don't want you to leave."

Dane threaded her fingers through Emma's hair and kissed her again, pouring her heart into the joining. She held Emma tight against her, ignoring the stab of pain in her back as Emma's weight pressed against her injured arm. Emma met her stroke for stroke, her fist gripping Dane's shirt. Emma groaned and sank against her.

Dane deepened the kiss. The days of worry and fear combined with memories of her fingers inside Emma, fueling her already combustible need. She had so many doubts about her life, her future, but the one thing she believed in was Emma.

She broke the kiss. Emma was breathless as she peered into her eyes.

Emma's brows furrowed, the question heavy in her eyes before she spoke. "Dane?"

"Do you see now?" Dane asked. "You are a part of me. I'm not leaving you."

Tears glistened in Emma's eyes. She let out a shaky breath. "What are we going to do?"

Dane pressed her lips to Emma's forehead. "There are some things I have to do. I just need a little time."

Emma could see that Dane was holding back. "And?"

Dane shook her head.

Emma took a deep breath and steeled herself against the loss that would overwhelm her the moment she let Dane go. She swallowed the lump of sadness growing in her throat. "Can you tell me where you're going?"

"I'll tell you all about it when I get back. There's just some things I need to do."

"I understand. Your life is waiting." She pressed her hand against Dane's chest. "Just remember you have a life here too, if you want it." Emma pressed her lips to Dane's, kissing her lightly, a kiss good-bye. There was so much she wanted to say, but she didn't want to pressure Dane. "Promise me you'll be safe."

"You have my word."

The silence between them grew thick.

"Emma."

Emma met Dane's eyes, but only for a moment. She took a step back. "I need to get to work."

"Emma," Dane whispered.

Emma shook her head. "When will your ride be here?"

"Anytime now. Thank you for letting me leave my Jeep at the farm." She patted the sling holding her arm to her chest. "I'm not up for driving yet, especially a stick."

Emma wiped her cheeks with her palms, gathering her emotions, pushing aside tears. "It will be there when you get back."

Dane started to reach for Emma but stopped and seemed to think better of it.

"You are coming back, right?" Emma asked, her voice shaky.

"I'll be back. I promise."

Emma nodded. She took one step toward Dane, brushing a kiss against her cheek. "Good-bye, Dane."

Emma wiped tears from her cheeks as she watched the car pull up outside the hospital. Her breath hitched when Dane stepped to the curb and climbed in the back seat. The brake lights flashed twice, the red glare distorted through the rain-flecked windshield of her truck. Emma waited, hoping Dane would change her mind. A moment later the lights dimmed, and the car pulled away. And just like that, Dane was gone.

Emma let out a shaky breath. She should have listened to her gut all those weeks ago when a good-looking stranger sauntered into her bar. The fact that she had been attracted to Dane should have been enough warning for her to know better than to go anywhere near her. But it was too late now. She had broken all her own rules.

She had let Dane into her life, and into her heart. It seemed the people she loved were always leaving.

She took a deep breath. The truth was, letting Dane stay at her house had been the best decision she had ever made. There wouldn't have been anything left to her life if Dane hadn't been there. Dane had saved her life, and she had saved Curtis. She would never regret that.

Emma put the truck in gear and headed north to the only place she had left to go. She stood in the middle of the room looking at the empty tables and booths. She had spent most of her life in that room. The bar was clean and fully stocked. The old chairs had been tightened and polished, and the floors had been scrubbed so clean she could see the grain of the wood. There really wasn't anything she had to do.

She pulled a beer from the cooler and the bottle of Jack Daniel's from the wall. She took the seat at the bar where Dane had sat almost every day since the first night she had walked through the doors. Emma poured the drink. She lifted the glass and peered into the amber liquid. She knew there were no answers in a bottle of booze, but she had all the answers she could handle for a while. Tonight, she needed the numbing the whiskey would bring. "Here's to you, Tennessee Whiskey, wherever you are tonight." Emma tossed the whiskey back, draining the glass in one swallow. She took a drink of her beer to chase away the burn.

She wasn't sure how long she'd been sitting there in the dark when she heard a knock at the door. Jeez. "We're closed," she yelled at the door.

"It's me, Emma."

Emma closed her eyes and slapped the bar with a thud. "Not now." She groaned. "Can't I have one night to just do nothing but feel sorry for myself?"

She poured another shot of whiskey and ignored the pounding on the door.

"Come on, Emma, I know you're in there. Your truck is outside."

Emma rolled her eyes. "And you obviously just heard me yell at you," she mumbled.

The knocking continued. Emma sighed. "A week ago, I was freaked out because he wouldn't come home, and now I just wish he would go away." She slid off the barstool and ambled toward the back door.

"What do you want?" she asked, pulling the door open.

Curtis stood at the bottom of the steps and looked up at her. "About time. What are you doin' in there all by yourself?"

"Trying to be by myself," she answered curtly.

"Oh." Curtis looked wounded. "Where's Dane? They said she left the hospital today."

Emma swallowed. "She went home."

Curtis pushed through the door, oblivious to the intrusion. "Home where?"

"She didn't say exactly."

Emma followed Curtis to the bar. She slid back onto her stool and picked up her glass.

Curtis plopped down on the stool next to her. "Can I have a beer?"

"Get it yourself."

Curtis looked at her, stunned. After a moment his expression fell. "Are you serious?"

"Yes, I'm serious. I'm done being the servant, the maid, and the caretaker. You want something, you can get it yourself."

Curtis stared at her for a few long moments before getting up and going to the cooler. He pulled out two beers and set one in front of Emma. "You're mad."

"No, Curtis. I'm not mad. I'm tired and I'm hurt. I am tired of working my ass off and not having a life of my own. You decided you could make your own decisions, and it almost got us all killed. If you want to be a grown-up so bad, you can start by waiting on yourself for a change."

Curtis peered into his beer. "I'm really sorry. I know I messed up. But I never wanted anyone to get hurt."

Emma sighed. "I know that, Curtis, but there's a world of difference between wishing and reality."

Curtis thumped his elbows onto the bar and sipped his beer. After a moment he turned to Emma. "I don't know what that means."

"It means that just because you want something to be true doesn't make it true. You wanted Trevor to be your friend so badly that you wouldn't listen to me or anyone else who tried to tell you the truth. You threw all of us to the wolves just because you wanted to believe a lie."

"I really thought Trevor was my friend. I never believed he would hurt us."

"That's exactly what I'm saying."

Curtis nodded. "Is that why Dane left?"

Emma ground her teeth. "No. She's hurt and needs to take care of herself. She can't do that here. Dane was always just passing through. She was looking for something and just happened to get wrapped up in our crap."

"Is she going to be okay?"

Emma really wanted the Twenty Questions game to end. How did she know anything about what Dane wanted or where she was going? "I'm sure she'll be fine."

"Is she coming back?"

Emma closed her eyes. "I don't know." She tossed back the shot of whiskey and chased it with the beer.

"You love her, don't you?" Curtis asked.

"Does it matter?"

"I think so. I know I love her. Does she love you?"

Emma poured another drink. She held the glass in front of her, swirling the contents as she contemplated her answer. "Yeah. I think she does."

"So she'll be back," Curtis said cheerfully.

Emma shook her head. "It's not that easy."

"Why not?"

"It just isn't, Curtis. Dane has a different life away from here. Why would she want to come back here when she could have so much more?"

Curtis looked thoughtful as he considered the information. "Maybe you could go there."

Emma stared at him. "How?"

"Just go."

Emma sighed. "What about you, and the bar, and all the other things I have to take care of?"

Curtis shrugged. "I have Lily and James and all the others. We're already working at the bar. Why couldn't you go? Like you said—I have to grow up. Maybe if I can take care of myself, you could do all those things you never got to do."

Tears pricked Emma's eyes. What if she didn't have to do everything? Could she dare to have her own life? If she stripped away all that responsibility, what would be left? She had believed there was nothing left for her. Maybe there was still a chance. Maybe she could still dare to do something different.

"You know I love you, right?"

Curtis grinned. "Yeah. I know."

CHAPTER SEVENTEEN

Dane pushed the button on the elevator and waited. She drew in a deep breath, trying to calm her nerves. It had been years since she'd stepped into this building. Not much had changed. The lobby had been updated with a more modern look, but the feel was the same.

A set of heavy glass doors slid open as she approached, giving her a clear view into the office. She stopped at the front desk where a twentysomething redhead with paper-white skin sat with a phone pressed to her ear as she typed something into a computer. Some things never changed. She clasped her hand over the sling cradling her other arm and waited.

"Can I help you?" the young woman asked when she hung up the phone.

Dane smiled. "I'd like to see David Foster please."

"I'm sorry, I don't have anyone on the schedule. Do you have an appointment?"

"No. Just tell him his daughter is here to see him."

The young woman's mouth fell open. She peered at Dane in disbelief. Dane was certain the young woman didn't even know her boss had a daughter.

To her credit she didn't ask any further questions. "One moment." She picked up the phone. "I'm sorry to bother you, sir, but there's a woman here to see you. She said she's your daughter."

Dane wished she could see the look on her father's face at that moment. But she hoped she hadn't just given him a heart attack. She was certain she was the last person he would expect to visit at the office.

"Yes, sir." The woman placed the handset back on the base. "He'll see you now. I can take you in."

"That's not necessary." Dane looked down at the nameplate on the desk. "Thank you, Charlotte, but I know the way."

The woman's eyebrows rose in surprise. Dane wondered how long she had been employed by her father. She could feel the young woman's gaze burning into her back as she stepped into her father's office.

Her father stood, moving toward the door as she entered. "It's been a long time, Dane. What brings you to town? After your call a few weeks ago, I figured you had gone back to New York." He almost sounded happy to see her.

"Hello, David."

His eyes fell to the sling holding her arm and the bandage around her hand, and then to the tender burns still healing on her face. "My God, what happened to you?"

"It's a long story. Can we talk?"

Her father motioned to a leather sofa and a set of chairs. "Okay. Have a seat. I don't have much time. What do you need?"

Dane looked at her father, really looked at him. She could see the young boy from Lily's pictures in the eyes of the man sitting in front of her. His hair was grayer than she expected, and his shoulders seemed less prominent than she remembered.

"I know I should have called."

"Nonsense." He looked at his watch. "I'm glad you're here. It really has been too long."

Dane nodded. "How have you been?"

He shrugged. "I can't complain. Business is good." He leaned forward and rested his arms on his knees. He searched her face, as if cataloging each line, bump, bruise, and burn. He shook his head. "Why don't we start with you telling me what happened to you."

Dane wasn't sure where to begin. She needed answers he had never been willing to share with her. She was certain this time would be no different. She pulled the old photograph out of her shirt pocket and handed it to him.

He stared down at the photo. His face paled as if he'd seen a ghost. "Where did you get this?" He ran his finger across the image of her mother's face.

"I've been in Jellico. I needed to know about her."

His head jerked back as if she'd struck him. "Why the hell would you go there? You had no business going there. Why couldn't you just leave it alone?"

Dane studied her father, surprised by the anguish she heard in his voice. "A lot has happened in the last couple of years. I needed answers. You would never talk about her, so I decided to go there myself."

"This is insane." David shook his head and peered down at the photograph. "Who gave this to you? Was it Ann?"

Dane shook her head. "Ann is dead. I got this from her sister Lily."

He nodded. His eyes became distant as if he had gone back into the past.

"Why didn't you tell me?"

"Tell you what? You were a kid. You don't know what you're talking about."

"I'm talking about Thomas."

David shot to his feet. "Did he do this to you?"

Dane was surprised by the reaction. She'd expected him to be upset with her, but his reaction was more protective than angry.

"No, this wasn't him."

David stared at her. "But you have talked to him."

She nodded.

Her father returned to his seat. His hands were shaking. She'd never seen him like this. "I'd like to hear it from you. I won't know what the truth is until I hear it from you."

"The truth." He shook his head. "We left there for a reason. We raised you away from there for a reason. Why couldn't you just respect that?" David looked like he wanted to climb out of his own skin. He opened his door and instructed Charlotte to hold his calls and not to let anyone disturb him.

He walked to the bar and poured himself a drink, then reached for another glass and added one for her.

His hand shook as he handed her the glass. "You'll want this."

Dane took the drink and braced herself for the truth.

"Your mother and I were barely more than kids when we met. I'd never been in love, but I knew the moment I saw her, that was what it was. From that moment on she became my world. We planned to leave Jellico and go off to college together. Her family had other ideas. They didn't like her seeing me. They thought because my parents were not from there that I wasn't worthy of her. They tried to keep us apart, but nothing worked. We always found a way."

His eyes took on a dreamy faraway look, and Dane imagined he was right back there as if he was sitting in that booth next to her mother.

"You and Thomas didn't get along."

David took a drink. "No. Thomas thought he owned your mother. He got out of control. Jenny was afraid of him. He was a beast."

Dane stared at her father. "He raped her."

David shut his eyes, the pain written in the lines of his face. He nodded. "I had already left for the city to get us a place to stay and get a job. I was to pick her up that weekend, so we could go away together. As soon as she called me, I came for her. We knew we had to get her out of there. We knew he'd kill her before he would let her go."

"Why didn't you go to the police?"

David laughed. "You've been there. Do you really think that forty years ago they would have done anything? They probably would have handed her over to him. She wasn't even eighteen. They would have seen her as a runaway, and I would have been the one trying to steal her. No one would take the side of a young girl trying to run away from home."

"When did you stop loving her?"

David flinched. "What?" He set the glass down hard on the table between them. "I never stopped loving your mother."

"What happened then?"

David shook his head.

"It was me, wasn't it? You couldn't bear to look at me. I was the constant reminder of what Thomas had done to her."

David frowned. "What are you talking about? Why would you remind us of Thomas? Your mother and I couldn't wait to have you."

Dane shook her head. "That's not how I remember it."

"What are you getting at, Dane?"

Dane drank her whiskey in one swallow. "I need to know. Are you my father?"

David looked confused, but then realization hit him. He rubbed his hand across his chin. "Look, Dane, I know I haven't been a good father, but I wanted to provide for you and your mother. I worked a lot. I wasn't around as much as I should have been. When she got sick, I didn't know how to handle it. I failed her. I couldn't protect her all those years before, and I couldn't save her from cancer. I didn't know any other way to raise you but to give you what you needed to be strong and make it on your own."

"Is that what you call it? You married Christine not even a year after Mom died. I was treated like a trespasser in my own home. You let that woman degrade my mother's memory. I couldn't even talk about her. You taught me how to be on my own, all right. You taught me that I had no one."

"You weren't the only one who lost her," David said, his voice raised in anger. "I loved your mother. You have no idea what it was like to lose that." Dane hadn't considered what her mother's illness must have been like for her father if he had been in love with her. But that didn't change the one question she needed answered.

"Are you my biological father?"

David looked her in the eye. "Why are you asking me that?"

"I met with Thomas. He was under the impression that he is my father."

"Son of a bitch." David slapped his hand down on the table. "Listen to me, Dane. You are my daughter and I am your father. That piece of shit will say and do anything he can to hurt me."

"How do you know?"

He shook his head. "I know because your mother didn't get pregnant until six months after we ran off together. Not that any of that would matter. *You* are *my* daughter." He punctuated each word by driving his index finger against the table. "This is precisely the kind of thing we wanted to protect you from. Jenny never wanted her family to be able to hurt you. That's why she shut them all out."

Dane took in every word her father said. She had no reason to doubt him.

"You understand why we never told you. Who wants to keep a memory like that alive?"

Dane thought about everything he had said. "Thank you for telling me now." She thought about all the old hurts, the wedge that had been driven between them. "If you loved her, why did you get married so soon after she died?"

David took a deep breath. "I'm sorry about that. I know what you must think."

"Why did you do it?"

"It wasn't like that, Dane. I didn't know what to do. I was so lost and hurt. I didn't know how to raise a kid on my own. And I didn't know how to be alone. Your mother's illness, her death was more than I could handle."

"I spent four years trapped in that house with a woman I hated. Don't tell me you married her for me."

David shook his head. "No. No, you're right. I can't explain to you what it was like loving your mother. I just knew I'd never have that with anyone else. I never tried to replace her. I was just trying to figure out how to live without her. I'm sorry."

Dane looked into her father's eyes and wondered why he never just talked to her. "Why now? For years you wouldn't talk to me. Why now?"

He shook his head. "I don't know. There was just something in your eyes when you walked in here. I was caught off guard. You look so hurt. You didn't really give me much choice. You've made me realize a lot of things."

"Like?"

"Like I've missed you. I can see things have been bad for you, and I wasn't there. I suppose it was time."

Dane had tears in her eyes, but she wouldn't let them fall.

David poured them another drink. "Now. Do you want to tell me what happened to you?"

Dane took the glass. "It's a long story."

He sat back against the sofa and rested his glass on his thigh as if he had all the time in the world. "I'm listening."

CHAPTER EIGHTEEN

"Where are you? How is your shoulder?" Emma's voice sounded weary and guarded through the phone.

"It hurts like a son of a bitch, but it's getting better. I'm in Knoxville. I have some things I needed to work on here before I go back to New York."

"How long before you start physical therapy?"

Dane sighed. "It will be a while. The scapula isn't mending as fast as I had hoped."

"Will you do that in New York?"

"No. I don't think so. I'm not sure when I'll be able to travel."

"Oh."

Dane heard the disappointment in Emma's voice. "How's everything going there?" Dane asked, wanting to change the subject. It was hard to talk to Emma on the phone. It was almost like talking to a stranger. She had trouble reading Emma when she couldn't see her eyes.

"Everyone has been great. Paul and Sue have been helping at the bar. Curtis and his girlfriend are spending a lot of time together, so that gets him out of my hair. I had the old house cleared away and I've started thinking about rebuilding. I think if I do rebuild, I want to move to a different spot on the property. Maybe a smaller place that won't be so much work. Oh, and the sheriff isn't going to pursue charges against Curtis. So that's at least one worry off my plate."

Dane closed her eyes. She knew she was adding to Emma's worry. "That's great news. When I get back, you can show me everything you've done."

Emma didn't respond right away. "Are you sure you're coming back?"

Dane sighed. "I made a promise, didn't I?"

"I know. But things change."

Emma was right. A lot had changed already. She missed Emma, but she had no idea how they would make a relationship work. Other than Emma, there wasn't anything for her in Jellico.

"We'll figure this out."

Emma sighed. "I need to go. Will you call tomorrow?"

"Yeah, I'll talk to you then."

Dane hung up the phone, feeling strangely disconnected. Emma had been the first person in her life to make her feel like she belonged. That all seemed like a dream now. Each time they talked, it was as if she could feel that dream slipping away.

Dane woke to a strange buzzing sound. She opened her eyes, not recognizing the room. She blinked, then remembered her father dropping her off at the apartment he kept downtown. The buzzing continued, and she struggled to her feet to answer the door. A young man in a black leather jacket, jeans, and motorcycle boots stood at the door.

"Can I help you?"

"Mr. Foster sent me."

Dane nodded and opened the door, motioning for the young man to come inside.

"My name is Adam."

Dane checked her watch, marveling at how fast her father worked.

Adam placed an envelope on the sofa table before pulling a laptop from his bag.

"How long have you worked for my father?" Dane asked, curious.

Adam looked unfazed by the question. "I've done a few things for him over the last couple of years. I'm good at finding things. He told me to tell you everything you requested has been arranged."

"That was fast."

The young man smiled. "Shall we get started?"

Dane stared at the computer screen. She didn't know how he did it, but in a matter of hours Adam had managed to compile everything she could ever want to know about Thomas Stewart and the slew of children he had produced, with detailed criminal records for each. She was sure her father was eager to present her with more proof that her mother's family was not worth her trouble.

Dane blew out her breath as she read over some of the offenses they had amassed over the years. "Damn, some people really shouldn't breed."

Adam laughed. "No kidding."

"You're really good at this."

"Thanks." He turned his attention to a file compiling her complete family genogram. She now had more information than she ever could have imagined for both sides of her family.

Adam printed out the last reports and shut down the computer. "Is that all you need?"

"Yes. I think that's it."

He glanced to the bandages on Dane's arm. "Mr. Foster filled me in on the situation. Looks like I don't need to warn you about these people and the kinds of things they're into."

Dane lifted her bandaged arm in acknowledgment. "Trust me, I've had my fill of playing the hero. I just want to get enough information to the authorities to put all of these guys out of business."

Adam reached into his bag and pulled out a black pouch. He unzipped the bag, revealing a 9 mm handgun.

Dane stared at the gun.

"Do you know how to use this?" he asked.

She nodded. "Yeah. But that doesn't mean I want to."

He zipped the bag closed. "Mr. Foster wanted to make sure you could protect yourself." He patted the bag. "Your registration and carry permit are inside." He stood, and Dane followed him to the door.

"What about your computer?"

He shrugged. "A gift from you father. He said you needed one."

Adam stopped at the door. "Be careful." He handed her his card. "Let me know if there's anything else you need."

She shook his hand. "I will. Thanks again."

Dane closed the door and stood with her back against the wall. She felt like she was in the twilight zone. She hated feeling vulnerable. She dialed her father's number.

"Did you get what you needed?" he said the moment he answered.

"I did. Thank you."

"Listen, I know you have a lot to do, but I'd like you to have dinner with me."

She frowned. What else was there to say? She thought about it for a long moment and decided she had nothing to lose. "I'd like that." She hadn't had a relationship with her father in years, but he had come through for her in force. He'd treated this like a business transaction, and everything was in place. She hadn't expected anything else from him after their confrontation. She hoped when this was over, they would have a chance to get to know each other.

"I'm downstairs now. I'll be up in a minute."

Dane raised her eyebrows in surprise. "Really?"

"You have that doctor's appointment. I thought I'd drive you."

For the first time since losing her mother, her father was acting like he actually gave a damn. They still had a long way to go, but it was a start.

❖

Dane watched her father's hands as he cut into his steak. She watched the way he kicked one foot behind his chair as he sat forward when he talked. Movements she knew she mirrored in her own behavior without even thinking. There were so many things about him she had never been willing to see because she had been so caught up in not wanting to be like him. She found these simple gestures comforting now. At least he wasn't Thomas Stewart.

"So," he said as she took a bite of his steak, "tell me more about this woman you met. Ann's daughter."

"Emma," Dane said reverently as if just saying her name could somehow summon her.

"Sounds serious."

Dane shook her head. "I don't know. The first time she met me, she told me I was trouble. She was right."

David picked up his wine and took a drink. "What is that supposed to mean? Do you think you're the only person guilty of making a mistake? Sounds like you need to lose this self-imposed guilt trip before you lose the girl."

Dane shook her head. "It's more complicated than that."

David sat back in his chair and watched her. "I wasted a lot of time when your mother was alive doing what I thought was best. I've spent years wishing I could get that time back. Don't overthink this, Dane. Get out of your head and follow your heart."

She met his eyes, wanting to see the truth there when she said her next words. "Even if that means I have to go back to Jellico?"

Something sad passed behind his eyes and she knew he was thinking of her mother.

"Jellico is just a place. Don't let a place get in the way of what you want. You're healing well, and you'll be able to travel soon— maybe it's time we put your plan in action. You can finish your therapy in Jellico if that's where you decide to stay."

"I'm scared," she admitted.

"Of what?"

Dane swirled the wine around in her glass, not certain how to answer. "Emma doesn't believe I'll come back. I left her there to deal with the fallout all by herself. What if she doesn't want the same thing I want? I can't see myself settling down in a place like Jellico, but I can't imagine anything else without her."

"You won't know until you see her. Have you talked to her?"

Dane nodded. "Yeah. But every time I call, I feel like she's worlds away. I don't know what to say. She thinks my life is too different from hers."

"That's just semantics. Little details to be worked out. What else is troubling you?"

Dane sighed. "In this condition, I can't protect myself, let alone anyone else."

"The sling comes off next week."

Dane nodded.

"If you love her, you have to try. Trust me, Dane—love isn't an easy thing to find. If you are waiting for life to be perfect or easy, that isn't going to happen. Love is something you have to fight for."

Dane sat back in her chair, studying her father.

"What?" he asked, narrowing his eyes.

"I was just thinking about how things could have been different with us."

He nodded. "I'm sorry about that. But I'm going to do better now."

Dane smiled, believing him. "Me too."

She knew they had a lot to work through, but she wanted to know him. She had gone to Jellico to learn about her mother, but in the end, it was her father she was getting to know. And he was right about one thing—she had left Emma waiting long enough. She was worth fighting for.

CHAPTER NINETEEN

Emma looked up from the box she had just pulled out of storage when she heard music playing in the bar.

What now? "We're not open," she called as she pushed the door open with her foot. She stopped suddenly and almost dropped the new bottle of whiskey she was carrying when she saw Dane sitting at the bar. Something in her heart mended itself at the sight of her. She hadn't heard from Dane in days, and when they had talked, Dane hadn't said anything about coming back.

"Hello, beautiful. What do I have to do to get a drink around here?"

Emma smiled. Her heart felt lighter than it had in weeks. Dane looked good. Her burns had healed, she'd gotten a haircut and new clothes, and the bandages were gone, and so was the sling. She looked like Emma imagined her in her other life. She no longer had the appearance of someone trying to fit in. She looked like someone who owned who they were without apologies to anyone. She was a sight for sore eyes. "What would you like?"

The hunger the question brought to Dane's eyes was dangerous. Emma's stomach tightened, and her head buzzed. That one look was all it took for her to want to take Dane right there on the floor.

"Do you really want me to answer that?" Dane said, her voice dropping to a husky whisper.

Emma couldn't hide her smile. She placed a glass on the bar along with a cold beer.

Dane shrugged. "I guess that will do for now. But just the beer is fine."

Emma observed the crisp pressed gray button-up shirt that hugged Dane's body, accentuating the muscles and curves without being binding. Her eyes drifted to the exposed skin of Dane's chest where she had left the collar open. "You look good," Emma admitted. There was something different about Dane that she couldn't quite put her finger on. She looked lighter, as if some of the trouble she'd carried had been put down.

"So do you," Dane said, her gaze lingering on Emma's.

Emma shook her head. "You're a bad liar."

"You look beautiful to me."

Emma came around the bar and wrapped her arms around Dane's neck. "Where have you been? I was worried. You could have told me you were coming. I missed you."

Dane placed a tender kiss to Emma's lips as she wrapped her arms around her waist. She drew in a deep breath. "I went to see my father."

Emma pulled back. "What? Why didn't you say anything?"

Dane shrugged. "I don't know. I guess I didn't want to jinx it, and I wasn't ready to talk about it."

"How did it go?"

"Good, actually. We had a lot to talk about. I think we're finally beginning to understand each other."

"That's wonderful." Emma didn't know what to say next. This wasn't what she'd expected Dane to have been up to the last few weeks. If Dane had the answers to her past that she'd been searching for, there wasn't anything left to tie her to Jellico. "Why did you come back?"

"You have to ask? I made a promise, remember?"

Emma smiled. "I remember." She ran her hand along Dane's thigh, the smooth dark blue denim warm beneath her touch as the heat rose between them.

"How's Curtis?" Dane asked, leaning closer, her lips only inches away as she brushed a strand of hair off Emma's face, tucking it behind her ear. Emma's skin tingled along the trail of Dane's touch, sending goose bumps down her arms.

"He's better. As soon as he was strong enough, we had a long talk. He has set work hours here at the bar, and he'll live with Lily until I decide on the new build, and even then, he'll have a separate house. From now on he has to earn his own way as much as he can."

"Wow. That's a big change." Dane's eyes widened with surprise.

Emma shrugged. "I realized I wasn't doing him any favors. He needs to be able to take care of himself."

"How does he feel about it?"

Emma smiled. "He's good, actually. He's excited about his own place. I think he wants his girlfriend to move in with him, but that won't happen until he finishes probation and proves he's going to stick to the plan. She has her own limitations, but they're good together, and her parents have been good to help out too. I hope he doesn't mess it up."

"What about you?" Dane asked.

"I'm still figuring that out."

Dane tossed back her drink, setting the bottle down with a pop against the counter. "Are you done here? I have something I want to show you."

"Sure. I was just keeping busy mostly."

"Good." Dane took Emma's hand. "Come with me."

"Where are we going?"

"You'll see."

Emma stopped abruptly just outside the door, her eyes landing on the brand-new Jeep. A lot had changed since she last saw Dane, and her stomach flipped as she wondered what other surprises Dane had in store.

"Mind if I drive?"

"Sure," Emma answered, sliding her keys into her pocket. "Nice Jeep."

"Thanks. I made some changes while I was rehabbing."

"I can see."

Dane opened the door for Emma and waited until she was settled inside. "Close your eyes."

Emma had no idea what Dane was up to, but she was excited and a little worried. She was happy Dane was back in her life, but she wondered if this was just a stop for Dane, before she moved on. "Where are we going?"

"You'll see. Now close your eyes."

Emma closed her eyes and covered them with her hands. She felt every bump and turn of the road. If she had to guess, she'd say they were headed to the farm.

Dane stopped. "Don't look yet."

Emma heard the rattle of a chain and the creak of an old gate. She was certain they were at the farm. She could smell the familiar scent of the hay in the loft and the tang of the pigpen.

The next time they stopped, Dane pulled Emma's hands away from her eyes. "You can look now."

Emma's mouth fell open. She was stunned into silence. She stared out at a brand-new Airstream camper parked in the field behind the barn. She looked from the camper to Dane. "What's this?"

"I know you're still staying with Lily, but I thought you could use your own space. Something a little closer to home until you can rebuild."

Emma was speechless. "I don't know what to say."

"It's okay if you don't want to stay here. I'll understand. I just wanted you to have a place of your own."

Emma shook her head.

"It belongs to my father. He bought it last year but only used it a couple of times for hunting trips. I told him what happened, and he wanted to help."

Emma blinked away tears as she took it all in. "What about you?"

Dane shrugged. "If you don't mind the company in such a small space..."

Emma threw her arms around Dane's neck and kissed her. "Does that mean you'll stay? You aren't going to leave again?"

Dane laughed. "l just want to be with you. But to be honest, I'm not sure Jellico is where I want to settle permanently. I want to take my photography in a new direction, and since this is mobile, I thought maybe we could take it on the road for a while. That would give us time to figure it all out and decide what we want to do together."

"Together?"

Dane nodded. "Together."

Emma was speechless. She wasn't sure what to think or feel. She was flooded with happiness, excitement, and love. But her elation was quickly diminished by feelings of responsibility and fear.

"How is this real? You didn't say anything about any of this when we talked. I wasn't sure you would come back at all. I don't think I can just leave. I have the bar, and I have to rebuild."

Dane took Emma's hand. "I know I'm asking a lot. I had a lot to work through. I started seeing a therapist so I could start to work through my past. The one thing I am certain about is you." Dane took a deep breath. "I know this is scary, but you can do this. We don't have to see the whole world in one trip. We'll come back here. You'll still be able to do all the things you need to do." Dane hesitated. "I didn't want to say anything until I was absolutely sure. I don't plan to ever make a promise to you that I can't keep. I love you, Emma Reynolds. I want to show you the world. I want to see it all with you. You keep saying I have a different life, but it doesn't have to be different. I don't want to go back to my old life. I want to build a new one with you."

Emma wiped tears from her eyes. Had she heard right? Did Dane really just tell her she loved her?

"You don't have to answer right now. Let's go look inside." Dane took Emma's hand. "It may be small, but it has everything we need. There's even a bathroom."

"What do you think?" Dane asked as she watched Emma explore the nooks and crannies of the camper.

"It's perfect. I just can't believe you did this."

Dane felt some of the tension ease its grip on her nerves, and she took her first full breath since she'd stepped into Emma's bar.

She knew Emma was overwhelmed, but her anxiety was getting the best of her. She'd told Emma she loved her. She had put it all on the table. All she could do now was wait.

Emma took Dane's hand and pulled her onto the bed. "So your plan is for you and me to live in this camper and travel around the world?"

Dane lay down next to Emma and curled her arm around Emma's waist. "Well, we can't really take it around the world, but we can at least cover the United States and Canada. Maybe by then you'll be ready to get on a plane with me."

"A ship," Emma said firmly, her fingers moving along the buttons of Dane's shirt, exposing the delicate scars that still looked too fragile.

"What?"

Emma pushed away the pain that struck her at the sight of the reminder of almost losing Dane. She kissed Dane's nose playfully. "I want to go on a ship."

"Okay, we can go on a ship. Is that a yes?"

Emma rubbed her hand across Dane's chest. "Tell me again."

"Which part?"

"The important part."

Dane laughed. "Oh, that."

Emma slid her hand to Dane's breast, rubbing her thumb roughly across Dane's nipple.

Dane groaned as her eyes slid closed. She pulled Emma close, brushing her lips against Emma's ear. "I love you, Emma."

The words were like fire igniting Emma's desire. She kissed Dane hard, claiming her with her mouth. She had no idea how they were going to do this, but she was ready to follow Dane to the ends of the earth.

"Where should we start?" Emma groaned as Dane bit down gently on her neck.

"Right here seems like a good spot." Dane kissed and sucked the pulse in her neck. "You smell like a field of wild lavender. Your breath is like the breeze stirring, moving me, your touch like the warm rays of the sun against my skin." She kissed lower as she snapped open the buttons on Emma's shirt. "Ah, and here. The curve of your body, the soft mounds of your breasts are like the contours of the mountains promising adventure and hinting of secrets to be found." She brushed her lips over the thin lace covering Emma's breast. "Oh yeah, I think I'd like to stay here for a while. Would you like that?"

"Yes," Emma whispered, running her hand through the short strands of Dane's hair.

Dane teased Emma's nipple with her teeth before pushing the lace aside and taking her into her mouth.

Emma pushed against Dane, her grip around Dane's head pulling her against her breast, silently asking for more. Dane brushed her fingertips lightly along Emma's stomach, reaching for the button of her jeans as she sucked and teased her breast. Effortlessly, she had Emma's jeans open and slid her fingers inside, cupping her.

"Oh, and there's this very special place I love most of all. I've been dreaming about this place."

"Hmm." Emma cooed. "Show me."

Dane kissed her way down Emma's body until she was kneeling between her legs. She gripped Emma's jeans in her hand and pulled. Emma lifted her hips and allowed Dane to undress her. Dane tossed the jeans to the floor and slid lower on the bed, nestling between Emma's legs. She ran her tongue along the soft skin just above the line of lace covering Emma. She rubbed her fingers between Emma's legs, feeling her clitoris swell beneath the thin fabric, the moisture seeping through, damp and hot against her fingers. Dane pulled at the lace with her teeth. Emma's hips lifted, pressing harder against her mouth.

"This place is warm. The smell is like a mountain stream, fresh and clean, inviting me into pools of invigorating water. I thirst for this place."

Emma's fingers fluttered against Dane's cheek and brushed through her hair. "Drink," Emma whispered. "Put your mouth on me and drink."

Dane pulled the lace aside and slid her tongue through the soft wet folds, finding Emma's clit swollen and hard. She sucked it into her mouth, lapping her tongue against it, circling until Emma writhed beneath her. She let go, stroked her tongue up and down the length of Emma, teasing the opening before sliding back up to take her clitoris in her mouth again. Over and over she sucked and licked, driving Emma to the edge, then pulling back. Emma was so swollen and wet, Dane ached for her, her own clitoris hard and pulsing. She wanted to taste every drop of Emma, drink her in, let the sweet heat of her fill her until she could hold no more.

"Dane," Emma begged. "Please."

"Hmm." Dane sent vibrations of sound into Emma's clitoris.

"Oh God," Emma cried. "Do that again."

Dane hummed as she sucked.

"Oh God, yes," Emma cried out, her body stiffening. Dane continued to brush gentle strokes of her tongue against Emma's clitoris. Emma crested again, her legs trembling, body tingling, her heart soaring.

Emma clamped her legs around Dane's head holding her still. The power of the orgasm electrified all her nerve endings. She was certain she would shatter if Dane made one more move. "Don't move. Give me a minute."

She jerked as Dane chuckled, sending more vibrations through her sensitive clitoris.

Emma pulled Dane up and kissed her, filling her mouth with her tongue, tenderly nipping and sucking her lower lip. She pulled back and stared into Dane's eyes. "There is nothing left of me that isn't yours. You have me, heart and soul. I am hopelessly in love with you. I thought I would die when you left."

Dane kissed her tenderly, gently framing her face with her hands. "I didn't want to leave. I don't ever want to leave you again."

Emma pushed Dane on to her back and straddled her. "I'll follow you anywhere. I have a feeling I'm going to like the places you take me." She grinned. "But right now, it's my turn."

EPILOGUE

Emma hugged Curtis. "I'm trusting you to be good."

"I will. Don't worry," Curtis said with a grin.

Emma cupped his cheek in her palm. "I can't help it. But I know you can do this."

Curtis wrapped his arms around Emma and hugged her.

Emma turned to Lily. "Thank you."

"Oh, honey, I'm so happy for you. I can't wait to see those pictures you promised. And don't you worry about our boy. We'll all look after him, and you know if he gets too big for his britches, I'll have a piece of his hide. And don't you worry—the bar will be fine. It's a good change for Paul. He'll take care of things while you're gone."

Emma fought back tears. "I love you, Aunt Lily."

"I love you too, sweetheart. Now you get on out of here before I get my broom after you."

Emma wrapped her arms around Lily, comforted by her warm strength.

Dane opened the door to the Jeep and whistled. Samson lumbered around the camper and jumped in the back seat.

"Where's Delilah?" Emma asked, looking around for the newest member of the family.

Dane shrugged and whistled louder this time. A crashing noise sounded from behind the house. A moment later the beagle tore around the corner in a full run. She made a lap around the camper before realizing where to go. She leapt into the Jeep, knocking into Samson, who tossed a paw around her neck and began licking her face.

Emma slid into her seat and closed the door. Dane reached for her hand, lacing their fingers together. "Ready?"

Emma squeezed Dane's hand. "Very." She waved to her family as they drove off. It felt strange leaving. She had dreamed of this, but now that it was really happening, she was overwhelmed.

"They'll be okay," Dane said reassuringly.

Emma nodded and turned to Dane. Warmth and happiness flooded her. She wanted to pinch herself to make sure she wasn't dreaming. Dane's hand gripping hers reminded her that no matter where they went, no matter what came next, she was home. With Dane she would never again feel alone.

"I know."

Delilah groaned in the back seat. Emma glanced back to see her resting her head on Samson's back. He was sound asleep already. Delilah wiggled closer, almost lying on top of him. Emma laughed, understanding Delilah's need to be as close to him as possible.

"How long did you say it takes to get there?" Emma asked.

Dane considered the question. "To the first stop or the whole trip?"

"Just today."

"Six hours should do it. Why? Are you okay?"

Emma smiled. "I'm more than okay. I'm in love."

Dane pulled Emma's hand to her lips and kissed her fingers. "I like the sound of that."

"Me too."

Dane glanced to the sign at the side of the road, signaling they were leaving Jellico. She had come here looking for answers to her past. It turned out she found her future. She found her heart. Dane knew they had a lot to work through, but they would figure it out together.

"Do you think you can put up with me for three months?"

Emma squeezed Dane's hand and leaned across the seat so that her lips were only inches from Dane's ear. "Hmm, let me see." Emma slipped her hand up Dane's thigh.

Dane groaned. "Careful, I'm driving here."

Emma drew Dane's earlobe into her mouth and sucked, then released it with pop. "Three months of sleeping with you under the stars, watching sunsets together, cooking over a fire, exploring the world, mapping every inch of your body with my tongue." Emma laughed when Dane clasped her hand stalling her wandering fingers. "Oh, I think I can handle three months. As a matter of fact, I'm looking forward to much more than that."

Dane chanced a glance at her teasing lover. "What do you have in mind?"

Emma's smile was radiant. "I was thinking more along the lines of forever."

Dane pulled Emma's hand from her thigh and clasped it to her chest. "Forever works for me. I love you."

Emma kissed Dane's cheek. "I'm so glad you do."

A snort from the back seat, followed by a high-pitched yip, made Emma laugh. Delilah's paws twitched as if she were running, and she blew small bursts of air through her lips in tiny little barks.

Emma laughed and leaned her head on Dane's shoulder. Dane placed a kiss to the top of Emma's head. The road stretched out before them, leading them to endless possibilities, boundless adventures, and forever love.

About the Author

Donna K. Ford is a licensed professional counselor who spends her professional time assisting people in their recovery from substance addictions. She holds an associate's degree in criminal justice, a BS in psychology, and an MS in community agency counseling. When not trying to save the world, she spends her time in the mountains of East Tennessee enjoying the lakes, rivers, and hiking trails near her home.

Reading, writing, and enjoying conversation with good friends are the gifts that keep her grounded. Her book *Love's Redemption* was a 2016 Foreword INDIES finalist.

She can be contacted at donnakford70@yahoo.com and on Facebook at https://www.facebook.com/DonnaKFordAuthor.

Books Available from Bold Strokes Books

A Moment in Time by Lisa Moreau. A longstanding family feud separates two women who unexpectedly fall in love at an antique clock shop in a small Louisiana town. (978-1-63555-419-9)

Aspen in Moonlight by Kelly Wacker. When art historian Melissa Warren meets Sula Johansen, director of a local bear conservancy, she discovers that love can come in unexpected and unusual forms. (978-1-63555-470-0)

Back to September by Melissa Brayden. Small bookshop owner Hannah Shepard and famous romance novelist Parker Bristow maneuver the landscape of their two very different worlds to find out if love can win out in the end. (978-1-63555-576-9)

Changing Course by Brey Willows. When the woman of your dreams falls from the sky, you'd better be ready to catch her. (978-1-63555-335-2)

Cost of Honor by Radclyffe. First Daughter Blair Powell and Homeland Security Director Cameron Roberts face adversity when their enemies stop at nothing to prevent President Andrew Powell's reelection. (978-1-63555-582-0)

Fearless by Tina Michele. Determined to overcome her debilitating fear through exposure therapy, Laura Carter all but fails before she's even begun until dolphin trainer Jillian Marshall dedicates herself to helping Laura defeat the nightmares of her past. (978-1-63555-495-3)

Not Dead Enough by J.M. Redmann. A woman who may or may not be dead drags Micky Knight into a messy con game. (978-1-63555-543-1)

Not Since You by Fiona Riley. When Charlotte boards her honeymoon cruise single and comes face-to-face with Lexi, the high school love she left behind, she questions every decision she has ever made. (978-1-63555-474-8)

Not Your Average Love Spell by Barbara Ann Wright. Four women struggle with who to love and who to hate while fighting to rid a kingdom of an evil invading force. (978-1-63555-327-7)

Tennessee Whiskey by Donna K. Ford. Dane Foster wants to put her life on pause and ask for a redo, a chance for something that matters. Emma Reynolds is that chance. (978-1-63555-556-1)

30 Dates in 30 Days by Elle Spencer. A busy lawyer tries to find love the fast way—thirty dates in thirty days. (978-1-63555-498-4)

Finding Sky by Cass Sellars. Skylar Addison's search for a career intersects with her new boss's search for butterflies, but Skylar can't forgive Jess's intrusion into her life. (978-1-63555-521-9)

Hammers, Strings, and Beautiful Things by Morgan Lee Miller. While on tour with the biggest pop star in the world, rising musician Blair Bennett falls in love for the first time while coping with loss and depression. (978-1-63555-538-7)

Heart of a Killer by Yolanda Wallace. Contract killer Santana Masters's only interest is her next assignment—until a chance meeting with a beautiful stranger tempts her to change her ways. (978-1-63555-547-9)

Leading the Witness by Carsen Taite. When defense attorney Catherine Landauer reluctantly becomes the key witness in prosecutor Starr Rio's latest criminal trial, their hearts, careers, and lives may be at risk. (978-1-63555-512-7)

No Experience Required by Kimberly Cooper Griffin. Izzy Treadway has resigned herself to a life without romance because of her bipolar illness but wonders what she's gotten herself into when she agrees to write a book about love. (978-1-63555-561-5)

One Walk in Winter by Georgia Beers. Olivia Santini and Hayley Boyd Markham might be rivals at work, but they discover that lonely hearts often find company in the most unexpected of places. (978-1-63555-541-7)

The Inn at Netherfield Green by Aurora Rey. Advertising executive Lauren Montgomery and gin distiller Camden Crawley don't agree on anything except saving the Rose & Crown, the old English pub that's brought them together. (978-1-63555-445-8)

Top of Her Game by M. Ullrich. When it comes to life on the field and matters of the heart, losing isn't an option for pro athletes Kenzie Shaw and Sutton Flores. (978-1-63555-500-4)

Vanished by Eden Darry. A storm is coming, and Ellery and Loveday must find the chosen one or humanity won't survive it. (978-1-63555-437-3)

All She Wants by Larkin Rose. Marci Jones and Tessa Dalton get more than they bargained for when their plans for a one-night stand turn into an opportunity for love. (978-1-63555-476-2)

Beautiful Accidents by Erin Zak. Stevie Adams and Bernadette Thompson discover that sometimes the best things in life happen purely by accident. (978-1-63555-497-7)

Before Now by Joy Argento. Can Delany and Jade overcome the betrayal that spans the centuries to reignite a love that can't be broken? (978-1-63555-525-7)

Breathe by Cari Hunter. Paramedic Jemima Pardon's chronic bad luck seems to be improving when she meets police officer Rosie Jones. But they face a battle to survive before they can find love. (978-1-63555-523-3)

Double-Crossed by Ali Vali. Hired thief and killer Reed Gable finds something in her scope that will change her life forever when she gets a contract to end casino accountant Brinley Myers's life. (978-1-63555-302-4)

False Horizons by CJ Birch. Jordan and Ash struggle with different views on the alien agenda and must find their way back to each other before they're swallowed up by a centuries-old war. (978-1-63555-519-6)

Legacy by Charlotte Greene. When five women hike to a remote cabin deep inside a national park, unsettling events suggest that they should have stayed home. (978-1-63555-490-8)

Royal Street Reveillon by Greg Herren. Someone is killing the stars of a reality show, and it's up to Scotty Bradley and the boys to find out who. (978-1-63555-545-5)

Somewhere Along the Way by Kathleen Knowles. When Maxine Cooper moves to San Francisco during the summer of 1981, she learns that wherever you run, you cannot escape yourself. (978-1-63555-383-3)

Blood of the Pack by Jenny Frame. When Alpha of the Scottish pack Kenrick Wulver visits the Wolfgangs, she falls for Zaria Lupa, a wolf on the run. (978-1-63555-431-1)

Cause of Death by Sheri Lewis Wohl. Medical student Vi Akiak and K9 Search and Rescue officer Kate Renard must work together to find a killer before they end up the next targets. In the race for survival, they discover that love may be the biggest risk of all. (978-1-63555-441-0)

Chasing Sunset by Missouri Vaun. Hijinks and mishaps ensue as Iris and Finn set off on a road trip adventure, chasing the sunset, and falling in love along the way. (978-1-63555-454-0)

Double Down by MB Austin. When an unlikely friendship with Spanish pop star Erlea turns deeper, Celeste, in-house physician for the hotel hosting Erlea's show, has a choice to make—run or double down on love. (978-1-63555-423-6)

Party of Three by Sandy Lowe. Three friends are in for a wild night at billionaire heiress Eleanor McGregor's twenty-fifth birthday party. Love, lust, and doing the right thing, even when it hurts, turn the evening into one that will change their lives forever. (978-1-63555-246-1)

Sit. Stay. Love. by Karis Walsh. City girl Alana Brendt and country vet Tegan Evans both know they don't belong together. Only problem is, they're falling in love. (978-1-63555-439-7)

Where the Lies Hide by Renee Roman. As P.I. Camdyn Stark gets closer to solving the case, will her dark secrets and the lies she's buried jeopardize her future with the quietly beautiful Sarah Peters? (978-1-63555-371-0)

Beautiful Dreamer by Melissa Brayden. With love on the line, can Devyn Winters find it in her heart to stay in the small town of Dreamer's Bay, the one place she swore she'd never remain? (978-1-63555-305-5)

Create a Life to Love by Erin Zak. When sixteen-year-old Beth shows up at her birth mother's door, three lives will change forever. (978-1-63555-425-0)

Deadeye by Meredith Doench. Stranded while hunting the serial predator Deadeye, Special Agent Luce Hansen fights for survival while her lover, forensic pathologist Harper Bennett, hunts for clues to Hansen's disappearance along the killer's trail. (978-1-63555-253-9)

Death Takes a Bow by David S. Pederson. Alan Keys takes part in a local stage production, but when the leading man is murdered, his partner Detective Heath Barrington is thrust into the limelight to find the killer. (978-1-63555-472-4)

Endangered by Michelle Larkin. Shapeshifters Officer Aspen Wolfe and Dr. Tora Madigan fight their growing attraction as they work together to destroy a secret government agency that exterminates their kind. (978-1-63555-377-2)

Incognito by VK Powell. The only thing Evan Spears is focused on is capturing a fleeing murder suspect until wild card Frankie Strong is added to her team and causes chaos on and off the job. (978-1-63555-389-5)

Insult to Injury by Gun Brooke. After losing everything, Gail Owen withdraws to her old farmhouse and finds a destitute young woman, Romi Shepherd, living in a secret room. (978-1-63555-323-9)

Just One Moment by Dena Blake. If you were given the chance to have the love of your life back, could you ignore everything that went wrong and start over again? (978-1-63555-387-1)

Scene of the Crime by MJ Williamz. Cullen Matthews finds herself caught between the woman she thinks she loves but can no longer trust and a beautiful detective she can't stop thinking about who will stop at nothing to find the truth. (978-1-63555-405-2)